THE LAST WISH

THE LAST WISH

by

M.A. Lanham

>â< PAROLA
PRESS

This is a work of fiction. Names, characters, places, and incidents either are the product of the author's imagination or are used fictionally, and any resemblance to actual persons, living or dead, businesses, companies, events, or locales is entirely incidental.

ISBN-13: 978-1-62225-6839 hardcover
ISBN-13: 978-1-62225-6846 paperback
ISBN-13: 978-1-62225-6853 eBook

First Edition: December 2024

Printed in the United States of America

10 9 8 7 6 5 4 3 2 1

Cover Design: A. R. Redington
Author Photo: Arpit Mehta

M.A. Lanham is the nom de plume of a number 1 bestselling, award-nominated author of novels, short stories, and more in diverse genres, including *The Lighthouse*, a small town, second chance romance. Lanham lives in small town Kansas with his two dogs and two cats making up stories and dreaming dreams and hopes to never stop. M.A. Lanham loves to read almost as much as writing. A fan of world travel, good music, good food, and good friends, you can find him online at www.malanham.com.

For Ramon and Glenda,
whose 60 year marriage taught me
the value of commitment and hard
work, and that relationships take both.

For M, K and K,
My family whom I love dearly.
I hope I also teach and show you the
same value, despite the fact I mess up
sometimes. I love you so much.

CHAPTER 1

LUKE MORRISON SIGHED as he stepped out of his office onto the sidewalk. The parking lot sparkled from all the colored lights his employees had strung over the shrubs and trees leading from the office to the main warehouse. The Christmas spirit obviously remained alive at the company in everyone except Luke himself. He hadn't felt Christmas spirit in three years.

Luke hadn't been looking forward to the holidays at all. Mostly, he was just biding his time, waiting for them to pass. Passing through town on errands or grocery runs, he'd been regularly assaulted by the familiar sights and sounds of the season—Santas on street corners ringing their bells, carolers singing loud enough to be heard over the Christmas music blaring from nearby loudspeakers, lights and tinsel strung from street posts. It all seemed so typical that any sentimental meaning was lost on him. The whole season simply served as another reminder of his failures. And Luke didn't need to be reminded. He knew he was a failure.

The office was in an old, converted brick warehouse on Olive Street—one of many older buildings being revitalized in that area. Surrounded by the Saint Louis skyline, many of the city's landmarks and popular venues, like the baseball stadium and football dome and the famous Gateway Arch, were all within walking distance. As with most cities, St. Louis loved to decorate for the holidays—mixing colored banners with phrases like *Noel, Happy Holidays,* or *Winter Wonderland* among the tinsel and lights—all designed to create a cheerful and unified spirit of the season.

Everything looked much the same as when Luke had come downtown ten years before, searching for a good location. The only thing that had changed at all was Luke himself. Even the bitter wind blowing across downtown off the Mississippi River seemed to affirm the coldness of his life.

He pushed his blondish brown bangs to one side with his left hand, as his right hand grasped the key ring in his pocket. Weaving in between rows of cars in the parking lot, Luke found it somewhat amusing that he'd once loved weather like this. It was one of the reasons he'd never wanted to leave the Midwest. He'd always liked experiencing the four seasons. Unfortunately, the season his own life was in made cold weather feel more oppressive.

He was about to unlock the door to his Subaru Crosstrek hybrid, when he heard someone call his name.

"Luke!" She called again, and he recognized the voice of his assistant, Elise Edmond, a charming blonde in her late twenties, who had worked for him for five years and proved invaluable.

Shaking off the chills, he took his hand off the door handle and turned, forcing a smile. "Did I forget something?"

Elise smiled back as she scurried across the sidewalk, keeping a careful watch for black ice. "Why don't you come to the Christmas party this year?" she suggested in that cheery, eager to help tone she always had.

He opened his mouth to speak, searching for another excuse. He hadn't gone for three years now, since the divorce. He just hadn't felt up to it.

"It's been three years," Elise reminded him. "I thought the point was to celebrate the Marshall family, not just at home but here at the office. You know everyone loves and respects you. It's not the same without you."

He closed his eyes and sighed. "You're way too kind. I can think of a few who don't think much of me."

Elise grunted as she stopped beside him. "They don't work for you so they aren't invited." She gently grabbed his arm and tugged toward the waiting warehouse. "You don't have to stay long, but I promise you'll feel better."

Two years ago, Luke had been happily married, father of three, a successful businessman, admired by neighbors and friends. Now, those same friends and neighbors turned away to avoid eye contact when he passed. People tended to avoid putting themselves in his path, taking great lengths to avoid any encounters with him. It was too hard to understand how someone who had everything could lose it all so quickly. He was living a nightmare.

When strangers smiled cheerfully and offered a bubbly "Merry Christmas" as they passed, it was like fingernails on a chalkboard. People who knew him rarely bothered. He had absolutely nothing to be merry about. It didn't help that Luke was one of those guys people always thought they knew. He was handsome, but not fashionable—his taste in clothes outdated, his hair tousled, tall, but not unusually so. He'd always felt well-liked and well-respected. Until the divorce.

The question that haunted them all—even Luke himself—was how could a man who had it all abandon his perfect family—wife and three kids and house—without so much as a fight. Anna wanted him to fight. She'd pushed him for months, and then exploded out of frustration. But Luke tired of fighting. He didn't like the person he'd become or the looks in his kids' eyes—the way it affected them. What she'd asked of him had seemed a sacrifice he couldn't afford to make and still keep the company going.

Anna accused him of being selfish. Taking on too much and forgetting he had responsibilities at home, too. He'd made some sacrifices on the home front to get the busy up and running for sure, to ensure he could provide for a nice future. But Anna wanted a husband who was there at home every night for dinner and helping with the kids. He had a hundred and fifty employees who counted on him. Customers and partners, too. He had responsibilities. He loved his wife and kids—they were his everything, and the company paid for it all. But Anna wasn't happy. None of them were. And he couldn't go on fighting all the time. Why couldn't they understand that everything he'd done had been for them?

In the end, despite every argument, he'd walked away from the greatest love of his life, because she was the greatest love of his life. He made her unhappy. God, he'd never wanted to be that guy. His kids were unhappy, too, and he hated himself for it. No, they were better off without him, he thought. But he'd never counted on the fact he'd be is miserable without them, too.

"I don't know, Elise," he began, but she cut him off.

"I do!" she insisted, pulling on his arm. "You need to stop punishing yourself and celebrate the success you've made here. The success we've all made. The reason we all work so hard and don't complain is because of you. You're a great leader and dedicated boss. You take care of us. I know you're sad and miss your family. And we all hate seeing what happened to you, but we love you and we want to celebrate the successes of another great year with the man who helped get us there, okay?"

Luke sighed again and surrendered. "Okay, but no longer than an hour."

"Great!" Elise said, sounding like a cheerleader as she led him onto the sidewalk and began winding her way toward the waiting warehouse.

IN THE END, he'd stayed almost three hours, and it was almost dark by the time he headed for the Subaru again. To his surprise, the party had been fun, with employee after employee congratulating him or thanking him or both, along with those coming to introduce kids or spouses who'd either never met him or hadn't seen him in three years. A lot had changed, of course. He made small talk the best he could with each one, telling the spouses and kids how invaluable the employee's contributions were and reminding them the company's success depended upon everyone, not just management.

For her part, Elise kept bring him eggnog, offering only a single glass of wine when it was time for the annual "toast." He somehow drank them all, imbibing more eggnog than he'd had in years. And the smile on his face quickly turned from plastered and forced to a genuine expression of the warmth, gratitude, and happiness he was feeling in his heart in the presence of those wonderful people.

He'd expected it to hurt to be among so many happy couples and families, but instead, he'd felt like the elder statesman, or grandfather, and despite being only thirty-six himself, it made him feel good. He'd caught the holiday spirit, or some form of it at least, and it was only when things started winding down and half the employees headed out themselves, that he'd excused himself and headed for the door with Elise's blessing.

She was all smiles as he bent to kiss her cheek and bid her goodnight. "Told ya you belonged here. Merry Christmas, boss."

"Merry Christmas," he said all grins, as he shook hands with her husband and began feeling for the car keys in his pocket, turning for the door.

As he pulled up at the gate to leave the parking lot, Luke noticed one of the guards, an older man in his late forties named Guy, looking exhausted and distant. "Hey, Guy," he greeted him. "How are you this afternoon?"

Guy looked up and seeing it was the boss, forced a smile and came to the window as he reached down to flip the button that activated the gate bar. "I'm okay, Mister Morrison. Long day."

Luke noticed his hair was disheveled and his uniform had

wrinkles, unusual for a guy who always took pride in his appearance. "Beat already? Is anything wrong?" he asked, keeping his tone lighthearted with hopes Guy wouldn't be intimidated telling the boss his troubles.

"My oldest son was arrested," Guy confessed. "Drugs. We're trying to get him in a program, but it's a tough time of year. Plus the wife and I both work long hours…"

"Go home, Guy," Luke said, lifting his cell to call his assistant, Elise. "I'll have Elise send someone to watch the gate for the rest of the day."

Surprise showed on Guy's face at Luke's kindness but then his shoulders sank. "Thanks, but I've got two more hours on my shift, Mister Morrison, and I need the money."

"Take the rest of the day paid," Luke said. "You've probably heard a little about my own family situation. Learn from my mistakes, okay? Put your family first. They need you a lot more right now than we do. Go!" He urged Guy off with one hand while he held his phone in the other, hearing Elise's voice on the line. It took only a few minutes to explain things and get a replacement headed out to the gate, and then Luke was out and onto the side street, continuing on his way.

As Luke pulled the Subaru onto Highway 64, the city's central corridor, he still couldn't believe things had turned out this way. There'd been no prior warning. He had traveled a lot for his job, but that's what it took to run a successful business these days. Anna had complained some. So had the kids. But their life was comfortable, and they were happy as far as he knew. Anna had always resented his travel schedule, but Luke had assured her it would only take a few years of sacrifice to build a strong, secure business. She complained, but their relationship was solid…or so Luke thought.

In the year prior, Luke had missed everyone's birthdays, and all of them had been hurt. But there'd been important meetings with large new clients on Anna's and Mandy's birthdays, and then weather conditions delayed his flight back for Kyle's. He'd missed Cassie's when a delivery crisis came up with the warehouse in Cincinnati, forcing him to make a last minute trip. In each case, it couldn't be helped. The marriage had soured but Luke hadn't thought it beyond repair. Marriages always changed over the years, he reasoned. Drifting apart a bit was only natural. Something all couples went through. It was just a phase. He'd never thought time would run out.

Then two years ago, Luke arrived home from a three day business trip to Cleveland. The plane had been on time for once, so he was looking forward to actually having a few hours with the kids before they went to bed. When the garage door opened and Anna's Volvo wasn't there, he figured they'd gone out for dinner, which they often did, and grabbed his bags from the trunk before entering through the side door. The house was dark and quiet, unusual enough. But then he'd noticed the appliances were missing. The furniture was gone, too. He'd dropped his bags and run upstairs. Empty bedrooms. Even the pictures were mostly gone. The only sign of their life together was a large family portrait left hanging over the fireplace in the family room, and judging from its crooked angle, Luke figured Anna had only left it because she couldn't get it down by herself. His family was gone.

Weaving his car through the late afternoon traffic, Luke still couldn't believe it. He and Anna were supposed to be together forever. That was what they'd always talked about. Years ago in college, they couldn't stand to be apart. His friends always teased him about it, but Luke knew they were jealous. None of them had anything close to a serious relationship, and Luke had found the dream: a perfect girl who really loved him. He'd gotten so lucky. Until he came home to find her gone, he'd still felt that way—the most blessed man alive.

The Jordan Kyrou bobble head bouncing on his dashboard broke his reverie. It was right where Kyle had insisted upon mounting it after they'd gotten it as a door prize at a hockey game two years before. He looked around to realize he was passing Enterprise Center, where the Blues played. He could almost hear the roar of the crowd, the slap of the sticks against the puck, the puck slamming into the sideboards. He'd finally given up his season seats in October. There wasn't any point now. He never went to games anymore. It just wasn't the same without his kids.

The two older kids were mad at him now. Cassie was only five and too young to understand much of what was going on. She just wanted her Daddy and Mommy back together. But Mandy and Kyle knew enough to figure the whole thing was their dad's fault. If he'd been home more, none of this would have happened. Kyle had taken it the hardest, being the only male in the house now. That was tearing Luke up inside. He had always been close with the kids, even when his relationship with Anna had drifted. Now he seemed to have lost that too, and it ate at him constantly. Which was why he was out trying to beat the crowds to buy their Christmas presents two weeks before the big day.

HE PULLED OFF the highway and into the parking lot of The Saint Louis Galleria, a large white mall located just north of Highway 64. A four-level parking structure sat to its west, connected to the mall by walkways, allowing shoppers to enter the regulated interior rapidly during the coldest and hottest days of the year. The mall was also surrounded by a huge outdoor parking lot, and both the lot and the garage were packed on weekends, but not today.

Luke entered from the parking garage and let the electric doors close behind him to shut out the chilly outside air. The Galleria seemed quieter than he'd expected—the calm before the storm. A few shoppers milled about, women dragging young children. A few older mall-walkers passed him on their daily laps. If he hurried, he could get in and out before the madness resumed. He preferred it that way. Luke hated shopping. Anna had always handled it for them. He wasn't even sure what the kids wanted; that was the problem. He had to improvise. And given that his kids were not happy with him, he wanted the gifts to be something special, something they would really like.

Cassie would be the easiest since she was at an age where she loved any toy, but Kyle had reached that grumpy preteen stage where a computer game would be the only acceptable thing for him. Mandy, ten going on sixteen, was as picky as her mother, so Luke decided to save hers for last. His administrative assistant had suggested he shop online, but Luke wanted to be able to tell the kids that he'd chosen the gifts himself—or at least he wanted to be able to tell Anna. She always accused him of taking the easy way out, but she wouldn't be able to do that this time.

Entering a toy store, he faced aisles and aisles of toys, games, and gadgets. It was overwhelming deciding where to begin. An entire wall of stuffed animals of all colors, shapes, and sizes imaginable stared back at him. As other shoppers hurried past on either side, he briefly entertained the thought of getting a stuffed koala for Cassie, but then shook it off as too obvious. She had so many stuffed animals already, and he needed something that showed he'd put some real thought into it.

He headed for the gaming section. So many choices with crazy names like *Street War Seven* or *SynRocket Three*. Some of the cover pictures were so violent he couldn't bring himself to even consider them. Most of them seemed to involve role playing. Luke had never understood the fascination with such games, and now that his own son was into them, he was all the more baffled.

"Looking for anything specific?" The teenaged sales associate smiled as she approached. The tan name plate on her blue vest read 'Allie.'

Luke smiled back at her. "No, just something for my son."

"What type of console?"

Was she speaking English? Luke's brow crinkled, his eyebrows rising in bewilderment. Her shoulder-length brunette hair reminded him of how Anna had worn hers in college. They had similar complexions, too, only the sales associate wore more makeup and had dark brown eyes.

"You know, PC, Xbox, PlayStation4, Nintendo 64, Wii?" She looked amused.

"Oh, Wii." He nodded as if he'd understood all along.

"Well, there's a lot to choose from." She motioned to the well-stocked shelves, starting to pull a couple games out, but Luke scowled at the violent images on their covers. She put them back and motioned to the opposite side of the aisle. "Here's something you both might like."

He followed her to a television surrounded by a guitar-style controller, an electronic drum set, and a microphone on a stand. She went to a console and hit a switch. The screen sprang to life.

"It's called *Rock Star Eight*. Every teenager wants to be a rock star, right? This gives them their chance."

Knowing Kyle was into music, Luke was intrigued. At least this game didn't seem to involve violence...

"Want to try it?" the sales associate asked as she grabbed a microphone off a table nearby, offering it to him. "You just read the lyrics and sing along into the microphone. It's easy."

Luke had never been much of a singer, and he didn't think this was the place to start. "Maybe it'd be better if you showed me how it works."

The girl shrugged. "Sure, no problem." She reached toward the console and hit a couple of buttons on a controller. Music began pulsing through two large speakers. She started rocking to the beat, really getting into the part. As the lyrics appeared on the screen, she started singing like the next American Idol contestant at an audition. She didn't have much of a voice but made up for it in enthusiasm, swaying and dancing, clearly enjoying herself.

Luke picked up the guitar controller, looking it over.

"You strum it," she offered, motioning.

Strum it, how? There's no strings. But the girl kept making strumming motions, so Luke held the guitar as players do, slinging the strap around his neck and began air strumming. The lights on the screen changed colors from red to blue in reaction.

The girl smiled, pleased. "That's it!"

Luke could understand the appeal of the game. With all the bright colors and effects on the screen, the pulsing music, you did feel the part. Kyle would probably love it. What teenage boy didn't want to be a rock star? "I'll take it," he blurted out.

The girl smiled. "Cool. Your son's gonna love it." She hit buttons on the controller and set down the microphone. The music stopped, and the screen reverted to the launch page again. "Let me have them bring one up from the dock."

Luke nodded, following her toward the checkout stands. "How much is it, anyway?"

"Two hundred fifty on sale. Twenty percent off!" she announced it as though it were almost a steal.

Two hundred fifty dollars for a game?! Luke fought the urge to sit down. He reminded himself that this gift had to be the best ever. Besides, he could afford it. He wouldn't have felt that way three years ago when he was still struggling to get the business on solid ground, and his client base was still small and barely established. But that was then; now things were good.

The business had started with an invention Luke's coworker had come up with for binding books. It was a machine that used a glue process similar to what large publishers used but of a smaller size and more reasonably priced for smaller publishers to afford. Luke had set up the marketing and manufacturing side of things and ended up running the company when his friend lost interest. They'd started the business from the ground up, and Luke had dedicated himself to making it work. In six years, they'd grown from five employees to twenty-seven, and four years later, they had almost a hundred employees and sales offices in five regional centers. Luke's hard work was paying off.

Last month, he'd finally promoted one of his long-time managers to vice president and put him in charge of things—a role that used to be Luke's sole responsibility. Things were going great, and, as a result, his income was the best it had ever been, and the business had garnered a solid reputation throughout the industry. Of course, there'd been sacrifices. He hadn't been there for the family the way they wanted him to be—the way he wanted to be. But he'd thought it was worth it to create a success that had provided them the life they'd always dreamed about. He'd thought Anna wanted it as much as he did. That turned out to be wrong.

Suddenly, finding himself with more free time than he'd had in two years meant a lot of time to think, and he knew why he'd lost them. He was determined to make every effort to prove he still cared about them. He'd win them back—whatever it took.

CHAPTER 2

INDING GIFTS FOR the girls turned out to be easier than expected. Luke arrived home confident that he had something for each of them that would show how much they still meant to him. They were all that mattered. Everything he'd done or was doing had been to make a better life for them; so he could give them everything they wanted. They might have given up on him along the way, but Luke hadn't given up on them. Now he had to prove it.

Even a year later, the place was practically empty–furnished with odds and ends he'd scrounged up at Goodwill and various garage sales. It hadn't made sense to buy new ones. To invest in something nicer would imply a permanent acceptance of his circumstances, something he refused to do. Setting the presents and the stack of mail he'd retrieved on the dining table he'd found at Goodwill, he glanced toward the phone console to check for messages. The light was blinking, and he wondered who'd called. There hadn't been many calls lately.

Grabbing a Coke from the fridge, he approached the machine and tapped the "Message" button. It took a few seconds for his brain to register the voice he hadn't heard in six months—Anna, reminding him not to forget the kids Christmas gifts. Given her scolding tone, Luke could tell her feelings toward him hadn't changed, but at least she'd called acknowledging he had a place in the kids' lives. Warmth surged through his chest at the thought, and he smiled. He debated whether to call back and let her know he'd not only remembered but found excellent gifts. Ultimately, he decided that given her mood, it could wait.

He sorted through the mail he'd carried in with him. Mostly junk mail as usual. Luke wondered how the post office could justify continually raising postal rates when they made so much money on the side getting paid to distribute junk. There were four or five pieces a day, it seemed. If he ran his company the way they ran the post office, he'd have gone out of business a long time ago. Maybe then he'd still have a family. He wondered how they could afford to pay employees so much. Anna's brother had been a postal worker for twenty-five years and was very well paid.

Tossing the bills he'd separated from the junk into the "To be paid" basket on his desk, he went to scavenge the kitchen for food. His sister stopped by once a month to make sure he got groceries. She made the list, and he went himself. Occasionally, either she or his brother had him over for dinner, but he hadn't been much fun to be around, so the invitations were few and far between.

Grabbing instant oatmeal packets from the cupboard, he dumped them in a bowl, poured in milk, and then put it in the microwave for four minutes. He'd reverted back lately a pattern he remembered from his bachelor days in college. That period had lasted barely two years, and then he'd met Anna. For Luke, it had been love at first sight, and his life had never been the same. How had he come to take it all for granted? He'd thought he was doing everything right. But clearly Anna and the kids disagreed.

The microwave beeped in time with the ringing of his cell. Luke opened the microwave as he reached in the pocket with his other hand for the phone. *Damn it.* He cringed as the bowl burned his hand. Leaving it to cool, he answered the phone. "Hello?"

"I thought I'd try one more time." It was Anna. She sighed.

"I'm sorry about earlier. I didn't need to say that."

"Actually, I was out shopping when you called. I got the kids some great stuff." At least, he hoped they'd be excited.

"Wow. You remembered. That'll mean a lot to them, Luke." She sounded really surprised. He smiled, pleased he'd done something right for once. "Look, I just wanted to call and remind you about Christmas. The kids miss you," she said.

"I thought they were mad at me." He sipped from his Coke, leaning against the kitchen counter as he pinched his aching hand between his thighs and grimaced.

"Maybe the older two. Cassie just wants her daddy back."

He paused a moment to keep his voice from cracking. "I miss them, too."

There was a long pause, and then: "So if you're not busy that day, maybe you could come over and open presents with us, then stay for dinner?"

Luke's belly fluttered, and he felt a lightness on his skin. It was the most unexpected thing she could have said. Had she finally had a change of heart?

"Luke?"

Don't blow this, his inner voice warned. "I'm here. I just...don't know what to say."

"Look. You're still their father. We're divorced, but we're still family. Your kids need you. The last two Christmases have been a disaster. Let's not let our issues ruin another Christmas for them."

She'd left him just after Thanksgiving. Luke had spent that Christmas avoiding festivities. He'd wanted no part of it. And though his sister had tried, he hadn't gone anywhere. Instead, he'd stayed at home with a case of beer feeling sorry for himself. He hadn't even answered the phone when the kids tried to call him. He'd regretted that ever since, feeling like such a loser. Why did he have to hurt his kids? He'd always adored them.

"Are you there?"

"Yeah. I'd love to." He finally managed to say. He pumped a fist in the air silently proclaiming "victory."

"Okay, I'll call you next week to confirm the time."

Luke smiled so big he thought his face might explode. He fought off the urge to jump up and down, instead saying, "Sounds great."

She hung up, leaving him floating on cloud nine. He went back and grabbed his oatmeal, dancing around the kitchen, humming. This was the second chance he'd been praying for but never thought he'd get. He couldn't wait. The reunion with Anna and his kids was all he could think about. Sure, she hadn't said anything about missing him herself, so it might not be an easy reunion, but at least she had made the effort. That alone seemed like a miracle. Luke was floored. He hadn't been this happy in a long time.

HIS SISTER, GRACE, came over that night to check on him and ended up wrapping the presents. He'd always been the worst at that. It had pretty much fallen on Anna. Watching him, humming, and moving around like he was walking on air, Grace seemed amused. "Not excited at all, are we?"

Luke danced toward her, handing her a mug of hot chocolate. "Can't a guy be festive at Christmas?"

Grace was shorter than her brothers and looked every part of the housewife she was. Her clothes were chosen for comfort and ease of mobility above all else. Her hair was always mussed in one way or another. But she was pretty with a great smile. She swallowed a sip of hot chocolate. "This is you, Luke. And besides, given how your life has been the past year, festivity isn't an obvious expectation."

"Okay, so maybe I am. Why shouldn't I be?" he asked, not letting Grace's practical caution dampen his growing hopefulness.

"Well, it's not like there aren't issues there to deal with. With the kids, I'm sure it'll be fine. They'll love the presents and seeing you again, even if they are mad at you. But you're almost acting as if you and Anna are getting back together." Her eyes were drawn to a pile of dirty dishes in the sink, as she opened the cabinet underneath to check for dish soap. A brand new bottle stood unopened in front.

"It could happen." Luke ignored the expression of disapproval she shot him showing her disapproval at his lack of attention to the dishes.

As she popped open the dish detergent, her expression turned worried. "Anything's possible. I just don't want to see you getting your hopes up, only to be heart broken when it doesn't happen."

"I'm a big boy, Gracie. She never said anything about us over the phone. But she made the effort. It's more than I've gotten from her in over a year." Luke gently pushed her aside and took the detergent, starting to rinse and scrub the dishes himself. Could it be enough time had passed for Anna to realize the mistake she'd made? Maybe his kids were coming around, too.

"Which is all the more reason to be cautious, Luke." Grace watched him, arms crossed over her chest.

"Point taken, little sis. I'll try and be realistic."

She chuckled at the serious face he made. She'd always been the serious one, when they were kids. Focused on her studies and thinking about the future, while Luke and Ray were always about having fun. Grace had seemed surprised to find Luke so dedicated to the business.

"Thanks for helping me out so much. I wouldn't have made it without you." He set the newly rinsed dishes in the dish drainer beside the sink. His swelling joy made even the slightest motion feel like a choreographed dance move.

Grace smiled as she grabbed a dish towel from the door beside the sink and set to drying. "Well, we're family. Who else would put up with you? Besides, I can't have you embarrassing the family by falling apart."

Luke made a face. "Who says that didn't happen?"

Grace chuckled. "I was trying to be nice."

Luke swiped the towel from her and motioned for her to stop. "That's all I get from people anymore. People walking on tiptoes trying to be nice. When they don't avoid me altogether, that is." It stung as he said it, but he knew it was true. Somehow it hardly mattered in the face of the upcoming reunion with his family.

Grace took one more look at the wrapped presents on the table and sighed. "Well, I'm through here. How're your cupboards?"

"I've still got the list from last month. I'm doing fine." He finished rinsing the last plate and switched to drying dishes with the towel he'd swiped from Grace.

She opened the cabinet by the microwave. "I swear Luke, you're keeping Quaker Oats in business all by yourself. Aren't you sick of oatmeal?"

Luke shrugged.

"Try eating some of this other stuff before it goes bad, okay? It wouldn't kill you to balance your diet, either."

"Now you sound like Mom." He knew he shouldn't have said it.

She scowled at him and shoved the cabinet shut. "Thanks a lot, jerk."

"Only kidding. She did always talk about balanced diets."

"Yeah, well, a lot of good it did her."

Their mother had been gone seven years, and their father wasn't taking it well. They'd been married thirty-three years, and she'd been his whole life. Like a lot of widowers, their dad just wasn't the same now. Grace had taken it upon herself to look after him. Two years ago, they'd moved him to a retirement community nearby. Luke hadn't managed to visit him in three months. Thinking about it made him feel guilty.

"You sure know how to bring people back down to earth, don't you, Gracie?" He said, frowning as she finished pulling on her coat and gloves.

"You're the one who compared me to Mom." Grace grabbed her purse off the table.

"Sorry." But the song his heart was singing didn't miss a beat as she slammed the door on her way out.

THE MINUTE SHE hung up the phone, Anna was filled with regret. She couldn't explain why she'd acted that way. It was just so hard to hear his voice again. She was glad the kids were at school so they hadn't overheard. They'd already witnessed enough drama between their parents. She didn't want to add more. Sitting in the kitchen of the Colonial house she'd inherited from her favorite aunt, she looked up to find her parents smiling back at her from a photo on the wall.

Anna certainly knew a lot about parental drama. At twelve, her parents had almost divorced. Her father was a successful lawyer, and as his practice grew, his time with the family shrunk. By the time he made partner, he was leaving for work by seven-thirty and not returning home until nine that night. Anna and her siblings had begun feeling like they'd lost their father. But for Anna's mother, it had been even harder. It was the first time she'd ever seen her mother cry.

After months of arguments overheard through their bedroom doors, her father stormed out of the house like a tornado through a wheat field. He'd moved an arm to push Anna aside as he stormed toward the stairs, but apparently thought better of it at the last minute and dodged to one side instead. Anna stood there not knowing what to say as her mother lay in bed, sobbing. The next day, her mother packed them all up and took them to their grandparents' farm. Her mother explained to them that while the time at the farm would be temporary, they probably wouldn't be going back to their house afterward. She was leaving their father, and she needed time to sort things out and find a place to start over.

Ten days later, the kids saw their father's Cadillac pulling up the dirt drive. Her father stepped out of the car looking like a stranger—hair disheveled, shirt untucked, face unshaven and covered in stubble. He resembled a cat who'd just been chased by a very big dog. He clearly hadn't slept much and had been very worried. Her mother and grandmother came out on the porch when they heard the car. None of the adults paid any attention to the kids playing in the yard to the north—all of whom stopped and watched as their father broke down.

"I've made a big mistake, Helen," he said. "I know I was wrong. Please, come back home." The last part of if it was barely discernable, because at that moment he disintegrated into a teary mass, falling to his knees on the dirt drive, hugging their mother's feet. This Richard Davis was not the high powered attorney his friends and colleagues all respected. He wasn't even the stern yet lovable father his children both feared and adored. This Richard Davis was a broken man. Anna watched her mother's heart melt at the sight of him. Watched as she gently grabbed his arm, pulling him to his feet and comforting him, then led him inside to talk.

When they returned home together, their father became a new man. He still practiced law, but he was home for dinner every night, and even the sternness he'd had in the past when disciplining his children had been tempered. He showed a renewed appreciation for his family in every moment he had with them.

Anna's own experience with her father made the situation with Luke all the more painful. One of the reasons she'd married him was a sense that he was the kind of man her father became after the crisis. He'd been so great when she was pregnant with their kids, waiting on her hand and foot, treating her like a princess.

"What do you need, babe?" he asked time and again whenever he felt her stir in their bed, no matter the hour. He'd sit up and flip on his bedside lamp, carefully looking her over to make sure everything was okay.

"I'm fine," she'd said most of the time, but on occasion, he'd done middle of the night hunts for some ice cream or other food item she was craving, each time with nary a complaint.

"Here, sweetie," he'd say as he came back home and delivered it to her in bed, complete with dish, utensils, and often a glass of water or juice on a tray. As she sat up and accepted the tray on her lap, he always leaned down and kissed her cheek softly. "I love you so much."

Just recalling it, shivers shot across her body. She'd been so in love with him. He was like the perfect husband. So Anna had watched with growing alarm and frustration as Luke instead became the kind of man her father had been before. It was not at all what she'd dreamed of. Now here she was watching her own children suffer the way she and her siblings had. After spending three years trying to make him see what was happening, she couldn't take any more. She'd had no choice but to remove them from that situation.

Unlike her father, however, even the separation didn't seem to be the reality check Luke needed. He complained about her destroying their family. He yelled in frustration, yet then went right back to the same life he'd been leading before she'd left— all work and no play. It wasn't what the kids needed in a father, and it definitely wasn't what Anna needed in a husband.

Now here she was, in the Webster Groves house, which finally felt like home, asking herself why she'd even bothered to invite him to Christmas with them this year. It had been a momentary softening in part because Cassie kept crying for her daddy and while Anna didn't want them living with a father who was never there, she didn't want them living without a father either. So, she thought maybe somehow getting them together would heal some of the pain they'd all been going through. It was Christmas, after all. The year before, Luke had missed it entirely, too depressed and down from the divorce to deal with it. But it was time to start moving on. The kids needed it. Anna needed it, and in her heart, she knew Luke needed it, too. She had called.

There was something about getting the answering machine that had just set her off—that and hearing his voice again after several months. Somehow, despite her best intentions, she'd found her anger rising. *Of course you're not there, as usual. God forbid you should ever be available to your family.* Had she really expected anything different? And when she heard the *beep,* she just couldn't restrain herself.

"Not there, huh? Big surprise," she'd said, not even attempting to hide her contempt. "I don't know why I even bothered, but I just wanted to remind you that your kids, for some reason, still ask about you. It might be nice, given that fact, if you remembered Christmas. For them. Try and find something they'll like, ok? I know you hardly know them anymore, but...just try, please. Bye." She'd hung up, and then sat in her warm kitchen, wishing she remembered the code for dialing in to check messages on the voice mail. Maybe then she could call and erase it. Only she couldn't remember the code—which left her with only one option. She had to call again.

She sat at the antique oak dining table for fifteen minutes, absent-mindedly curling her dark bangs around her index finger, when she noticed the baby purple finches outside the kitchen window chirping loudly. As she turned to watch, their mother arrived with fresh worms. Then she noticed the clock, sighing loudly. The kids would be home any minute. If she was going to do this, she had to do it now. She'd watched the finches for a moment longer, then turned and grabbed the phone.

CHAPTER 3

THE NOUVEAU ARTS Culinary Institute occupied the end of a strip mall off South Forty Drive and Log Cabin Lane in Ladue. Traffic on Highway 64 sped by on the other side of a fence from its parking lot. Luke arrived promptly at eight, per the instructions he'd received over the phone, and parked at the end of a row. As he got out of the car, a cornucopia of pleasant food smells invaded his nose, awakening his senses. Memories flooded him as he started across the parking lot toward the double front doors, and he smiled.

When he'd announced the office would be closing two days early on December twenty-third, his employees had a first reacted as if they didn't believe him. It was not that they didn't like him. Luke had always treated them like family—actually he'd treated them better than he'd treated his family, to be honest. He'd grown to respect and admire each of them, and it felt good knowing they respected him, too. The surprise came from the fact it was the first time Luke had ever closed the office early in the history of the company. He'd overheard a few mumbled comments wondering if he'd lost his mind. That made him chuckle. They'd worked hard to get to this level. Now it was time to share the benefits with his team.

Actually, he did have an ulterior motive. He'd decided to make the extra effort to contribute something to Christmas dinner. When Anna had called to confirm their plans, he made the offer, knowing he had never been much of a cook. Anna had laughed, saying if his object was to make peace with them, cooking might not be the best road to success. Luke didn't care. He was determined to make whatever effort was needed, so he'd enrolled himself in a two-day cooking class. It was a pre-holiday cooking special event offered once a year by the chefs in training.

He entered the brick building and found himself surrounded mostly by housewives with a few other men thrown in for good measure, including two pairs holding hands. The student chefs and their professors were mostly male also, however, so he didn't feel as out of place as he'd feared. In fact, Luke found the class quite enjoyable. The focus was on traditional Christmas dinner with all the fixings, from stuffing to mashed potatoes and gravy to preparing a turkey. It was all designed to target specifically non-professionals—people who just needed to prepare good food as quickly as possible.

Like most kids, Luke's children loved sweets, and whatever he made, he wanted it to be something they would be excited about, so he paid special attention to the lessons on pies. He wanted everything about this reunion to show the whole family that he was a new man, with new focus. He had to show them, not just tell them, that things were different now, that he wanted to be a part of their lives and would do what it takes.

On the way over, he'd driven past Pizza World, Cassie's favorite, which only reminded him of how much he had to prove. The last time Luke had seen the kids, it had not gone well. He'd run late, as he always seemed to, because of a late shipment he had to inventory. He'd arrived at Anna's around six-forty-five instead of five-thirty, and the kids looked crestfallen. They'd already decided he wouldn't show up. Luke didn't know why. That had only happened a few times lately. He guessed it was residue from his past mistakes. Since the marriage had broken up, he'd tried really hard not to miss time with the kids. He was usually late, but he always showed up. There had only been two times he'd missed, and it just couldn't be helped. He'd called both times. As a business owner, sometimes things just came up. The kids never understood, of course. Neither did Anna and they always managed to make him feel guilty about it.

He'd arrived at Anna's on one of those spring-like October days he'd always loved—gentle breeze, temperatures in the seventies, a brief respite before the coldness of winter. Luke was smiling and happy to see the kids, but was met at the door with somber faces. They were all cranky too.

Anna just had to comment. "We'd pretty much decided you weren't coming,"

"Of course, I was coming. Wouldn't miss this for the world." He'd had to work hard to hide his irritation at her dig.

He loaded the kids into the car and took them to Cassie's Pizza World, hoping the games and pizza would quickly erase their sourness, but he'd been wrong. Only Cassie had recovered at all.

Soon enough, the older two ran off together to play their favorite games, while Luke stayed with Cassie. She wasn't big enough to play most of the arcade games and was too scared of some of the motion rides. He couldn't leave her alone and chase after them, so he ended up spending the rest of the night with her. Unlike her siblings, Cassie just wanted the family together as it always had been. In her little girl world, that was the only life which made any sense, and the divorce had disrupted her sense of order. She'd cried and asked when he was coming home time and again. The question always left him with a knot in his throat—like he'd swallowed a golf ball and gotten it stuck in his esophagus. He always managed to find something to say, but never felt it was adequate—especially not when Cassie stood there looking up at him with those eyes. Little girls had eyes like angels, totally innocent and hopeful. When faced with them, Luke, like any father, melted, and when they contained the hint of sadness he now saw regularly in Cassie's eyes, it was melting from guilt.

Luke felt that way about all his kids. So why had he not made time for them? What kind of man forgot about his family?

How could he have let himself get too busy to think about how much he needed them—how much they needed him? The Bible instructed men to love their wives as Christ loved the church and to rule their children and their houses well. He'd failed on every count. What kind of Christian was he?

Kyle and Mandy made it back to the table on occasion to grab slices of pizza or refills of soda. They seemed to have no objection to eating the food he bought them, jamming their faces with pizza while chewing as fast as they could, like contestants in an eating contest. They finished by washing it down quickly with a glass of soda before racing off to continue playing games. A moment he could talk with them that never came.

Later, after he paid the bill and they all headed for the parking lot, he tried to initiate a conversation. "You haven't said much about school lately," he started.

Mandy shrugged and hurried on past.

"I really want to know what's going on in your life, honey. Can't we talk for a bit?"

She'd slowed and looked at back him as if she was surprised it mattered, then turned and continued on. Luke had stood there wishing he could think of something that would stop her, some better words to hold her interest or make her want to talk to him, but nothing came.

Kyle he couldn't wrangle at all. He hung back from his sisters, currently in the phase kids always went through of wanting less and less to be seen with your family —Luke had slowed to walk beside him. "Your uncle tells me your pitching has improved. He said you might go out for the team next spring."

Like Mandy, Kyle simply shrugged and kept on walking.

"You wanna throw me a few pitches sometime? I haven't batted in a long while. You'd probably strike me out in a flash," Luke went on.

Kyle just kept walking.

"I'm trying here, son. Can't we talk a little?"

Finally, Kyle looked at him, but it was the kind of look one gave a piece of rotting meat, not a loved one. "You can stop trying, okay? I don't want to talk to you," Kyle replied. "You don't care about us. I'm glad you're gone. I don't blame mom for divorcing you. You were never there when we needed you."

Luke had seeped back, frozen, like he'd been shot, a painful tightness in his throat. He couldn't remember the last time words had stung him more. It was as if his heartbeat had pause inside his chest. Kyle couldn't really mean that, could he? "I'm glad you're gone," the words echoed through his mind over and over. It was a terrible thing to hear from your son, and an even more terrible thing to say if you didn't mean it.

As Luke turned the car onto Anna's street, Cassie started to cry. "Please come home with us, daddy. We miss you." She kept repeating it over and over through sniffles and sobs.

Luke's heart just broke into a million pieces. He didn't know what to say. He wanted the same thing as she did. How could he make her understand?

LUKE SHOOK OFF the memory and concentrated on mixing the pumpkin with the spices, struggling to regain his focus. The Pizza World trip had been the last time he'd bothered to schedule time with the kids. After that, he'd just assumed a break would do them some good. What was the old saying: Absence makes the heart grow fonder? He sure hoped that was true. In any case, he'd focused on training the new vice president, and making sure the company had an especially good sales run for Christmas, so there was plenty to do. He found himself hoping that his kids had missed him during the two months as much as he'd missed them. He'd wanted to call them so many times, but restrained himself. He didn't want to hear those words again: "I'm glad you're gone." What if Mandy said it this time, or even Cassie? He couldn't bear to know that all three of his kids felt that way, haunted by the fact that just one might really mean it.

Luke pushed it out of his mind for now, refocusing his energy on pouring the newly mixed filling into the pie shells he'd prepared earlier. He found himself hoping there could somehow be more good times ahead than bad. Something far better than the last visit he'd had with his kids, or even with Anna. He said a quiet prayer. *Please God, help us to love each other just for one day the way we used to.* Was it too much to ask for? He did consider it a small miracle he was requesting. Still, it was their first Christmas together since the divorce. He hoped his family, as much as he, didn't want memories of another bad Christmas. Maybe they could put aside their differences for one day and just be a family again. For his part, Luke would try his hardest. He only hoped the rest of them would, too.

When the pies came out of the oven later, he was pleased with the results. His wasn't perfect, but it was edible. He'd known not to expect too much of himself. He was pretty sure he could make another one, and that his kids would want to eat it. For Luke, that was enough. The goal of taking this class had been accomplished. In two days, he had an even bigger goal to achieve.

CHAPTER 4

LUKE PREPARED HIS pies on Christmas Eve morning, carefully mixing the ingredients exactly as he had written it all down during his culinary class. Then, when he finished mixing the filling, carefully poured it into the premade pie crusts he'd bought at the store. He smoothed off the top of each pie with a spatula and then carefully covered them with wax paper before lifting them and setting them, one at a time, on the counter. When he was finished, he smiled, pleased with himself, then went to wash his hands.

After turning on the oven to let it warm up, he concentrated his energy on getting his Christmas cards ready to take to the post office. They wouldn't arrive until after Christmas, but at least he was sending cards this year, his first time since the divorce. Somehow each name he read off his list reminded him of some moment with the family—time spent with the friends to whom he was addressing a card. His list was small, but the people one it had been through a lot with them—good times and bad. He found himself hoping there could be more good times ahead again.

Luke hadn't done much decorating at home. For one thing, Anna had taken all their Christmas decorations when she'd moved out, and, like the furniture, he'd never bothered to replace them. The previous Christmas he'd been too depressed to want any part of the Christmas spirit, but earlier that week, he'd found a small pre-decorated Christmas tree at Schnucks Supermarket and put it up in the front window on a small table as soon as he'd unpacked the groceries. Plugging it in, the glow of the lights against the tinsel made him smile. He actually felt a warmth swelling inside—somehow the magic of Christmas didn't seem so distant today.

He stared at the tree for a moment, then began singing Christmas carols as he went to work on the pies. He started with "Jingle Bells" then followed with "Winter Wonderland," working his way through "O Little Town of Bethlehem," "Angels We Have Heard On High" and "O Holy Night," before finishing with his favorite, "Silent Night." He sang the first verse in both English and German. Luke knew he wasn't a very gifted singer, but with no one around to hear him, he belted out the songs like he was Frank Sinatra or Tony Bennett.

As he went to check on the oven, the phone rang. For just a minute, he worried Anna had changed her mind and was calling to cancel. He frowned, hesitating to answer, and then finally picked it up.

"Hey, big brother. How's it going?" It was his brother Ray.

"Fine, Ray. How are you?" The smile disappeared from his face.

"Good. So, I hear you're going to Anna's?"

Ray and Grace loved to gossip about him. It was something that particularly annoyed him, probably because he constantly seemed to be the last one to hear any family news, while they kept each other readily informed.

"Yes, I am."

"All right. Well, I hope it works out for you, buddy. But listen, I had Julia set an extra place for you just in case."

Luke frowned. Ray never did have any tact. He just said whatever was on his mind. "I won't need it, but thanks."

Ray had always been the family troublemaker, but he'd also been the kind of guy all the ladies loved. Blessed with good looks and charm, Ray always seemed to sail through the most perilous situations unscathed. On the other hand, Luke adored Ray's wife, Julia. She was from a small Brazilian city called Mariana. She had come over as a tourist and met Ray in a bar. Ray had sworn he'd never get married, but Julia had him talking about it in less than three months. They'd worked out the immigration and were married eight months later. Grace thought it would never last, but Luke figured anyone more charming than Ray stood a pretty good chance.

"Didn't mean to tick you off, Luke. I just wanted you to know we're there if you need us, okay?"

Luke rolled his eyes. Ray hadn't been much support this past year. It had been Grace who'd helped him through. Somehow Anna had managed to take to Ray though. She'd confided in him all their marital issues. Ray had been the first to know when she decided to leave Luke. And it was Ray who had come over to explain things, when Luke arrived home from his business trip to find his house empty and his life a shambles. Luke had never resented Ray's charming nature more than at that moment.

"Seriously. Julia would love to see you. She sends beijos," Ray added. Beijo was Portuguese for kisses, a common greeting among Brazilians.

Luke was so distracted by his thoughts that he almost spilled filling out of the pies as he placed them in the oven. He grabbed the spatula and calmly smoothed off the surfaces again. "I'm not mad. Tell Julia I appreciate the kindness. I'll try and stop by soon to see you guys, okay?"

"Okay. We've got big news to tell you anyway, so come by. Anyway, she's making that Brazilian flan you love."

As Luke set down the spatula and closed the oven door, he licked his lips. He could almost taste it—his favorite dessert in the world—the Brazilian caramel custard. He'd discovered it when Julia brought it to a family gathering a few summers before and it blew his mind. Since then she'd made sure to prepare it whenever Luke came over.

"I have to try to make things work with the kids, Ray. You know I'd love to see your charming wife any time, but I just don't know." He finished wiping up the spilled filling and draped the towel over the middle bar of the stainless-steel sink.

"Stop by on your way home, okay? We're always up late anyway."

"I'll try." Luke hung up the phone. Another thing about Ray was he never gave up. The word "no" wasn't in his vocabulary—at least not the vocabulary of his ears. He loved saying it. He just wouldn't accept it from anyone else.

Snowflakes glinted against thin rays of sunlight as they landed on the windowpanes like tiny crystals. It was starting to look Christmassy white outside. Luke heard carolers across the street serenading his elderly neighbor and smiled. Last year, he'd dreaded their arrival. This year, he sang along softly to himself. Maybe he could even help Cassie make a snowman. He used to love to do that with Kyle and Mandy when they were younger. He was sure they wouldn't be into it now, but Cassie would be.

He stared again at the presents he'd placed around the small tree. The packages were actually larger than the tree, but it made him happy putting them there. He couldn't help but imagine what his kids' expressions would be the moment they opened them. For a moment, he worried that Anna might have bought the same things, but then he dismissed that. He'd just try and get them to open his first. That way, if they got another from Anna, one of them could be exchanged, but the joy they'd experience would be for his.

He quickly chided himself for being selfish. It was unfair to Anna to think that way, even childish. But then again, Luke was the one who needed to heal things with his kids. Why shouldn't he get the chance to thrill them on Christmas? Anna was with them every day. He'd hardly seen them for a year.

By the time he got back from the post office, he was too tired to do any more cooking. The pies had turned out perfect and were cooling in the fridge. He'd finished a hastily ordered pizza just in time to head to church. The candlelight service had always been special to Luke, but he'd missed it the past two years—last year, because he was too depressed, and the year before because he'd been on a business trip and his flight had been delayed until almost midnight on Christmas Eve.

The church itself occupied a classic building from the 1940s, the kind that appear particularly traditional on the outside, but which had been renovated so many times, the inside failed to match. Still, the light-yellow walls and blue carpeting made it a pleasant place to worship. Traditional pews had long ago been retired and replaced with more comfortable padded chairs, easily moved and rearranged into a variety of configurations as the event or attendance required. Luke and Anna had liked it from the start, especially the warmth of the congregation, which was a collection of friendly faces and welcoming people, who had been surprisingly supportive for Luke after Anna left and started attending another congregation in Webster Grove with the kids.

That night, the worship songs praising God for His blessings took on new meaning for Luke. The musicians were good, and they'd brought in special instruments to add holiday flavor, like a harp and some trumpets, which made it particularly powerful. He'd always liked the contemporary praise melodies and simple words, but this time they really seemed to reflect what he felt in his heart. God had answered his prayers, and Luke was overcome with joy and thankfulness, recognizing, as never before, the blessings in his life were from God.

CHAPTER 5

ANNA AWOKE ON Christmas morning from a very restless night of sleep. Not only had she stayed up late wrapping last-minute presents and arranging things under the tree, but she couldn't stop thinking about Luke. He hadn't wanted the divorce, and there had been real distance between him and the entire family for so long. Maybe it was a mistake inviting him to Christmas Day. Her parents were dead, her brother and his family were at the in-laws, and her sister lived in Dayton, so she wouldn't have any other adults around to run interference. Still, Anna knew what it would mean to her kids, and she couldn't bear to cancel.

They'd first met during the birthday party of her friend Michelle at college. Luke had been immediately smitten with her. For Anna, it took some convincing. He was a bit of a loner and hadn't dated much. He'd only come to the party because his roommate's had razzed him about being anti-social. He was handsome enough, but not very good at making small talk. Anna was a freshman and Luke a junior, and she wasn't at all sure she wanted any kind of commitment. Luke had followed her around all night, bringing her drinks, a plate of snacks— anything she wanted. She hadn't minded that at all, and eventually, he won her over. Within a month, they were inseparable.

The things she'd always questioned at first soon became the

most special parts of Luke. He didn't have a lot of close friendships, so it was easy to get him to devote time and attention to her. He wasn't good at small talk, so she rarely worried about him flirting with anyone else. Besides, it was obvious Luke was crazy about her from the first time they met. Anna never felt more special than when she was with him. He made her feel like a movie star or a princess. What else could any girl hope for? On top of that, he was dedicated enough to want to make something of himself, yet not so serious that he couldn't have fun. Like any woman, Anna wanted security, especially since she'd never been particularly career-oriented herself. She wanted a good husband and great kids, and the stability to enjoy it. She quickly realized Luke was very likely to provide all of those things, and within a month or two she was as crazy about him, as he was about her.

Looking back now, she wondered how they'd gotten so off track. The marriage had lasted eleven years, six months. They'd long ago lost the closeness she'd always treasured. This wasn't the perfect husband and happy family she'd always dreamed of, and no matter how hard she pleaded, Luke wasn't hearing her. He'd gone from being obsessed with her to being obsessed with his publishing plant. She had lost the contest, and she didn't know how to live like that.

She decided the only way to get back some of the happiness her family had once enjoyed was to break it apart, so when Luke went away on a long business trip after Thanksgiving, she had prearranged for movers to come and move her and the kids to the two story Colonial she'd inherited from her favorite aunt in Webster Groves. The house was warm and homey, with a newly remodeled kitchen and the latest in appliances—the inside decorated in a way that complemented the Colonial exterior.

When they'd first moved in, Kyle had commented it was weird living in a museum, but it had come to feel like home now. Anna loved the way the house creaked sometimes, as if it was stretching after a long nap. Its older construction was solid, so it never caused her worry. Instead she'd come to consider it almost like the voice of the house crying out to remind her it was still there.

Although for most of the past two years she'd been angry at Luke, she didn't hate him. In his own way, Luke had done what he did to provide a better life for her and the kids. She hadn't resented their comfortable lifestyle at all, but she also hadn't been prepared for the sacrifices Luke would be willing to make of their time together and time for their kids. For the final two years of their marriage, she'd felt like a single parent, and whenever she took the kids to visit friends, their husbands were always there, participating, while hers was too busy at work. Being a married single parent got old really quick, and it wasn't at all what she'd bargained for. She'd started to feel more like a mistress than a beloved spouse. She resented him for losing track of his priorities. She resented him for losing the passion that had made them inseparable in the past, and it hurt that she wasn't interesting or beautiful enough to hold his attention anymore.

When Luke seemed to have lost interest in the kids, too, Anna just couldn't take anymore. She didn't want to watch her kids grow up with a father who didn't care about them, or at least thinking he didn't care. Deep down, she knew Luke loved all of them, but if he didn't realize that love needs to be demonstrated not just implied, then she wasn't about to let her kids suffer. He needed a wakeup call, like her father.

Oh, Luke had protested, of course. He'd yelled and complained and accused her of abandoning him. But he'd never once acknowledged his own role in it, as if in his mind everything had been perfect, and she'd imagined the whole thing. But there had been no sincere admission of guilt or apology. Nothing like what her father had offered on her grandparents' dirt drive twenty years before. The kids protested less than she'd anticipated. Kyle and Mandy acted as if it didn't matter, and Cassie just kept asking when her daddy would be coming to their new house.

She sat up on the side of the bed and slid into her robe and slippers, then glanced at the clock—seven forty-five and not a peep from the kids. That was unusual. She opened the door to her room and listened for any sound. The house was quiet. Usually the kids were up at the crack of dawn on Christmas morning. Last year's Christmas had been a disaster, because of the divorce, but she hoped it hadn't ruined their Christmas spirit forever. She'd told Luke to come over around nine for opening the presents and had anticipated having to struggle to hold the kids off that long. Now it seemed maybe she'd gotten lucky somehow.

They'd gone the night before to the eleven o'clock candlelight service at their new church. It had been hard for Cassie, but the kids usually didn't sleep well Christmas Eve night anyway, and she'd hoped it would encourage them to sleep in just a little longer. Apparently the plan had worked. She headed for the kitchen to get started warming and preparing their usual Christmas morning breakfast. For years, she'd been serving Swedish tea ring and an egg and sausage casserole. The kids really loved it and it was a special treat. Luckily, there was a bakery nearby owned by Swedish immigrants. Otherwise, she might have had to drive back to Clayton for the tea ring, which would have been out of the way.

Since the divorce, Anna had gone back to work. Her aunt and parents had been wealthy, and left her comfortable through their wills, but Anna didn't like to be idle. Though the kids kept busy with activities, she at least wanted to have something of her own to talk about when she saw her friends. Besides, the part-time job at Sam's Club had turned out to be a perfect fit. She enjoyed the employee discount, and they arranged her schedule so she only had to work while the kids were at school. It was enough extra income to provide a buffer, and enough activity to keep her from boring days by the pool reading or exchanging gossip with other women. Anna had never been much into gossip.

As she slid the casserole into the microwave and set the timer, she heard a rustling on the stairs. Shutting the microwave door, she stepped back and peered out into the living room to see Cassie yawning and moving quickly toward the tree. Anna's heart tingled watching her youngest looking so cute in her pajamas and bunny slippers. She hurried out to intercept. Most of the presents were wrapped but she didn't want Cassie getting too overeager since they were waiting for Luke.

"Good morning, sweet pea," she said, tussling Cassie's blonde hair.

Cassie had seen the doll house and was clearly about to start squealing, so Anna captured her in a bear hug and began ticking her. "Mommy! Stop! I want to see!"

"We have to wait for daddy. Don't you remember?"

"Ah, Mommy. Just a little, can't I?"

The smell of warm eggs and sausage teased Anna's nose as the casserole heated. "Why don't you come help me with setting the table? We have to wait for Kyle and Mandy, too. Besides, aren't you hungry?"

Cassie rolled her eyes. Clearly she would rather play, but she acquiesced as Anna took her hand and led her toward the kitchen. "Is Daddy coming soon?"

"He'll be here in thirty minutes, okay? Would you like a candy cane and some eggnog while you wait?"

"It would be so much easier if Daddy just lived here, Mommy."

Anna couldn't help but smile. The blunt innocence and endless hope of children always amazed her. "You know Daddy doesn't live with us now, honey. That's just the way it is."

"Bah humbug," Cassie muttered, accepting the candy cane Anna offered and waiting patiently as Anna poured eggnog into a plastic cup.

Anna chuckled. They'd gone to see Kyle in 'A Christmas Carol' at his school the previous week. Kyle had played the Ghost of Christmas Future, and Cassie had picked up some of the phrases, offering them up whenever she felt they were appropriate—sometimes with quite comical results.

As Anna arranged the plates and silverware, Kyle and Mandy

appeared in the doorway, both dressed in t-shirts and pajama bottoms. Mandy had on pink slippers with High School Musical: The Series logos on them. Of all the kids, she was the one who looked the most like Anna, with long dark hair and pale skin. Kyle had Luke's eyes and body type, but he had darker hair like Anna and Mandy. He was starting to show signs of puberty and looking less the little boy like his parents still thought of him. Both had clearly already taken their own peek at the Christmas tree and moved past her looking to get breakfast started as quickly as possible. Luke and Anna had always insisted on sitting down for breakfast before the kids opened presents. The older two knew the routine and were clearly determined to get breakfast over with and move on to the good stuff as quickly as possible.

"Good morning, Mom. Merry Christmas, Mom," Anna said teasingly. They were clearly not awake yet.

"What time's dad coming over?" Kyle said, mid-yawn.

"In thirty minutes," Cassie chirped, taking her own seat at the table.

"We aren't waiting for him for breakfast, are we?" Mandy asked quietly, her shoulders curling forward as her face formed a frown.

"No, sweetie. We can go ahead and eat," Anna replied. All three looked pleased, as she began slicing the tea ring.

"Do you think Daddy remembered presents?" Cassie wondered.

Kyle and Mandy shot her a look. "You know how he is, Cassie. Don't get your hopes up," Mandy said.

"If he does, it's only because Mom reminded him," Kyle said bitterly.

Anna shook her head as she served them all tea ring. "Your dad loves you guys. I know it's hard to believe that sometimes, but he does. He's only worked as hard as he does to make a good life for us." She still felt guilty at the message she'd left on his machine.

"If you believe that, why'd you divorce him then?" Kyle asked as he grabbed the pitcher and poured orange juice into his glass. He'd always had a way of saying just the right thing to make her previous assurances seem false and manufactured.

"It's complicated. You know that." She was saved by the microwave beeping, and hurried off to get the casserole and bring it to the table.

"You guys aren't going to fight all day, are you?" Mandy asked as she poured her own juice.

"Why would you think that?" Anna returned and set the casserole dish on the table, slicing and carefully sliding a piece on Cassie's plate.

"Come on, Mom. You two haven't exactly gotten along the past two years," Kyle said. Of all the kids, he seemed to have taken the divorce the hardest, which made sense to Anna. After all, he was the oldest, and he was a boy, so more immediately affected by the lack of male influence.

"Well, I'm sorry you guys had to see that. The divorce had a lot more to do with having different priorities than it did about fighting, though. I'm sure we can bury the hatchet for Christmas, okay?" Anna hoped she was telling the truth.

"Why'd you invite him anyway?" Kyle frowned, tearing the casserole apart with his fork and moving it around his plate.

"He's your father. He should be with you on Christmas."

"Are you going to feel that way some day when you get remarried?" Kyle shot her a look.

She furrowed her brows at him and rolled her eyes. "Who said anything about getting remarried? I'm not even seeing anyone. You sure have an active imagination today." Anna didn't like hearing him talk this way in front of his sisters, especially at Christmas. "Why don't you use some of that energy to eat your breakfast, okay?"

"Yeah! I want to open presents!" Cassie cheered.

Mandy and Anna laughed as Kyle stabbed a piece of casserole and lifted it toward his mouth.

AS HE ROLLED out of bed Christmas morning, he stumbled to the kitchen, rubbing his eyes as he went, and fixed himself some cereal, then grabbed the morning paper and read through the local news and business section as he waited for the coffee to brew. After he was more awake, he flipped on the Christmas tree lights and watched his elderly neighbors' grandkids build a snowman on her lawn. They seemed to struggle getting one ball on top of another. He was half tempted to go pitch in, but remembered that Evelyn had been very cold to him since Anna left and decided not to go near her grandkids.

The kids finished after a forty-five minutes, decorating the snowman's face with a large carrot nose and two button eyes. They even added a scarf and hat, always an ironic touch Luke thought. Like a man made totally of ice would be bothered by the cold. *Maybe he has issues with his family, too,* Luke wondered.

Luke shook off the negative feelings quickly. Things seemed to be turning around. He had a happy day to look forward to. Between the presents and the pies, and his own heart, he knew his family couldn't help but see he was a changed man. Proving that to them would be his Christmas present to himself. There was absolutely nothing he wanted more.

As he finished breakfast, the phone rang.

The minute he answered he heard his niece Sara's voice, Grace's daughter, whispering, "Do we have to do this?"

"Yes, then we'll open presents," Grace whispered back, causing Luke to smile.

"Okay," Sara said, then counted, "Three...two...one..." She and her siblings, Tod and Charlie, launched into "We Wish You a Merry Christmas" and serenaded him for a moment, finishing with a round of "Merry Christmas, Uncle Luke's" before handing the phone to their mother.

"Merry Christmas, bro," Grace said.

"Merry Christmas, Gracie," he replied.

"How'd the pies come out?"

"Pretty good," Luke said.

"You made new ones, right? You didn't just save the ones from class." From Grace's tone, he could tell that's exactly what she thought he'd done.

"Of course not, brand new," Luke said, rolling his eyes.

"Good," Grace said then paused before adding, "So you're ready for this?"

"Yeah, I'm fine. Feeling great."

"Okay, I hope it goes well," she said. "You can always come over here if you need us."

"Stop torturing your kids and let them open presents. I'll be fine," Luke said, chuckling. She was such a mother hen.

"Okay, see ya," Grace said and hung up.

Luke swung into high gear, rinsing his dishes in the sink and heading for the bedroom to dress before loading the car. The whole time his body buzzed with a warm flow within. It was Christmas and he was off to see his kids. Nothing could be better.

CHAPTER 6

LUKE ARRIVED PROMPTLY at nine, carrying two beautiful looking pumpkin pies. Anna's eyed widened as he lips pursed, looking impressed. The kids, however, were less enthused.

"Didn't you bring any presents?" Cassie wondered.

"I thought you guys loved pumpkin pie. Did you know daddy could make pies, sweetie?" Luke asked, as Anna carefully took the pies and carried them off to the kitchen. His nose caught the scent of rose and something else. She'd switched from the perfume she'd worn since college, Eternity, which was more of a fresh citrus mixed with violet and musk. For a moment, he wondered why the change. Was she seeing someone?

"But I'm not hungry 'cause I just ate," Cassie explained as Luke hugged her, chuckling. She was so adorable. He missed her a lot.

Kyle and Mandy stood further back from the door, shooting him glances while avoiding eye contact. Mandy at least offered him a forced smile when he looked over. Luke remained hostile—arms crossed, eyes narrowed, his brow wrinkled and is jaw set. Luke had hoped the months apart might have softened them a bit, but obviously, neither was overly excited about seeing him.

"No hug for your dad on Christmas?" Luke asked.

Mandy finally met his eyes and sauntered over for a quick hug. Despite the fact her arms hung down stiff at her sides and he did all the work, he felt the warm fuzzies he'd had hugging Cassie, and he found himself hoping for a hug from Kyle, too. "I miss you guys," Luke said.

"Did you remember presents or not?" Kyle said. Obviously he still had hard feelings. He pulled away when Luke approached and tried to hug him.

"They're in the car. Want to help me with them?"

Kyle shrugged and followed Luke back out across the driveway. He opened the back door of the Subaru and handed Kyle a present, then grabbed the other two along with a plastic grocery sack on the seat beside them and swung the door shut. Kyle led the way to the house as Luke followed behind.

Cassie jumped up and down excitedly upon seeing the presents. "I knew Daddy'd remember," she smiled, looking straight at Kyle, who shot her a scowl.

Anna appeared in the doorway again, smiling. "The pies look and smell delicious, Luke." She looked pleased, her voice even friendly.

"I told you I wanted to bring something."

"I had no idea you knew how to cook," she added as he handed her a plastic grocery sack. "What's this?"

"Cool Whip for the pies." Anna nodded her approval as he went on, "I should've gotten something for you, but I didn't think…"

"You already brought more than was expected of you," Anna said, her smile never faltering. Despite the warmth she showed, the words stung. She realized almost immediately, and her eyes offered an apology, but it was too late to take it back. They continued to stare at each other for a moment.

Luke hadn't seen her in months, and seeing her now

reminded him how she'd taken his breath away the first moment he saw her. With her dark eyes, long, dark hair, and pale complexion, she was beautiful in a way that might not have led her to the runway, yet always made her stand out from the crowd. She glowed when she smiled, and Luke had always thought she was just as stunning without makeup in jeans and a ragged t-shirt.

Cassie fidgeted beside him, pulling on his sleeve. "Can we please open presents now?"

Anna and Luke laughed and followed the kids into the living room toward the tree.

The next three hours passed like a dream. The kids reveling in opening their presents just like the old days, while Anna and Luke looked on with delight, taking a few pictures, sipping eggnog. It was a happiness Luke hadn't experienced in too long—like they were a whole family again.

Cassie loved her Easy Bake Oven. It had been rereleased for Toys-R-Us a few Christmases ago, and he'd remembered it from when Grace had one as a kid. She was already clamoring for Anna to help her bake something. Mandy liked the electronic keyboard he'd gotten her. He knew she'd been talking about wanting to learn before the divorce, and he'd hoped Anna hadn't gotten around to getting her one. She was already off in a corner, fiddling with the keys.

The real test had been Kyle. Preteen boys are hard enough to please under normal circumstances, but when they're mad at you, the odds are not in your favor. When Kyle opened the game, his eyes went wide with amazement, his smile so big it could have bridged the ocean. He looked straight at Luke and said: "Wow. I never thought you could come up with something this awesome." And then he'd come over and actually hugged Luke. The uncertainty on Kyle's face as he pulled away after the hug hadn't lessened Luke's joy. Warmth flooded him again, and it was all Luke could do to hold back tears. Anna hadn't even tried. She wiped hers away with her sleeve and smiled at him, offering a thumbs up.

The kids even had presents for Luke. After they'd opened theirs, they each brought them over to him one at a time, and waited while he opened them. Cassie's was a cartoonish tie with a sun and a moon dancing on it. He smiled and hugged her, kissing her cheek.

Mandy's was a new leather wallet. Luke had been carrying the old one around as long as any of them could remember, until it had openings and flaps in it that weren't part of the original design. In fact, he had to use a rubber band to hold it together. Mandy hugged him, too, and kissed him gently on the lips, smiling. "I love you, daddy."

Kyle had bought him two CDs of the rock group KANSAS, one of Luke's childhood favorites. "Supposed to be their newest," he'd offered. Luke wanted another hug, but Kyle moved away quickly again, signaling he wasn't offering.

Just hugging each of them, had required taken extra strength from Luke to let go. He wanted to just keep holding on. It had been so long since he'd held them. He'd realized he missed them before, but now he knew how much. He'd really messed up with his kids, and he knew he had a lot of work to do if he wanted to make it up to them; to repair what had been lost.

The biggest surprise of all came from Anna, when she handed him a gift from herself. "You got me something?" Luke said, totally surprised.

She shrugged. "It's not a big deal. Just something I thought you should have."

He opened it to reveal a bound set of color copies of the kids' school projects from the past year—Cassie's colored drawings, a couple of poems from Mandy, and a short story from Kyle.

"These were the highlights, and you missed them, so I thought you should have a chance to see," Anna explained.

Once again, Luke found himself fighting back tears. He couldn't believe she'd been so thoughtful after the way they'd been fighting. They'd been mad at each other for what seemed like forever, but now all that faded away as he remembered why he'd fallen in love with her in the first place.

Anna had always been good at remembering the details. She always took note when one of the kids or Luke saw something in a store they liked but didn't buy, so she could buy it for them later. She remembered the food, music, and other things he or one of the kids mentioned. She made an effort to share those things with them and appreciate them herself. She knew how much the kids had always meant to Luke, and here she was offering him a little piece of their lives from the time he'd missed.

"It's the best present anyone ever gave me," Luke said, meaning it, as he sat on the couch, flipping through the book. "This whole day has been the best present." *A second chance*, he thought.

Anna leaned back into the couch and sipped her coffee. "I'm glad you like it. I kind of threw it together last minute."

"Now I really feel bad that I didn't get you anything," he said.

She shrugged. "I didn't have to worry about pies."

Kyle chortled. "She made backups just in case."

Anna's and Luke's eyes met and they both laughed. Luke had been pretty sure she'd do that, now Kyle had confirmed it. That was just like her, but the graciousness to pretend meant a lot to him all the same. It was the nicest moment they'd had in a long time.

Anna and Mandy went into the kitchen to prepare the meal as Luke, Kyle, and Cassie gathered up the wrapping paper, bows, and other remnants and threw them in a large barrel trash can. Kyle worked hurriedly so he could get on with playing his new game. Cassie hugged Luke when they were finished, then went over to play with her doll house. Luke simply enjoyed watching their delight. It had been so long since he'd gotten to do that, he'd almost forgotten what it was like. There was nothing in the world quite as wonderful as watching your kids' joy.

He thought back on their lives before everything fell apart. The times they'd played together. He'd done all the usual sports stuff with Kyle—tossing baseballs, practicing batting, soccer, football. Mandy had been big into tea parties from around age five until a couple of years ago. She'd gotten a tea set from Anna's parents, and she adored setting up a miniature table with her dolls and inviting her daddy to join her. Each doll had a name, and she made up such intricate stories about their lives and activities that Luke had a hard time keeping up with it all.

Cassie had always delighted in swings and blocks and dolls—all simple things. She was three when his work started taking over his life, and only four when Anna left him. Seeing her now, he knew he couldn't bear to miss all those special years ahead. He'd seen Mandy and Kyle growing up into their own little individuals, and he wanted to same thing with Cassie, too. Plus, there was a lot more left to experience with Mandy and Kyle as well.

Anna's parents had died six months before she left him. They'd been run over by a semi-truck while waiting to merge onto highway 270 off 64. The truck driver had been distracted by his cell phone and ran over a whole line of cars, crushing eight vehicles and causing several deaths. Thirteen people had gone to the hospital with critical injuries. It was a horrific accident—the kind of thing you never thought would happen to anyone you knew. Anna had been devastated, and her grief had only been compounded by a husband who was too busy at the office to give her the support she'd needed to grieve.

With his own mother gone, too, more than ever, he wanted to be there for his kids at those special moments that families should share. He wanted that for himself, too. Somehow he'd let himself become one of those fathers who didn't know his own kids, and he didn't like it at all. He said a silent prayer to God to help him stay on course. He prayed he would always remember these moments and treasure them as inspiration for whatever lay ahead. Now, here he was getting a second chance, and he was determined to let this day mark the beginning of a fresh new start.

Anna called them to dinner about forty-five minutes later as the wonderful cornucopia of holiday smells from turkey and gravy to hot buttered rolls and green bean casserole filled their noses and made Luke's mouth water. The turkey had been cooked on a timer over night, so Anna had just had to reheat it and prepare the gravy and vegetables.

When they gathered around the table, Luke took it all in with amazement. Anna had always been a fantastic cook, and he knew his tongue and stomach were in for a wonderful treat. They held hands and prayed as a family, with each one offering words about something they were thankful for. Luke said many more words silently to God than he shared around the table.

Cassie kept it simple: "I'm thankful that my daddy came home for Christmas." Once again, Luke fought back tears.

The food was as delicious as expected, and though they mostly ate, a pleasant chit chat passed between them as they shared the table. When they'd finished, Luke insisted on prepping the pies himself, so everyone waited while Luke disappeared into the kitchen. He returned moments later with two pies, the plastic container of Cool Whip, and serving utensils then began asking each family member what they'd like.

After Luke had served them all and rejoined them at the table, Kyle took a bite, his eyes bulging with pleasant surprise as he fought back a smile. "It's actually really good."

Anna and the girls laughed as Luke shrugged. "Hey, what'd you expect?"

"Sorry, Dad, but you never cooked before," Kyle said, stuffing his mouth with another bite.

"Well, people can change. Besides, I wasn't home much." Luke watched as the girls and Anna also enjoyed his creations. Kyle and Mandy even asked for seconds.

"Who taught you?" Anna couldn't resist asking, as she finished her last bite of pie.

"I took a class at a culinary school," Luke explained.

"Really? Just one class? When?" Anna looked even more impressed.

"Monday and Thursday," he replied.

She reacted. "This past Thursday, December twenty-third?"

Luke raised his palms like a game show model, and they both laughed.

"Good job, dad," Mandy said, licking her lips. He reached over and tousled her hair. "Maybe you can show me sometime."

Anna chortled, shaking her head. "Never thought I'd hear our kids say that."

"Me neither," Luke confessed, chuckling with her as they each finished their pie.

CHAPTER 7

WHEN DINNER WAS over, the kids ran off to play with their presents again, while Luke helped Anna clear the table and load the dishwasher. "I'm really glad you came over, Luke," she finally said.

"I'm really glad you invited me," he responded as she gently set a stack of plates on the counter. "It took me by surprise."

Luke had really surprised her. The presents he'd gotten were perfect, and the pies! She'd never imagined Luke making Christmas pies, especially ones that tasted so great. Even now, she was still blown away. Luke had clearly decided to make an effort to set things right, and she was more than happy to encourage it. When she'd first considered inviting him, her friends had warned her she was asking for trouble. Now she was pleased with how it had gone. She knew she'd done the right thing.

"I really want you to be a part of the kids' lives, Luke. They still need you, even if things didn't work for us," she said as she finished saran wrapping bowls of stuffing and cranberry sauce.

"I need them, too," he said, rinsing the plates before placing them in the dishwasher.

"You really did a good job with the presents today. And you did and said all the right things. To be honest, I'd almost thought you'd forgotten how to do this."

She meant it as a compliment. He saw that in her eyes and smiled. "I thought so, too."

She was pleased hearing him admit that. In the past, whenever she'd confronted him about it, he'd acted as if he hadn't done anything wrong. But today had been like an admission of guilt, an apology. Could he really have changed so much so quickly? For a moment, she considered telling him everything. So much had happened the past few months. Her entire life had been transformed, yet somehow, she couldn't bring herself to do it. What if he just been lucky? What if it didn't last? He seemed sincere enough, but she couldn't take the chance. She needed to know this was real.

Luke watched her. In the old days, he could almost read her mind, but this time he simply looked at her, as if he wondered what she was thinking. "Anything you want to talk about?"

Anna had been thinking about what she would say for a long time. She finished putting the leftovers away in the refrigerator then turned to him and nodded. "I was just thinking about how different you seem. Wondering how you could have changed this much?"

"Well, I've had a lot of time to think."

"Apparently it's done you good," she teased.

Luke's face formed a scowl and they both laughed. It was good to enjoy time together again. "If you want to spend time with them, you should," Anna added. "I think it's good for them to know you still care and start healing the rift between you."

"I never meant for there to be a rift," Luke said, wincing as he stared down at his hands.

"We both never meant a lot of things, but they happened. Now we have to deal with them."

Luke nodded. "I'd like that." It had been a long time since they'd been able to talk like this.

"Your children need you. They need to have a relationship

with you, and even though we're not together. I want to make it work for you to spend time with them and rebuild that bond you once had."

Luke pondered her sincerity as if he wasn't quite sure what to make of it.

Noticing his puzzled expression, she asked, "You're wondering why I'm being so nice?"

"Exactly. It wasn't what I'd call an amicable divorce," Luke responded, wiping his hands dry on the dish towel.

"I left you because I had to, for me and for the kids. Because I couldn't take being ignored any more. Because I knew we could never go back to the way it was when we first met," she explained. "I was mad at you for a long time, but now...the kids need their father. And I can't punish them any longer for my issues."

"I'm sorry, Anna," he said, meaning more than just about the kids.

"I know." She reached out and laid her hand gently on his forearm. "And if it hadn't been so obvious today that you're willing to make an effort, we might not be having this conversation. But you were great today, and the kids needed that, so I want you to know I'll support of your spending time with them, if you want that."

"You know I do," he answered. After a moment, he went on, "I never meant to hurt any of you. I never meant to ignore you. I wanted a better life for us..."

Her eyes locked on his as she gave an understanding nod. "I always knew that, but your priorities were out of whack. It wasn't the life I wanted for me or the kids." She knew in her heart that he hadn't wanted that life for them either.

For a moment, their eyes met and she could tell he had a question but was hesitant to ask. Finally, she prompted him, "What is it?"

"I noticed you've changed perfumes," he said hesitantly.

Then, after another pause, "Is there any significance to that?"

The question startled her, but then she realized he thought she'd met another man, that she was seeing someone else. Her first reaction was anger and she tensed, wanting to tell him it was none of his business anymore. But then she realized she was being silly. If she'd noticed something similar, she'd have asked, too. "No," she finally said. "I just wanted a change."

Their eyes met again and Luke seemed to accept that she'd told him the truth.

"It's nice," he said.

They finished the cleanup in silence and Luke turned on the dishwasher. Suddenly, they both realized the house was awfully quiet. They exchanged a look and hurried into the living room. Cassie had fallen asleep on the floor beside her doll house. Mandy was asleep on the couch, television remote still clasped in her hand, while cartoons flickered on the television. Kyle was still busy playing his game with headphones on, oblivious to everything else.

Luke watched the kids for a while, while Anna went upstairs for a nap. When Cassie and Mandy awoke, he played the game Sorry with them. Kyle stayed wrapped up in his video game. Later, after Anna got up, Luke said goodnight, hugged the girls, and headed for Ray's.

After feeding the kids leftovers for dinner, Anna poured herself a cup of coffee and sat in her favorite chair to read a book she'd gotten as a present. It was a new Nicholas Sparks novel she'd been waiting to get in paperback. She opened the book, but her mind was still racing with thoughts of all that had happened that day. Luke had handled everything so well, and she thought about how it had made her feel to see him again, how the kids reacted. It had all gone much better than she'd ever anticipated. He wasn't out of water with the kids or her yet, but today he'd given them a glimpse of the old Luke, the one they'd missed for so long—the Luke she fell in love with. For the first time in ages, she'd felt a bit of the old magic she'd thought was long past. She wasn't falling in love again. For her, their life together was over. But it was a nice memory, and it softened some of the hardness toward him she'd been carrying in her heart for so long.

She could tell when Luke left that he'd been a little disappointed. Except for the immediate reactions to their presents, the older two hadn't given Luke much attention, and he'd obviously been hoping for more. But Anna was sure it would take a number of visits to positively reinforce the fresh start Luke had made. It was altogether the best day they'd had as a family in a long time, and she hoped it had changed things for the better for all of them.

Even the kids had reacted better than she'd hoped for, especially Kyle. He'd been quieter and more introverted since they'd separated. She knew he missed his dad, and it had to be hard for a boy that age to not have the male influence. Ray, Luke's brother, had taken him out once a month, and that helped, but he needed more. She knew he felt rejected and blamed himself, and she'd tried to convince him that wasn't the case, yet every time she brought it up, he just got angry. Luke's gift had clearly pleased him, but Anna knew it would take a lot more than that to heal their relationship.

With the girls, it was easier, because they still had their mom, and Cassie was so young she didn't deal with things on the same intellectual level as the other two. But it had been Cassie's tears which had finally pushed Anna to invite Luke over. Her school had had a father-daughter event, and her friends were all going. Cassie had wanted to go so badly. Anna had sent Luke the information by email at the office, but he'd never responded, so when the night came, Cassie sat at home, crying and asking, "Why doesn't my daddy want to be with me anymore?" How did you answer a question like that from your child? It was unbearable.

Mandy had always been the most introverted of the three. She rarely spoke out loud about her feelings or thoughts, keeping them to herself. But Anna knew she was old enough to feel the same guilt and fears that Kyle did about things being her fault. Anna had talked to her about it, too, telling her that sometimes adults had problems they couldn't fix, and even though mommy and daddy loved their kids very much, their marriage didn't work, but that wasn't the kids' fault. Mandy had nodded and hugged her as if she understood, but Anna never really knew what was going inside her mind. From the way she'd interacted with Luke today, though, Anna felt confident progress had been made.

The ringing phone interrupted her thoughts. She walked into the kitchen to answer it, seeing Mandy and Cassie playing nicely with Cassie's doll house beneath the tree. She smiled as she said, "Hello?"

"I'm dying to know how it went." It was her best friend, Brenda. A dark-skinned brunette who dressed, looked and talked like a businesswoman, despite the fact that she was a housewife, Brenda had it all together, and Anna admired her for it.

Anna glanced back in the living room to make sure the kids wouldn't be listening, then took the cordless phone and moved further into the kitchen. "It went better than I had ever thought it could," she confessed.

"Really? Luke was on his best behavior?"

"It was more than that," Anna answered. "Luke was like a different person."

"Really? Wow. Details." Brenda had clearly expected to hear the worst.

"The gifts were perfect. The kids went nuts for them. And can you believe he actually made two pumpkin pies, and they were delicious?"

"Are you serious? Luke in the kitchen? That had to be a sight!"

They both laughed at the thought.

"He was kind, thoughtful, fun—like the man I fell in love with. He even helped me clean up after," Anna said, still amazed by it all herself.

"Oh honey, I'm so happy for you. That's encouraging," Brenda said, sounding pleased, but then her tone changed as she asked, "Did you tell him?"

Anna had known that was coming. The truth was she'd almost wanted to tell him, but it wasn't time yet. She needed to be sure. "No. I didn't tell him that. But I did tell him I welcome him spending time with the kids, that they need him, and I would like to see him restore the relationship."

"He should know, Anna," Brenda said, sounding like a scolding older sister.

"I'll tell him when the time's right," Anna responded as she leaned against the counter near the sink. The diagnosis was something she still struggled coming to terms with, but to share it with Luke would mean she would mean she was that much closer to telling the kids, and the thought of hurting them again was so hard to bear. "I have to know this change is real first. That it's going to last."

"You can't afford to wait too long," Brenda reminded her.

"I just need a little more time to see what he does with this second chance, okay?" Anna wasn't annoyed, just trying to explain.

Brenda chuckled. "Sounds like you've got things under control, then. I'm glad it went well. Merry Christmas."

"Merry Christmas to you, too," Anna said, relieved Brenda didn't push her further. "You haven't told me about your Christmas yet?"

As Brenda filled Anna in about her family's gathering, Anna silently said a prayer of thanks for the blessing of good friends. Without Brenda and their friend Bekah, Anna would have never had the strength to do what she'd had to do the past two years. They had been such a good support for her, and their kids adored each other. Even their husbands, Dave and John, had been supportive, helping her with moving, handyman work—whatever she needed. Both families included her and the kids in their outings. Really, they were more than friends for her. They were like family. Recently, more than ever, family had been foremost on Anna's mind.

When Brenda finished her story a few minutes later, Anna yawned and mentioned she had to get the kids headed for bed soon, so they promised to get together in a few days and said their good nights before Anna slid the phone back on its charger and went to check on her kids.

CHAPTER 8

ON THE WAY to Ray and Julia's house, Luke continued thinking about all that had happened that day. He was thankful that things had gone well and said a prayer of thanks for blessed time with Anna and the kids. He knew it was only the beginning and that a lot of work would have to be done to restore the relationships, but the whole thing had gone so much better than he'd ever anticipated, leaving him feeling encouraged about future possibilities.

As he climbed out of the car and headed up his brother's drive, he took in the world around him. Stars glittered in the night sky like tinsel through Christmas lights, and the cold, clean air rushed through him like the breath of a new day. The welcoming glow of Christmas trees from windows around him sent rays of happiness through his heart. He'd been living in such a daze for so long, it felt good to have these sensations again. Anna had looked at him today like he was a totally new man, and in moments like this, Luke truly felt that way. At least he was trying to be a better man. He figured that was a good place to start.

His brother's house was a one level with three bedrooms in an older neighborhood. It was a good starter home, the kind many young couples invested in. Julia greeted him at the door with a big smile and a kiss on each cheek, a Brazilian tradition. She was younger than Ray, mid-twenties, short like Grace, and dark-skinned, but that just made her beautiful white smile shine even brighter. She led him inside to where Ray and Grace were playing with Grace's kids, while Grace's husband, Karl, stoked the fire nearby. Ray was taller than Luke, and skinny as a rail. He had tattoos on his upper arms from some past night of too much drinking. He still dressed like a frat boy most of the time, despite the fact that he was past thirty. Karl was an ex-quarterback who had played for Missouri State. He'd turned thirty last year and now worked as a manager at Target.

They all looked up and shouted greetings as he walked in. The youngest child, Charlie—short for Charlene—ran to hug him as he took of his coat and gloves. He shook hands with Ray and Karl, and then Grace hugged him, while searching his eyes to determine what might have happened that day.

"Well," she finally said, "are you going to tell us about it or what?"

Luke shrugged. "It was a good day."

Ray and Karl laughed at the way Grace squirmed. She was dying for the full scoop as always. She scrunched her face and stared at him again. "Is that all you're going to say?"

"The kids liked the presents," Luke added with a smirk.

Then Charlie grabbed his arm and dragged him over by the tree to show him her presents. Grace and Ray exchanged a look and Ray shrugged, as if to say 'give him time.'

In the meantime, Julia motioned to Ray. "Fala, amor," she urged him. Luke knew his brother loved when she spoke Portuguese in that sexy accent of hers.

"I'm waiting for the right moment," Ray replied.

Grace rolled her eyes and moved toward Luke. "Luke, Julia's pregnant."

Ray ran toward her as she hurried away, just out of reach. "You never could keep a secret," Ray said, annoyed.

"You were going to tell him anyway. And you were being

such a chicken about it," Grace responded as Luke looked at Julia and Ray with a big smile on his face. Julia hugged him again, and Ray shook his hand even more firmly the second time.

"Congratulations, you two, I'm so happy for you," Luke said. "What a nice Christmas present."

"It is, isn't it?" Julia said, beaming ear-to-ear.

"Baby brother's growing up and becoming a responsible man, I guess," Karl said, teasing.

Grace made a face. "Like that's even possible."

Ray resumed chasing her around the room as she laughed loudly, narrowly shifting her body to miss Sara, who was playing on the floor.

Luke, Karl, and Julia watched them running around and laughed. "Will those two ever grow up?" Julia asked.

Karl and Luke shook their heads and laughed again.

"Where's Dad?" Luke asked.

"He went home to rest. It was a long day for him," Julia explained. Luke's father, Lee, hadn't been the same since their mother's death. It was almost as if he'd aged ten years over night—his hair graying, skin wrinkling. He looked like an old man now, Luke thought, every time he saw him.

Luke watched as Karl knelt to play with his son, Tod, who had a new Tonka truck. It brought back memories of years ago, playing with Kyle. Sometimes, Luke wished he could go back and do those days over; appreciate them a little more. But he knew he couldn't. He had to figure out a way to reconnect with the twelve-year-old who had long ago left those things behind. No matter what it took he wanted to be a part of his kids' lives again the way Karl was now and Ray would be.

He spent a lovely couple hours with his family before heading home to bed. He had to work in the morning, and he it had been a good but exhausting day.

THE END OF the year was always a busy time for at the office. Between working with the accountant on end of year bonuses and wrapping up the books, the days between Christmas and New Years were some of the longest of the year for Luke. For once, he didn't even notice. He was so relieved to have succeeded in reconnecting with his family that the days floated by like a leaf on the wind. Cassie called twice to hear her daddy's voice, but both times he'd been on another call and couldn't talk. He did manage to call the kids on Wednesday and ask what they were doing for New Years, thanking them for their presents again. The girls sounded happy to hear from him, but Kyle was harder to read over the phone.

Luke arranged to pick them up on New Year's Day and take them skating at the rink in Forest Park. It was something they used to do together as a family, and he figured starting with the traditions was a good way to rebuild. He'd invited Anna to come along, but she'd declined, claiming she had Christmas cards to finish and end of the year bills to deal with. Luke was surprised at how much it disappointed him that she wouldn't be there. Despite the fact his heart was still broken over their failed marriage, he'd been focused so much on what had happened between him and the kids that he hadn't taken much time to think about what had happened between him and Anna.

One of the largest urban parks in the entire country, Forest Park contained, among other things, the State History museum, the city Art Museum, and a collection of buildings built for the 1904 World's Fair, now being used for various other purposes. It also was home to the city zoo, a respected institution known for being family-friendly and one of the more innovative zoos in the nation. In recent years, the zoo had renovated its exhibits to include an area incorporating glass walled viewing stations and more natural habitats for many of the animals. They had also been blessed with the birth of baby elephants and other newborns sure to delight and draw crowds.

Luke and the kids' destination was Steinberg Skating Rink, a fifty-year-old outdoor oval lined with a black mesh fence, advertised as the largest such rink in the Midwest. The oval itself was large enough to accommodate a sizable number of skaters, and during summers, the ice had been replaced with sand to create two regulation size beach volleyball courts. Next to the fence was the patio of the concessions facilities, which occupied a long, rectangular building that had windows of multifarious sizes lining two sides, including the one facing the rink to better allow parents not wanting to skate or play beach volleyball to keep an eye on the rink.

The kids brought along their own skates. He and Anna had started them out when they were very young, having read in a parenting book such skills were easier to learn the earlier you started. Luke rented some for himself, feeling nervous to get on the ice again, because Anna had always been the better skater. He stayed close to the wall and tried not to go very fast, dreading the embarrassment of falling in front of his kids. Cassie and Molly skated in circles, staying with him as they made their way around the rink wall. Kyle spotted some friends from school and skated off to hang with them.

Luke knew his son was entering the preteen years, when such a thing was more and more common, but he was a little disappointed to see Kyle disappear so quickly. He had hoped that the way he'd loved his Christmas present might soften some of the resentment, at least long enough for Luke to prove to him that he still cared. But Kyle had been the least enthusiastic of three about going with him, and it was frustrating that he might not get the chance to talk with him the way he was with Mandy and Cassie.

When the girls asked for some sodas from the concession stand, Luke handed them money and skated over toward Kyle to see if he wanted anything as well. Kyle saw him coming and winced, his ears flushing as he avoided eye contact. Luke waved, wobbling his way over clumsily like a man who'd never had skates on before.

"We're taking a break to get some snacks. Did you want anything?" he asked as he drew close enough for Kyle to hear.

"That's okay," Kyle said, angling his body away and shuffling on his skates as his friends watched.

"Are you sure? I can give you some money, if you want to go yourself."

"Mom gave me some money," Kyle said, then skated quickly away with his friends.

Luke watched him go, shoulders drooping. Didn't all this trying count for anything with him? He hoped he'd get the chance to talk with him later before he dropped the kids back at Anna's.

Turning and making his way toward the concession stand, he hit a slick patch and fell on his rear. A couple of kids nearby chuckled at him struggling to get back up. When he finally managed, he glanced over to see Luke and his friends pointing and mocking him. Luke ignored the stabbing in his chest, finally managing to make his way over to where Mandy handed the cashier the money as she and Cassie sipped from sodas. He noticed a bag of popcorn and some chocolate bars on the counter as well.

"Did you get anything for me?" he asked.

Mandy looked down at her feet, afraid he was upset with her. He smiled and hugged her. "I'm just kidding, sweetie. I'll order for myself."

Mandy looked relieved as she grabbed up the popcorn and chocolate and followed Cassie toward some benches and tables nearby.

LATER, AS THEY made their way back to the car, the girls ran on ahead, while Luke took the opportunity to hang back with Kyle. "Did you have fun with your friends?"

Kyle didn't even look up as he continued walking. "They're cool."

"Well, I wish we'd gotten to skate together some. I'm a little rusty and could have used some pointers," Luke said, hoping a joke might break the ice.

"Yeah, well, you're so busy with your work. Besides, I'm a little old to be hanging out with my dad these days."

"I guess you are growing up for sure," Luke said, stung. "But still, I want to spend some time with you. It doesn't have to be skating."

Kyle turned and looked at him like death warmed over. "Look, just because you got me the game, and it was cool, doesn't mean that we're all buddy, buddy again like we used to be."

"I know that, Kyle," Luke said, trying his best to meet his son's shifty eyes. "But I'm doing my best here."

Kyle grunted. "Why even bother after so long?" And he hurried on ahead with Luke struggling to catch up without slipping on the path.

As soon as they reached the car, the girls started arguing over who got the front seat. When Luke unlocked it, Kyle climbed into the back, preventing Luke from attempting further conversation. Luke put all three kids' skates in the trunk, then settled the girls' argument by flipping a coin. The drive home consisted of Cassie describing in detail all the new skating moves her sister had shown her that day. Kyle just put his ear buds on and lost himself in his iPhone.

"Daddy," Cassie asked, as they pulled onto their street, "can you go the movies with us tomorrow night?"

Tomorrow was a Sunday, but Luke shook his head. "Daddy has to finish some work with the accountant at work. I'm sorry, sweetie."

Cassie looked disappointed. Mandy wouldn't even look at him. He noticed Kyle had taken out one of his earbuds to listen, but popped it back in, when he saw Luke looking at him, still avoiding eye contact. Luke knew then he'd disappointed them again—same old dad. How could he balance his responsibilities at the office with his desire to rebuild a life with his kids? He'd gotten weekends and Wednesdays in the custody settlement but between traveling for work and the strained relationships, he'd been forced to forfeit too many of them. Obviously the first thing he needed to do was prioritize that. He knew he could count on Elise to help coordinate his schedule for that.

When they pulled into the drive at Anna's house, the girls hugged and thanked him, while Kyle headed inside. Anna came out and waved, mouthing "Thank you," then followed the girls into the house.

Luke drove home wondering what he could do to break through with his son. He'd always stayed close with his own father, in spite of a few rough spots during his teenage years. It had meant a lot to him having his father around for advice whenever he'd needed him all these years, and he wanted to share all that with Kyle as well. But as happy as he was about the chance to spend time with his kids again, these times also reminded him how much he'd screwed up the past few years. He'd been so blind and foolish.

He spent the evening going over and over in his mind all the fun things he and the kids used to do together, ruling out anything they would find boring now, and making a list of some activities he could plan with them. With Mandy and Cassie, it was much easier, not only because they both liked similar things, but because what he'd done with Mandy at Cassie's age, he could now do with Cassie. Kyle had become much more interested in things Luke knew less and less about. He was going to have to ask Ray and Anna for suggestions. Maybe he could also ask some of the guys with teenage sons at work? Either way, he was determined to recapture the fun of the past with each of them.

CHAPTER 9

ANNA HELPED CASSIE off with her skating clothes as she listened to Mandy describe their skating that day. They'd both had a blast and were clearly happy to have resumed a family tradition. Anna felt bad for having not taken them the past couple of years herself, though they had gone a few times with friends.

Later, she went to check on Kyle and found him in his room sulking and streaming music on his iPhone. She didn't have to ask what was wrong to know it had something to do with Luke, but the girls had really had a great time with their dad, so she wondered what was bothering their brother.

He noticed her peering in the door and took out one of his earbuds. "You need something, mom?"

"You wanna talk about it," she asked, trying to sound casual despite her concern.

"Not really."

"Did you have a good time with your dad at least?"

From his pinched expression, he knew she was probing. "I mostly hung out with some friends from school." The earbud went back into his ear, and that was the end of their conversation.

After she'd put the kids to bed, Anna sat down and thought

back on when the kids had first been born. Luke made such a great father, so good with them, always handling their tiny bodies like precious China. She never worried about him like other mothers she knew did about their husbands. He talked to the babies, gave them lots of attention, and clearly adored her all the more for having given him such precious gifts. As they grew older, he loved to play with them and help them with their homework. All of that was before the invention, before he started down the path to revolutionize publishing. Back then, he was a Business Administration grad just trying to find where he fit. He'd spent some time working for his father's company, but when that got bought out by a larger competitor, he floated for a while.

As long as she'd known him, Luke had been good at business, skilled at marketing and sales, and with managing people. That made it all the more ironic that he'd failed so completely to manage his priorities. Anna knew well that business acumen didn't always translate into parenting or family skills, but he was so good with his employees that many of them would work extra hours with no complaint. They'd do anything for him. He had passion, and they had caught the fire. She wished he could have brought some of that passion and leadership home once in a while. Maybe the same skills could translate now into helping him rebuild his relationship with the kids, because despite their anger and hurt feelings, she knew they loved him and needed him. Ultimately, they just wanted their dad back. She was sure they were even more afraid than she was that he would soon forget about them all over again and go back to his old ways.

Anna and Luke had both grown up in Christian homes, and they both believed in the power of prayer. For as long as she could remember, she'd prayed every day, sometimes more than once. When she and Luke got married, they'd started praying and doing devotions together. Until Luke's schedule seemed to make that impossible, that is. It was their special time, and one of the things she'd missed most, when things started to go sour. Now she realized that quiet time with God had been her salvation through the difficult months and days. God had been her companion, when she had no one else to turn to, and once again, she was thankful He had also provided good, supportive friends to help her through. Her faith had remained through all the trials of the past three years. Between the disintegration of the marriage, the death of her parents, and being on her own for the first time at thirty-three years old, there were so many times she could have doubted and turned away.

But Anna never blamed God. She never felt He'd abandoned her. She always knew He was there, supporting her and giving her strength. He especially felt close in times of trial, and she knew that was due to the great foundation of faith her parents and pastors had established for her growing up. Some of Anna's friends didn't have that, and she knew they even thought it a little odd to place so much trust in a being you couldn't even see. For Anna, her faith underscored everything she did—every thought, every action. It was the lens through which she viewed life, not just a set of rituals and rites.

THE NEXT MORNING, after the kids headed off to school, Anna went to her doctor's office for an appointment. She arrived at eight-thirty, right as the office opened, and didn't have to wait long.

After he'd examined her, Doctor Sousa smiled and patted her on the arm. "How have you been feeling?"

"Just fine. Same as always," she replied.

Doctor Sousa was a dark-skinned man in his forties with kind eyes and the beginning traces of grey in his hair. He spoke with traces of an accent left from his native Brazil. "Nothing out of the ordinary?" he asked.

"Nope. Same old routine," she said, smiling.

"Well, there's no new lumps, and the tumors we spotted on your last visit are not growing, so that's good news."

Anna breathed a sigh of relief. "But we won't really know until we get the results?" she said. A question filled with so much anxiety and mixed emotions. She found she couldn't meet his eyes as she said it.

Doctor Sousa waited until she looked up again. "Yes, we'll have to wait for the lab results, but I'm glad see there are no changes. That's encouraging. How're the kids?" He hung his stethoscope around his neck as he pulled a stylus from his right front pocket and made notes on her iPad chart.

"Just fine, thanks. They had a nice Christmas with their dad," she explained.

"Really? They went to his house?" Doctor Sousa knew the situation well.

"No. I asked him to join us, and he did. He found perfect presents for them, too."

Doctor Sousa chuckled, pleased. "That was a good idea, Anna. I'm glad it worked out. The kids need a father."

She nodded. She felt the same. "Well, he's trying hard."

Doctor Sousa pursed his lips with understanding. "I'll call you in a couple days with the results of today's tests, okay?"

She nodded again, as he opened the door. She drove home in silence then went to her bedroom window and lit the prayer candle she always kept there. The flickering flame acted as a beacon reminding her that God was always present, in trials and good times, and the comfort that brought had provided her strength for years.

DR. SOUSA CALLED on Wednesday, just after she'd dropped the kids at school. Afterward, Anna sat in her favorite chair in silence, slowly sipping her coffee. She didn't know what to do.

At noon, she met Brenda and Bekah for lunch at their favorite bistro in Brentwood. The moment they saw her, they knew something was wrong.

"What happened?" Bekah asked. A short haired Asian of Filipino roots, who looked the part of the housewife and mother, Bekah always seemed a bit bedraggled and worn down from the business of shuttling around her kids and taking care of the household. But she made up for it with her warm sense of humor and friendliness. She was the easiest person to talk to Anna had ever known. One of those people who's friends with everyone.

"It's in my pancreas," she responded. She didn't need to say anymore. They already knew the rest, and the agony mixed with grief on their faces spoke louder than words. Anna took a deep breath and shrugged. "I can't help hoping. It's part of my optimistic nature."

"We know," Brenda said, gently placing a hand on her arm. "It's part of what we all love about you."

That brought a genuine smile. "I couldn't have made it through these past few years without you guys, you know?" Anna said, her heart full to overflowing. "God really blessed me when He gave me friends like you."

"You're the blessing, girlfriend," Bekah said putting on an accent, and they laughed. It was fun to have people you could be silly with. After you became an adult, those opportunities were hard to come by. You could do it with your kids, but that was expected. Anna, Brenda, and Bekah had found something special—true friends they could say anything to and relax completely. They knew her better than anyone. Sometimes, it was almost like they could read each other's thoughts, and at this moment they both knew she was thinking about Luke.

"Have you heard anything from him, since the big

Christmas?" Brenda asked as they followed the hostess to a table.

"He took the kids skating on New Years," Anna said.

"How did that go?" Bekah asked.

"The girls loved it. Kyle seemed to be having a harder time. Apparently, he spent the whole afternoon hanging out with friends from school."

"Well, he's been through a lot. It'll take time," Brenda reassured her.

"At least Luke's finally making an effort," Bekah said, sounding relieved. "Maybe he's actually learned something."

"He seems so different now," Anna said, images of Luke and the kids flashing through her mind again. "I don't know much about what he's been up to. We've hardly spoken, but he's not the same man."

"Thank God," Brenda said, sarcastically.

They all laughed.

The waiter came by and noticed the menus sitting unopened on their plates. He shot them a look, eyebrow raised before shuffling off again.

"Do you think we might actually order some food here, girls? I'm starving!" Bekah said when he'd gone, making them all giggle as they began flipping through the menu.

On the way home, replaying their conversation, Anna knew they were right. She hadn't told anyone outside their friend circle about the tumors, but if the results came back for cancer or some other illness, she had to prepare herself. She'd have to make plans, and Luke would have to be part of that. She'd have to tell the kids, too. God how she dreaded that. There were so young. Hadn't they been through enough already? It was so hard to think about, but they all had to know… and soon. They were still too young to really understand. She barely understood it herself. She was only thirty-three. She was too young herself, she'd always thought. So much about this was a mystery.

She stopped by the church on her way and knelt in the chapel to pray. Again, she asked God for wisdom and strength to do the right thing. She asked Him to hold her in His arms, too, and felt the warm glow she'd come to know as the Holy Spirit, filling her body. It was a wonderful feeling, like a real physical presence of another being, only from the inside, instead. For anyone who hadn't experienced it, it was always hard to explain, but for anyone who had, it was always one of the key experiences which cemented their faith. It was impossible to experience the true presence of God and the Holy Spirit like that and not know He was real.

When she called her brother, Paul, who'd always been the rebel of the family, he couldn't understand why she seemed so at peace with God given the diagnoses. "If it was me, I'd be pissed, wondering how God could be so cruel," he confessed.

"God didn't make me sick, Paul," she countered.

"Oh yeah? Is this the God who's supposedly in control of everything?" Paul replied.

"It's a fallen world, and sickness and pain are part of that," she said.

"If God wanted you well, he'd heal you. He has that power. Why would he allow tumors in the first place?" She could almost hear Paul shaking his head. "Stop letting him off the hook. Your kids need you. We need you. You're still so young."

Anna understood his feelings and knew Bekah and Brenda had similar doubts, but she just couldn't feel the way. God wasn't punishing her or singling her out. She had cancer, and it scared her, but God could still choose to heal her, and if he didn't, it was part of a greater plan. Everything would be okay.

The difference between her and Paul was she truly believed that. For some reason, Paul just couldn't. For Anna, it gave her a sense of peace through trials. For Paul, it was a source of constant torture, so she prayed for him often, hoping he'd find peace someday.

I just trust you, Lord, she said to herself. And she always had, just like her mother. It was just the way she lived, whether those around her understood it or not.

As she drove home, she wondered if she'd had enough time to impart such faith in her kids and hoped somehow, some way they'd have enough foundation to find strength in their beliefs no matter what happened the way she did.

That night, she lit her prayer candle in the window and reached for her Bible.

CHAPTER 10

THE FOLLOWING SATURDAY, Luke came over to Anna's again to spend time with the kids. He had planned on taking them out to a movie and then for pizza, but it started snowing an hour before he arrived, and according to the weather forecast, it wasn't supposed to be a fun day for driving. Instead, they ordered pizza and stayed in. Anna and the girls joined Luke at the kitchen table in a game of *Life*, while Kyle listened to his iPhone, and then played *Rock Star Eight*. He'd barely acknowledged Luke's presence.

Luke wondered how long it would take for Kyle to come around, or if he ever would. He'd exhausted his mind searching for activities they could do together that Kyle might actually be excited about but so far hadn't come up with much. Most were the old standbys like playing catch or going to a sports event or even helping him with his homework, but none of these seemed very fresh or exciting. They were more like things every father was expected to do with his son. Luke wanted to surprise Kyle, and maybe even be more of a friend than a dad. Finally, he decided to ask Anna about it.

On a break from the game, while the girls ran off to the bathroom, he and Anna stood alone in the kitchen, as she poured some coffee. "Kyle sure loves that game I bought, doesn't he?"

"Yes, he does. Even when you're not here, he plays and

plays." Anna said, handing him a mug. "The girls love what you got for them, too. Cassie keeps making this cute little pies and cakes. I have to hand it to you. You nailed the presents this year."

Luke's heart skipped a beat at hearing her praise, but he quickly frowned again as he thought about Kyle. "I just wish I could figure out how to reconnect with Kyle. I've been searching my mind for ideas, but they all seem so ordinary and expected."

"Maybe he'll show you how to play the game with him sometime," she suggested.

Luke hadn't even thought about that. "Good idea. I knew I married you for a reason all those years ago."

Anna chuckled as she poured cream and sugar in her coffee and grabbed a spoon to stir it. "Give it time. To be honest, I'm surprised the girls are doing as well as they are. You really hurt them."

Luke looked away. He already knew that, but hearing her state it so directly stung. "I never meant to. And I'm trying to give them the father they deserve."

Seeing the hurt in his eyes, she sighed. "So far you're doing a lot better, but you didn't expect them to just open their arms as if nothing happened, did you?"

Luke looked at her, his neck suddenly stiff, and for some reason he felt hot. Why did she keep stating the obvious? "I'm smarter than that, and you know it."

"You asked my advice, Luke. I'm not trying to be hard on you, just honest," she said. Clearly his defensiveness bothered her, too.

"You know I've always loved those kids. They're like a gift from God for me," he said.

"You used to tell me I was a gift from God, too, Luke, and look what happened," she said.

Luke scoffed. "It probably didn't help that you had all kinds of nice things to say about me when we separated either, did it?" He set his mug down hard on the counter, spilling his coffee. In truth, he had no idea what she'd said or not said to them, but he could imagine it hadn't been flattering. That was usually the case.

Anna tensed. "I've always tried very hard to avoid airing our problems in front of the kids and you know it," she said, cheeks flushing. "Don't accuse me of things you're imagining in that warped mind of yours!"

"I know enough divorced people to know how it works, Anna!" he replied, almost yelling.

"Don't take your frustration out on me! You thought you could just walk back in here and everything would be like it was before, like it would be easy, and it's not. Cassie called you twice after Christmas, sitting by the phone for hours, waiting for you to call, and you didn't. You were late today. You turned down taking them to a movie." She ticked them off with her fingers like items on a list. "Do you know why I called you? Do you know why I bothered to even invite you for Christmas? Your five-year-old daughter was crying because her daddy was the only father who wouldn't come with her to Father-Daughter Night at school, that's why! I sent you the invitation and everything, but you never responded. Like that's a surprise."

"You sent that to me," he said, calming down. He had no memory of it. "I don't think I got it."

"I emailed it to you at work, Luke," she explained. "Do you know what Cassie actually asked me? 'Why doesn't my daddy want to be with me anymore?' I just didn't want your kids to keep thinking you were a jerk, so I invited you over and look at the thanks I get."

Suddenly, they glanced over and their faces dropped. All three kids were frozen in the doorway, staring at them. Cassie was already sniffling.

Anna smiled as if nothing had happened and grabbed her

coffee. "Hey, guys. We were just headed back to finish our game, you ready?" She put her hand on Cassie's shoulder and lead all three back into the Living Room.

Luke stood there frozen. He couldn't believe what had just happened. He hadn't come here to fight with Anna. He'd merely been hoping for some suggestions, but some of the things she'd said really hurt, because he already knew them. He didn't need to hear it from her.

He stood there, trying to collect himself, but couldn't find the strength to go back out there and face the kids. The girls and Anna were waiting for him to finish the game; he just didn't think he could handle the looks he knew he'd see in the girls' eyes as they waited for another explosion.

Finally, after a few long minutes, he grabbed his jacket and keys from a chair by the kitchen table and slipped out the back door.

ANNA HEARD THE back door slam and wanted to kick herself. She hadn't intended to say hurtful things. She'd only meant to be honest about the situation, to tell Luke what he needed to hear—that his expectations were too high. Fixing things with the kids would take time, and she didn't want him making things worse by pushing the kids too hard. She should have kept her mouth shut about the obvious. If she were him, she wouldn't have wanted to hear it from her either. But somehow the words had come out before she even realized what she was saying. She'd been going over and over what to tell him about her health crisis and procrastinating all night. A part of her wondered if maybe picking a fight had been her way of putting it off further.

The girls sat at the table in the Living Room for twenty minutes, hoping their dad would reappear. Anna tried to get

Kyle to finish the game for him, but Kyle wasn't interested. Finally, the girls gave up and ran off to their room, Cassie in tears. Anna sighed, sipping her coffee. Add another abandonment to the list. *Way to go, Luke.* But the truth was she was relieved he hadn't stayed, not if they were going to fight like that. The kids had seen enough of that in the past. Right now, they needed a sense of calm stability. He'd be back. It was obvious he wasn't going to give up. He needed time to think and that was something she understood all too well.

As she cleaned up the game, folding the board and tucking the pieces back in place on the cardboard tray inside the box, Kyle stood in the doorway and looked at her. "Dad's a real jerk, isn't he, Mom?"

Her eyes met his and she shook her head. "No, Kyle. Your dad's a wonderful man who's made some mistakes. We just got to talking about some painful things that were hard for him to hear. Hard for both of us."

Kyle handed her a piece that had slid to the opposite side of the table.

She took it and put it back in the box.

Kyle's shoulders sank. "I don't know why he's trying so hard. He already proved he couldn't care less about us. I mean, if he cared so much about us, where was he the past three years?"

"Look, Kyle. Your dad messed up. He forgot for a moment what really matters. When you get a little older, you'll find out how easy it is to do that sometimes. Your father's not the only one who's ever done that. Remember what the Bible says about honoring your father and mother?"

He looked away, nodding. "I remember."

"Well, I'm pretty sure the author didn't mean calling your dad a 'jerk' when he wrote that," she said. It came out more harshly than she'd intended, just like with Luke. Kyle started to walk away. "Honey, I'm sorry. I didn't mean to scold you. It's just that, someday you're gonna want your father, and I just really don't want you to miss out on that."

"I don't want anything from him anymore," he said, looking back at her for a moment before heading up the stairs.

That's what I'm afraid of, she thought to herself. *And your father is, too.*

WHEN LUKE GOT halfway down the drive, he wanted to scream. How had he let things get out of control like that? Anna hadn't said anything he didn't already know. Yes, it had irritated him that she'd brought it up again when things were going so well, and he was trying so hard. But why had he let it get to him so much? Now he'd overreacted and abandoned his kids yet again. It was just one more wrong move he'd have to make up to them.

He thought about stopping and going back, but his heart was still racing and his body tense. He needed time to cool down, and Anna probably did, too, so he kept on driving.

He and Anna hadn't fought like that in a long time. He knew Anna hadn't been trying to hurt him with her words, but she was so dramatic. Taking advice from her just wasn't as easy as it used to be. He had no idea what to do next, so he flipped on the radio and just drove. Finally, a preacher came on the radio.

"Children, obey your parents in all things: for this is well pleasing unto the Lord. Fathers, provoke not your children to anger, lest they be discouraged," the preacher read.

Luke thought it might be from Colossians. It spoke right to his heart. For years he'd always remembered the obedience part, but not the part about not provoking your children. He'd been so concerned about his children's obedience and respect for him that he'd failed to show them the respect they deserved. Now he saw clearly that their anger with him had been provoked by his negligence. They'd stopped believing in their own father, and deep down it was all his fault. He deserved whatever anger they had toward him, but he hoped that time would heal the wounds. That his efforts and dedication would show them he was a changed man; that things would be different from now on. He'd set a terrible example of what love and responsibility are for his family. He had to accept that there wasn't going to be any quick fix. He'd have to earn their trust and prove himself all over again.

As he drove home, he silently prayed for strength and wisdom and endurance. He asked God to make him the kind of father that God Himself is for His children. When he was finished, a peace came over him that he hadn't felt in a long time. He felt refreshed and ready for anything. As he made his way to the house, he started to sing a song he'd just heard on Sunday. By the time he'd turned the key in the lock, he was singing at full volume.

Tomorrow, he'd go over and apologize to Anna and his kids. Make the effort to show them how sorry he was for screwing up again. Maybe if he faced up to his faults openly, it would show them how hard he was trying to change. Maybe that would be a step toward winning their trust again.

If he wanted to raise his kids to do better than he had, he had to start by doing better himself. So, Luke would demonstrate humility and repentance in both his words and his actions. Then they'd see for themselves his sincerity and determination to be a better man.

By the time he'd changed into a t-shirt and fresh boxers and brushed his teeth, the anger he'd felt leaving Anna's house had faded, replaced by determined resolve. "You can do better, Luke, you really can," he said aloud.

And an hour later, he fell contently asleep.

CHAPTER 11

THE NEXT DAY, Luke drove across town to Webster Groves, headed for Anna's. He arrived to find his three kids out building a snowman in the yard. It made him smile. He'd always loved making snowmen and had fond memories of helping them do just that when they were younger.

As he climbed out of the car, Kyle spotted him and glared, focusing his attention on trying to make the middle ball bigger and smoother at the same time, an obvious mistake. Instead, the ball grew lumpy and harder to roll. The temperatures were in the upper twenties but fortunately the wind was light and Luke's down jacket kept him warm. The kids were all bundled up as well in thick coats, scarfs, stocking caps, and mittens, although Kyle had taken his off to make the snowball.

"Daddy!" Cassie called and ran to hug him. Mandy watched him warily but stayed where she was as Luke continued struggling with the ball.

After he'd hugged Cassie and kissed her on the forehead, Luke strode across the snowy lawn toward Mandy, smiling and leaning over to kiss her on the cheek. "Hi, sweetie."

Then he stood watching Kyle. "Aren't your hands cold?" Luke asked, hoping to ease his son into conversation, but Kyle ignored him. So he tried again. "It's easier if you smooth it out afterwards," he suggested.

The look Kyle shot him could have cut through ice. "What do you know? I thought you always ran off when things got hard."

Luke swallowed a wince. It was harsh but fair. "Yeah, I'm sorry I left like that. I should have stayed."

"We were in the middle of a game," Mandy said, her eyes sad.

Luke nodded. "I know, and I'm sorry. I was just so embarrassed that your mother and I fought like that. I'm trying so hard to do better. And I hated you seeing us that way."

"She only told the truth," Kyle snapped.

"Yeah, she did," Luke said. "And I shouldn't have gotten mad. I'm sorry. I messed up."

Luke had never been good at apologizing, and it was clear his response had taken the kids by surprise. Mandy shot him a puzzled look, while Kyle refused to look at him, still focusing instead on the snowball.

Cassie rushed toward him, throwing her arms around his middle. "It's okay, daddy. We love you."

"I love you, too," Luke said.

Apparently watching her sister do it made Mandy feel free to do the same. She hurried over and hugged her father. "We forgive you," she whispered.

"Oh honey, I promise to do better," he said.

Kyle had finished the ball and was smoothing off the edges, but he was hesitating and favoring his hands which were pink from cold.

"Let us do that," Luke offered. "You put your gloves back on and warm up those fingers."

He moved toward the ball and Kyle squared off, pushing him back with two hands against his chest. "It's our snowman! No one invited you!"

"Kyle Lawrence Morrison!" Anna scolded from the doorway.

Kyle turned to see his mother shooting him one of those motherly looks that froze any child in their tracks and made them reconsider what they were doing "Just go away!" he yelled, then turned and ran for the house, brushing past his mother and disappearing inside.

Luke looked up at her and sighed. "I just wanted to help."

"I know," Anna said, shooting him a look that asked 'why are you here?'

Luke's eyes met hers. "I'm sorry, Anna. I should never have gotten angry. You were just telling me things I already knew about myself. I came to apologize for that. To you," he motioned toward Mandy and Cassie, "and to them."

Anna relaxed against the doorframe. "Well, you're trying. That's what counts. We all make mistakes."

"Can daddy help us finish?" Cassie asked.

Anna smiled at her daughter. "Why don't you all come in for cocoa and wait for your brother? He really wants to be part of it."

Cassie grinned, rubbing her mittens together, then reached out to grab Luke's hand as she headed for the door. "Cocoa! Yay!"

Luke followed his daughters toward the house. "With little marshmallows, right?" he said in a kid-like voice that made Anna chuckle.

"I think I can rustle some up," she said as Mandy slid past her into the house and Cassie followed, leaving Luke facing her on the front stoop.

"I really am sorry," he said quietly.

Anna nodded again. "Kyle will come around."

And then Luke followed her inside and headed for the kitchen.

THE WEEK FLEW by as the kids went back to school and Luke returned to the office, but the following Saturday, he made plans to take them skiing with Ray and Julia at Hidden Valley Ski Resort in Wildwood, Missouri. Located thirty minutes southwest on Interstate 44, and as odd as it seemed to even have a ski resort there, Luke found its facilities fairly impressive.

Luke, Ray, and Grace had been raised by parents who were skiers, so they'd spent many a childhood day or week navigating slopes at both Hidden Valley and out in Colorado, or even east in Vermont. Julia and Luke's three kids, however, were all beginners. Luke and Anna had discussed taking them before the divorce, but they'd seemed too young then, so this was his first opportunity to share with them the sport he loved.

Comprised of three mountains, Hidden Valley offered twenty-three runs of varying skill levels, with a good selection of easy and beginner slopes as well as an entire section devoting to tubing. They arrived right before eight a.m. Of course, once they saw tubing, Mandy and Kyle immediately wanted to head straight for it, but Luke and Ray insisted they try skis first.

"Julia needs someone to ski with," Ray said.

Mandy frowned. "But you can ski with her."

"She'll have more fun with you," Ray said. "Your dad and I ski at a much higher level."

"He means they don't want to get bored going slow with me," Julia said, smiling.

Kyle crinkled his face. "Well, yeah, let's do something where we can go fast. It's more fun."

"You have to learn first," Luke said as they reached the ski rental building and he opened the door. "Come on. You guys will love it once you know the basics."

"We were skiing like crazy when we were your age," Ray added.

Julia led the kids inside, but none of the three looked convinced. Luke and Ray followed.

He lowered his voice and said to his brother, "Such enthusiasm."

"They're scared of something new," Ray said with a dismissive wave. "We were too at that age. They'll be over it as soon as they discover how cool it is."

Once the kids and Julia had been properly outfitted with skis, boots, and poles, Ray and Luke retrieved their own skis and poles from atop the car and their boots from the trunk, slipping them on, and then snapping on their skis.

Ray pointed the way to the lifts. "The middle mountain has the beginner and learning runs."

"Do we have to take lessons?" Kyle whined as several younger kids zipped past him on skis like experts.

"Yes," Ray said. "But we got you a private instructor, so it'll just be you guys and Julia."

"There will be people of all ages learning," Luke said. "Don't be embarrassed. Try and have fun." He kept his tone chipper and upbeat, but Kyle wasn't buying it. Mandy still looked hesitant.

Only Cassie looked excited. "But we want to ski with you and Uncle Ray, daddy," she said.

"We'll do that for an hour or so until your instructor is ready, then again after lunch," Ray said.

Luke nodded. "We're going to have a great time, I promise."

"If we don't like it, we can still tube, right?" Mandy asked, Kyle grunting beside her, hands crossed over his chest.

"You're gonna love it!" Ray said like a cheerleader.

"Just give it a chance, honey, okay?" Luke added.

Mandy nodded, still looking nervous.

The steady drone of snowmaking machines and the hydraulic lifts filled the air as they made their way to the bunny slopes, Ray and Luke alternating between leading, cajoling, and assisting the others. Julie seemed to take to the rhythm fairly naturally, alternating between pulling herself with poles and the sort of slide-walk skiers learned to master.

Snowplows worked the slope up the mountain from them as they stepped onto the green-flagged runs.

"Okay, this is where everyone starts," Luke said.

Kyle rolled his eyes and motioned to the lift, where benches filled with skiers glided up the mountain. "Not everyone."

"Where they're just starting out, he means," Ray quickly added, and Luke shot him a grateful look for the backup. Kyle was clearly determined to make this difficult, so he'd take all the assistance he could get.

"Okay, let's try it," Luke suggested.

They lined up at the top of the run, skis pointed downhill, and Mandy and Cassie each grabbed on tight to their dad's arm while Julia held onto Ray. Kyle stood off to one side, refusing help.

"Here we go," Ray said and pushed off, Julia doing the same and they started sliding down the slope.

"Ready?" Luke asked, and when the girls nodded, he pushed off too, with them imitating his every move. They began sliding together, the girls' grips tight on his arm. Luke used the angle of his skis to control the speed and keep it slow and steady, but the girls' skis were straight and soon they were tugging on his arms.

"You have to point the tips of your skis toward each other a little, like a triangle," he gently coached.

Mandy glanced down at his skis and slid hers quickly into

similar formation while

Cassie struggled to coordinate. "Daddy!" she called out, her face scrunching in fear.

Luke slid his right ski over and knocked her right ski to an angle. "Like that, see? Can you do the other one?"

Cassie clumsily managed and the girls' speed slowed to even with their dad's.

"We did it," Mandy said, grinning. Cassie brightened also.

"You did. Good job," Luke said. He glanced over to check on Kyle and saw his son headed downhill with increasing speed. "Kyle! Angle your fronts to slow down," he called out, but a moment later, Kyle hit what looked like a minor bump and fell onto his rear, sliding downhill as he struggled to stop himself.

Mandy and Cassie laughed, and Luke smiled. He'd done that so many times as a boy.

Ray and Julia angled over toward Kyle to offer assistance. Kyle managed to stop himself and was retrieving his skis and poles from nearby snow drifts as he sent glares at his giggling sisters.

"It's okay, Kyle," Ray soothed, "it happens to everyone when they're learning."

Kyle ignored his uncle, fuming, then struggling to get his skis to stay still long enough to slide them back on. Ray glided over and held them as Julia continued on down the hill slowly on her own.

By the time Luke and the girls hit the bottom and he'd high-fived them both, Ray and Kyle were skiing down to join them.

"Okay, wasn't that fun?" Julia said cheerfully.

"Yeah," Cassie and Mandy agreed. Kyle just grumbled.

"Do you want me to try it with you one time?" Luke suggested, skiing toward his son.

Kyle shook his head and turned away, angrily brushing

packed snow off the butt and legs of his snow pants.

"How about Uncle Ray shows you how to control your speed?" Ray suggested.

Kyle nodded and Ray went to work showing him some techniques.

"Let's go again!" Mandy said anxiously.

"Okay, let me show you how this lift works," Luke said.

They maneuvered over to the mini-chair lift bordering the bunny slope. Luke showed them how to slide in front of it as it turned and let it push them back up the hill. He rode with Cassie and Julia with Mandy.

This time, Mandy wanted to try by herself, so Julia skied beside her as they headed downhill together. Luke hung back with Cassie, who held tight to his arm at the start, but grew more confident as she controlled her speed this time and let go part way down. Both girls made it to the bottom without falls and beamed with pride.

Kyle made another run with Ray as well and made it unscathed, allowing himself a grin at the bottom as his uncle shook his hand.

"Way to go, kiddo," Ray praised.

"Good job, Kyle," Julia chorused.

"Okay, you're all getting the hang of it," Luke said, trying to sound encouraging rather than pushy, "so keep practicing."

Ray and Luke made a few more runs with the beginners before a pretty blonde ski instructor with a nice tan and Swedish accent skied over to introduce herself. "I'm Katarina. I'm here for your lesson today."

"Yay," Cassie, Mandy, and Julia chorused. And even Kyle eyed the attractive instructor with surprising interest.

Ray chuckled. "Someone has a crush."

Luke shushed him. "Okay, so we'll leave you in Katarina's

good hands then meet up after for lunch."

Cassie and Mandy opted for quick hugs while Kyle was too cool to acknowledge his dad and Julia offered Ray a quick kiss, then the two brothers headed off together for the larger lift up the mountain.

AFTER THEY MET up again, Luke and Ray escorted the newbies across the bottom slopes to the log cabin-esque main lodge where they'd rented equipment earlier and joined the cafeteria-style line. They put food on their trays, Luke helping Cassie, then found a table together and ate before heading up the larger lift to the top of the middle mountain to try some runs.

The kids had clearly thrived at their lessons and Julia as well. There were a few falls when one or the other tried something too ambitious or hit an unexpected mogul or heavy patch of snow. But at the end of day, they were all smiles and laughter as they headed back to the car together, and Luke knew it had been a successful outing.

That night, they stopped at Grace's for chili and had fun hanging with the cousins and Grace and Karl before Luke took the kids back to Anna's.

"How'd it go?" Anna asked as the tired-looking kids traipsed past her into the house.

"Success, I think," Luke said.

"How was Kyle?"

"Hateful but he took a liking to the sexy Swedish ski instructor," Luke said with a grin.

She laughed. "He's at that age, all right. Just what we need, huh?"

"They want to go again," Luke said. "Maybe you can come with us."

Anna's brow furrowed as she thought it over. "I haven't skied in ages. We'll see."

Luke could see she was very hesitant about the idea. "I just thought it might be fun," he said. "Think about it."

Anna nodded. "I will."

"Okay, well, good night," he said and offered a wave as he backed down the stoop.

Anna stood there watching as he headed for the car and pulled out of the driveway before disappearing inside.

At least I still intrigue her, Luke told himself, but it was clear he had the most work cut out for him winning back Anna and Kyle both. So be it. He would never give up.

CHAPTER 12

"SO HOW'S IT going with Luke?" Brenda asked as Anna gathered with her friends for tea at Pantera Bread a couple Mondays later.

During the previous two weeks, Anna had noticed that Luke had a different attitude during his visits. He'd obviously done a lot of thinking after their blow out, and the kids had all three said positive things about the ski trip. The following weekend, he'd taken the kids to a Saint Louis Blues hockey game. Even Kyle had been happy to go along for that. He loved hockey, just like his dad. The Blues won, too, which only made it better. Their track record had been pretty dismal lately.

Anna saw it as a thawing of sorts, and that was encouraging. "He's been attentive to the kids, taking them skiing and to a hockey game."

"And they had fun?" Bekah asked.

"Seemed to," Anna said with a nod.

"Good," Brenda replied, looking pleased.

Anna had invited him to come with them the next weekend to an outing at the zoo. The weather was supposed to be unusually warm for January, and the girls had been begging to go, so it was the best opportunity they would have to go for a while.

"We're going to the zoo this weekend," Anna said.

"All of you?" Brenda seemed surprised.

"Yeah, I invited him along," Anna confessed. "The girls really want to go, and even Kyle enjoys the animals."

"Sure—Lions, tigers, and bears, grrrrr," Bekah joked, forming claws with her hands in the air. The ladies laughed.

"He's been asking me to join them," Anna said, "so I figured it would be good to see the dynamic, but this is safe and very non-date-like."

"Good luck," Bekah said as she and Brenda exchanged skeptical looks.

"It'll be fine. Plenty to distract us," Anna said. She really wasn't worried about Luke at all. More about all the walking they'd have to do and hoping the zoo staff had cleared all the paths well.

"And how's the chemo?" Brenda asked, finally broaching the subject she knew they'd be asking about.

Anna sighed. "It's misery. I started it while they were skiing. They did this operation to put what's called a Venus port in my neck below my clavicle. All that technical stuff."

Brenda nodded. "I had a cousin who went through this with breast cancer."

"I started radiation, too," Anna said. "So basically, I am exhausted, and I forget what I'm doing now halfway through a task."

"Yeah, they say that's common, honey." Bekah reached out a hand o gently clasp Anna's wrist and squeeze.

"And my hair's failing out," Anna said. "Thank God for wigs."

"You told the kids and Luke, right?" Bekah asked.

Anna looked away. "I can't find the words."

Brenda and Bekah looked somewhere between exasperated

and worried.

"You don't have a choice, Anna," Brenda urged. "If you want us to come over and be there when you tell them, we can, but you have to talk to them. Pancreatic cancer is serious."

"Six months at most," Anna said. "That's what they said."

"Oh my God! So fast!" Bekah said as a tear rolled down her cheek. Brenda teared up too.

"I'm still hoping for a miracle," Anna said.

"They're gonna see the signs," Brenda said. "It's time to let them in."

"I know it's hard. But they deserve to know," Bekah added.

"You're right!" Anna said, too loudly, and blushed as a couple women at a nearby table glanced over with furrowed brows.

Anna's own tears started then and the three of them clasped hands and cried together, ignoring the other customers, overcome with emotions.

THAT SATURDAY, LUKE met them in the zoo parking lot right on time. The sun was out, its bright rays warming the air through a cloudless blue sky, so they enjoyed the chance to be outside. Some of the animals had even been let out by zookeepers for fresh air. Anna wondered how animals from places like South America and Africa could survive the winters here. But then she heard some zookeepers talking about how the penguins had been let out on a particularly cold day a week before and realized it was all relative.

"My feet are tired, mommy," Cassie said as they made their way past the chimpanzees.

"Stop being a baby," Kyle said as he and Mandy traded off making faces at the apes and giggling. The chimpanzees went on playing as if they weren't even there.

So much for family unity, Anna thought.

"I am a baby," Cassie said proudly, sticking her tongue out.

Anna and Luke laughed. Anna smiled as Luke picked up Cassie and carried her on his shoulders. Even Kyle was being friendlier to Luke today. They took their time exploring the various inside exhibits. It was warmer than outside, and there were some newly redesigned habitats the kids particularly enjoyed.

It was as they were moving toward the exit of the Jungle of the Apes that she first felt it. It started out as a slight discomfort in her abdomen and then grew into a sharp pain. It became harder to breathe. She almost couldn't walk, stopping for a moment to see if it would pass.

Luke and the kids took a moment to notice she had stopped and turned back.

"Everything okay?" Luke asked.

She nodded, forcing a smile. "Yeah, my feet are tired, too." The doctor had warned her she might start having more incidents like this, but the sharpness of the pain caught her off guard. The earlier times had been much less intense.

"Do you want daddy to carry you, too?" Cassie chirped.

Anna and Luke laughed.

"No, sweet pea. Daddy can't carry both of us," Anna said, smiling. The pain had subsided, and she moved to rejoin them.

Luke looked her over a minute, clearly wondering if there was something more to it than her feet, but she shook her head and kept smiling as if nothing was wrong.

"Can we get some Dippin' Dots?" Mandy asked.

"Me, too!" Cassie chimed in.

"You guys want cold ice cream on a day like this?" Luke asked, amused.

"It's not ice cream. It's Dippin' Dots," Mandy insisted.

"They're really good, daddy," Cassie added.

"It's ice cream, stupid." Kyle said.

"Don't call her 'stupid,' Kyle." Luke scolded.

Kyle rolled his eyes and looked at Anna.

"You guys can have it if you really want it," she said.

"Really?" Mandy said excitedly. She must have been expecting a 'no.' She raced toward the food booth ahead as Cassie cried out, "Hey! Wait for us!"

It surprised Anna that vendors were even selling cold items today. The afternoon sun had heated it up into the mid-fifties for a change, but still, it wasn't the time of year when most people would be interested. But as Luke pulled out his wallet, the zoo employee smiled and asked the girls which flavor. Even Kyle wanted some, too, to Anna's amusement.

"Let's find a place inside to eat it, okay?" Anna suggested, motioning toward a dining building nearby.

"Aw, Mom, it's not that cold," Mandy said, wanting to eat it as quickly as possible.

"It'll just take a minute to get there," Anna reminded her.

Mandy and Cassie ran on ahead, spilling a few dots on the sidewalk as they went. Anna watched as two birds swooped in right away to eat what had fallen. "Be careful not to spill," she called after them as the pain suddenly struck her like a lightning bolt. She almost stumbled, stopping where she was to catch her breath.

This time, Luke saw the pain on her face and hurried over, concerned. "What's the matter, Anna?"

"It's nothing. Just a little pain," she said.

"A little pain? You almost fell over," Luke said, his brow

wrinkling as he put a hand on her forearm.

"I'll be fine in a minute. I just need to sit down," she said, moving slowly toward the dining building. Luke took her arm and helped her as they saw the kids, through the window, settling in around a table inside.

"Do you get these pains often?" he asked.

"Every now and then," she said, dismissively.

"You better go to the doctor," he urged her.

"I have, Luke," she said, as he opened the door and helped her inside.

The pain came back again, suddenly, and she fell against Luke as he tried to help her to the table where the kids were eating. She cried out as it intensified. Luke looked really worried now. The last thing she saw before she blacked out was his ashen face, his eyebrows drawing together, as he tried to keep her on her feet.

BARNES HOSPITAL WAS located off Kingshighway and Highway 64 just east of Forest Park and the zoo. A major teaching hospital with ties to Washington University Medical School, Barnes consisted of a complex of buildings, including a children's hospital, multiple ERs, and huge parking structures. It was the signature hospital for the entire city, a leader in research and development as well as top new surgeries and techniques. It was also a leading cancer center and so Anna's doctor had directed her there after her diagnosis for the best local treatment available.

Anna awoke in a treatment room as Doctor Sousa and a nurse examined her. Luke paced the floor behind them. Not feeling any pain now, she looked around for the kids. "Where am I?"

"You're in the hospital, Anna. Luke brought you here after you passed out," Doctor Sousa explained as he signed orders on an iPad and passed it to the nurse.

"Passed out? What happened?" she asked, groggily.

"You experienced some pain. The chemo and radiation weaken your immune system and drain your energy," Doctor Sousa explained. "Have you experienced nausea, diarrhea, or vomiting?"

"No," Anna replied.

Doctor Sousa nodded. "Ok, well, you probably will. It's common. I'm afraid it's going to get worse. Sooner rather than later."

Anna looked at Luke. He knew now. He'd heard everything. He hurried to her side. "Why didn't you tell me?"

Doctor Sousa smiled, supportively. "We'll be back to check on you in a little bit." He and the nurse moved out, shutting the door behind them.

"Didn't you think I should know?" Luke asked.

"I tried to tell you a couple of times," Anna confessed. "Once right before we had that fight, and then I just couldn't."

Luke winced, his voice cracking. "How long have you known?"

"They found the tumor three months ago. By the time, they found it, it was fully metastasized," she explained. "I've only known myself for a few weeks."

"My God, Anna, you're only thirty-three!" Luke's eyes narrowed and his face took on a pained expression. She knew how he was feeling. She hadn't wanted to believe it either when Doctor Sousa first told her. But having done the research, she'd discovered that about nine percent of breast cancer cases—and one in eight women experienced it—were under the age of forty-five. She just had the bad luck to be among them.

"Well, there's cancer in my family, and there have been a lot of cases," she said. She had read everything she could get a hold of since then, listened to dozens of podcasts, read hundreds of websites—all seeking answers, knowledge, anything to give her hope. She didn't want to miss the kids growing up—graduations, weddings, so many magical moments.

"How long?" From the look on his face, Luke clearly didn't want to hear the answer.

"They told me six months, when they found it," Anna said, "but I've only been short of breath a few times since I started treatment. I really hope it will get better. God is with me."

"I deserved to know," Luke said, sounding almost angry.

"To be honest, I wasn't sure if you cared anymore. I just have pain sometimes. And I'm handling it"

He looked flabbergasted. "I always cared!"

She could tell he was experiencing a similar gamut of emotions to that she and her siblings had experienced when they first learned the diagnosis.

"So, this is why you invited me for Christmas?" he said, angrily, his arms sweeping the room as he turned away to stare at the medicine cabinets lining a nearby wall. Their opaque glass doors revealed they contained a cornucopia of bottles and vials.

"It's not the only reason, but yes, you need to rebuild things with the kids, Luke. They're going to need you. Call it a last wish maybe..."

"Don't say that," he said, cutting her off. "It makes it sound like you're not going to fight this."

"We can hope for a miracle, and I tell myself that but pancreatic cancer works quickly. They're doing everything they can" she said, resigned. "We need to be prepared."

"You're thirty-three-years-old, damn it! You have to fight to live!" He turned back, putting his hands on her shoulders as if he wanted to shake some sense into her.

"I've been getting chemo twice a week and radiation as well, whatever the doctor says to do. It may slow things down, but they gave me the option to not even try. There may be nothing they can do. We have to face the fact that I may not have much longer."

He pulled away, looking out the window. Anna knew how he felt. She'd been struggling to process it all herself, and it surprised her to find that now that she'd told him, she was sounding so strong and certain when she really felt lost and filled with questions inside. She stayed silent, allowing him to wrestle with his own emotions. "My God, what about the kids?" he finally said, pulling his hands back.

She took a deep breath before smiling. "You're going to do fine."

"Kyle can hardly stand me! I still have to run the business!" She knew his mind was a rush of scattered thoughts as he tried to wrap himself around what her illness meant.

"When I called you to come for Christmas, I was worried, Luke," she explained. "For the same reasons you are. I didn't know if you could do it, and I had to see for myself, to be sure. So, I could make plans, while I still can." She locked her eyes on his, slowly closing and then opening them again. "But I've seen a new you, this past month. And it's been so good to see that. I always knew you could be the man I married, and you're doing fine."

"I can't do it by myself," he said, shaking his head as he squeezed his hands together.

"You'll find a way, Luke," she offered. "Besides, I'm not gone yet. We just have to be ready in case..."

Luke's eyes darted away, but not before she saw the pain there. He still didn't want to think about it. Anna reached out and gently put her hand on his. "I know you'll do whatever is necessary, Luke. I have faith in you. If I didn't believe that I wouldn't have let you back in."

Luke took a slow breath, fighting back tears. Anna was

touched to realize how much he still cared about her. Her heart fluttered as she sniffled. "Don't make me cry, okay? I'm already sick here..."

Luke chuckled. "You're supposed to be the weepy one."

Anna offered a mock scowl. "Don't pretend you didn't used to cry at those sappy movies we used to see in college. I saw you trying to hide the tears from me."

Luke looked at her as if he hadn't realized she'd noticed. "You saw that?"

"Yeah, Luke. It's one of the reasons I fell in love with you, my sensitive man." She reached out and squeezed his hand in hers as they both chuckled at the memory.

"Do the kids know?" Luke asked as he looked at her again, his eyes red.

She'd expected the question and shook her head. "No. I haven't figured out how to tell them yet."

"They deserve to know, Anna." But as he said it, he looked away. Clearly, he had no idea how to tell them either.

"I've been thinking a lot about that. I kind of wanted you to be there when I tell them."

Luke softened a bit, his shoulders lowering as he nodded and squeezed her hand back. "Of course I will be." He took a deep breath. "But Anna, we have to tell them soon. They're already worried after today," he stated the obvious.

"Let's just get me out of here first. I don't want to tell them looking like I'm already half-dead, okay?"

Luke nodded. Anna felt so relieved to have finally told him. It wasn't the best way to find out, she knew, but he'd handled it well, considering. She said a silent prayer of thanks for the strength they'd both had the past few hours. Then she asked God to help them through this—especially the kids.

Half an hour later, Luke left to check on the kids, and she felt herself dozing off. She hoped this wasn't the start of the long hospital stays she'd been dreading. *Please God, just a little more time.* She wanted to help Luke prepare for being a single dad, and she wanted to be sure her kids were ready to accept him back fully before she went.

Thoughts of how to facilitate that flooded her mind as she drifted off to sleep again.

CHAPTER 13

LUKE STILL COULDN'T wrap his mind around what he'd just learned. Anna couldn't be dying. She was too young! Hearing the doctor and Anne discussing it with no warning had left him weak and dizzy. He'd managed to stay upright in the chair, but his chest grew tight, and for a moment, he wondered if he might be having a heart attack. As he'd sat there, forcing himself to keep taking breaths, watching her in the hospital, he'd been overwhelmed by the realization how much he still loved her. The way her curly bangs flopped across her forehead when she rolled onto her side, the warmth that radiated from her smile and her beautiful eyes, her alabaster skin. He realized he'd never fallen out of love with her—not after the break up; not after the divorce. Even now, she was the love of his life, and the love of his life was dying. All the pain of the divorce, the anger, the kids' resentment faded away, replaced now by a sense of despair that felt so much worse.

How could she wait almost a month to tell him? Had she hated him that much? And what would happen to the kids? How would he take care of them alone? Luke couldn't sleep that night, sorting through it all in his mind. He understood how much she must be going through, trying to figure it all out herself. He had been uncaring, and she had been more than decent to him since Christmas Day. More decent than he deserved.

How could God let this happen? What had she done to deserve this? What had their kids done to deserve losing their mother? Life was so unfair. God's will was such a mystery. Snippets of verses came back to him—something about "God never gives you more than you can handle" and God having a plan for a future full of hope. He'd heard them a thousand times, even repeated them to others, but now they just seemed meaningless. Empty platitudes. How was this plan not destruction? Where was the future and the hope for Anna? He just couldn't understand it. He prayed for wisdom, but it felt empty, because his heart wasn't in it. He was too furious with God.

In the morning, Luke called in to work and took the day off. He told his secretary to only call if it was an emergency. Family crisis, he'd told her, as if the boss needed a reason. He couldn't focus on that right now. He needed time to think, pray, be alone. How could someone who had it so together at work be such a mess with his family? And now they'd lost three precious years they could never get back.

He knew Anna didn't love him that way anymore, but she was and had always been the first and greatest love of his life. He wasn't ready to lose her. Luke remembered the way her hand always fit perfectly into his. The way her smile had this magic that erased any worries or stress the minute he saw it. He'd jokingly dubbed it 'the miracle cure.' "Could you give me the miracle cure, please, Anna?" he'd say, and she would laugh.

That was another thing he'd missed. It had been so good to hear her laughter again. How could he face the future knowing that soon he would never be able to hear it again? He longed to take her in his arms and hold her one more time. He knew if he did, he might never let go. He'd learned the real meaning of love from the way she loved him. He might never get to know what that felt like again.

What about all the moments with the kids she would never get to share? Or all the moments with the kids she would never be able to handle for him, when he couldn't handle it? Anna had always been better with the kids in certain situations. Luke thought about the future. Soon he'd be teaching Kyle to drive. After that, the girls would start dating. His head hurt at the thought. There'd be graduations, weddings, their own kids. He knew he wasn't going to be ready for all that. How could a good, loving God let Anna miss all that? It was the reward for having and raising good kids to get to share that one day. So many questions. So few answers.

That night, he took the kids to his dad's condo at the retirement community for a family barbecue. Uncle Ray was at his best entertaining them, and Luke was grateful. His mind was somewhere else. As he stood on the patio watching Ray playing with the kids—his and Anna's kids—he fought back tears.

Finally, Grace left Karl to entertain their own kids and came over to him. "What's the matter, Luke? You've been quiet all night."

Luke didn't know where to begin. Their dad, Lee, came over and patted him on the arm. "You okay, son?"

Luke looked at their concerned eyes and just started to cry. They hadn't expected it, and it made them worry more.

"My God, what is it? Anna? The kids?" Grace asked.

Luke couldn't speak for a moment. His father hugged him for the first time in years. "Come inside, son. It's going to be okay."

Luke followed as Lee led him into the kitchen. His father had just turned sixty, but he looked ten years older. His health had really gone downhill after their mother died, and every time Luke saw him, he was still surprised. But Lee was kind, gentle, and a great father. The whole family adored him. Luke and his dad took a seat around the table as Grace slid the patio door shut to make sure the kids wouldn't overhear before joining them.

Finally, Luke collected himself enough to say: "Anna's dying. Pancreatic cancer. Probably only a few months left."

"Oh my God," Grace sighed. Her face fell.

Lee put his hand firmly on Luke's arm. "You'll get through this, son. It first hits you like the end of everything, but you'll get through it." Lee himself had lost his wife, Glenda, their mother, from cancer only four years before. He had been devastated at first. They had discussed it amongst themselves and expected him to die soon after. Their parents had been married for thirty-three years. Their mother was his whole life. Lee had never expected to live without her, and they thought he probably would lose the will to live, but somehow, he'd made it through and found strength to carry on.

"She's only thirty-three-years-old. She's too young to die," Luke said.

"Sometimes, cancer can appear so much earlier these days," Lee said. "When your mother was ill, we were shocked by the age range of the patients on her ward."

"They can fight this, Luke..." Grace began, but Luke cut her off.

"It was too late when they found it. She hadn't been to the doctor in almost a year," Luke said and turned his eyes away, feeling a pain in the back of his throat.

"It's not your fault, son." Lee said, knowingly.

"Of course it's not his fault, Dad. Why would you say that?" Grace scolded.

Lee grunted. "When your mother died, I knew it was my fault—all those years of smoking," Lee said. "It was my smoke that clogged her lungs. I poisoned her. I killed her."

"Mom died of liver cancer, Dad," Grace reminded him.

"I know what she died of, but it was my smoke that caused it. I knew it," Lee said. "I was certain of it." He looked at Luke.

"I should have been a better husband and father," Luke finally said.

"Yes, son, you should have, but it's not your fault—the cancer," Lee said. "I was so angry at God and with myself when the doctors told us. It took me a few weeks to realize I was wasting precious time. God doesn't owe us any explanations. Your mom had limited days, and every one of them was precious to me and to her. I could waste them being angry and feeling sorry for myself, or I could do something to make sure every moment she had left was among the best moments of her life."

Luke and Grace had watched their father's attitude change. He retired early and took their mom on a whirlwind trip across several states in the RV. They came back with pictures and souvenirs from Yellowstone, Mount Rushmore—many places they'd always talked about but never seen. It was the trip of a lifetime, and they both treasured every minute of it.

After the trip, Lee had devoted himself to taking care of her. He did all the shopping, anything she needed. And he made sure she was happy and comfortable, treating her like a queen. Their mom had joked that if she'd known he'd react like this, she'd have told him she was sick a long time ago.

Grace had had a tough relationship with their mother. Glenda Morrison was the envy of everyone—the perfect wife, perfect mother. Everyone wanted her for their PTA or committee. Everyone sought her out for advice. She was the kind of woman who would put aside everything, including feeding her kids, at the drop of a hat if someone needed her. She could never do enough for you. You never knew what unselfish love was until you'd met Glenda. She was adored and loved by anyone who ever met her, and Grace could never live up to the expectations that came with being her daughter.

It's not that Grace didn't share qualities with her mother, or wasn't kind and loving like her. But Grace was quieter, more shy and reserved in public. She just didn't have the gregariousness to be so open to everyone, and so she just couldn't fill the shoes expected of her after people met her mother. To add to the pressure, Glenda apparently had decided after the diagnosis that she had limited time to give her kids the best advice she could to see them through the rest of their lives. For whatever reason, she'd offered the most advice to Grace, and Grace ended up resenting it. She didn't want her mother to run her life anymore. She was almost thirty. She had her own kids and family. She got tired real quick of hearing how she could be doing things better or differently. She fought with her mom a lot, and no matter how Luke or Karl tried, she couldn't seem to tolerate the advice that came from a truly loving, non-judgmental place. To Grace, Luke heard her say later, it seemed like an indictment of her. She couldn't receive it any other way.

But Lee also knew his kids well, and he'd nailed it. Luke did feel guilty. He felt responsible for so many bad things that had happened the past three years with his family. Anna's cancer was just the icing on the cake. Maybe if he'd been there, she would have checked herself out in time to do something about it. She'd been so busy with the kids and her new job, she didn't have time to do everything she used to do. She had always been fervent about doctor visits for all of them, and yet, she'd admitted at the hospital that it had been hard to be as vigilant after the divorce. So yes, Luke absolutely felt responsible.

"You have to decide how it's going to be, Luke," Lee went on. "For you, for Anna, and for the kids. Are you going to spend her last days angry and sad, or are you going to help her celebrate her short life with her kids, so that they always remember her through the happy times you have left?"

Grace turned away, wiping away a tear.

Luke looked at his father. The words made sense, but the whirlwind of emotions—especially anger—still raged inside. Saying it seemed easy but doing it—he didn't know how. "I just feel so lost, Dad."

Lee nodded. "You take it a day at a time, Luke. Live for the moment. Make the most of each one as best you can. You're a good man, son, and I've always been proud of you. I'm sorry I didn't speak up when I saw you working too much and not paying enough attention to your family. I knew what it was doing to them, but I was so distracted by my own grief, and then, you were hardly around enough to talk...I should have been a better father."

Luke wiped away his tears. "You were a great father, Dad. You were always a great father. I wasn't there for you either. I'm so sorry. I was selfish. I hope you can forgive me."

Lee stood and held his arms out.

Luke stood and let his father wrap him in the kind of bear hug a son never outgrows.

"I love you, son."

"I love you, too, Dad," Luke said.

Grace couldn't hide the tears now. "You two are killing me," she teased. They opened their arms and she joined the hug.

"You guys always leave me out," Ray said from behind them. They turned to see him grabbing two beers from the fridge. "Karl wanted a fresh one. What's going on?"

Grace and Luke exchanged a look. "Anna has cancer," Luke said.

Ray looked shocked. "My God, Luke. She's not even forty!"

"They have cancer in kids, Ray," Grace said. "It's a lot more common these days."

Ray swallowed, still coming to terms with it as they all were. "When did you find out?"

"Yesterday."

"Is she in treatment? She's young enough to fight it, right?" Ray looked around and saw the answer in everyone's eyes.

"They caught it too late, Ray. It's months at best," Grace answered, sparing Luke the pain of repeating those words again.

Ray leaned back against the counter, shocked. Clearly, he didn't know what to say.

"Wanna join the hug, Ray?" Grace asked, teasing. It was just what they needed. They all laughed.

"Whatever you need, bro. You just call, day or night. We'll do whatever we can," Ray said, putting his hand firmly on

Luke's arm.

Luke nodded. "I'll be taking you up on that."

Then they all heard the sound of children's giggling outside and Ray glanced toward the windows. "Do the kids know?"

Luke started crying again. Finally, he managed to shake his head. "We don't know how to tell them. They're so young for this..."

Grace and Lee hugged him again. Ray looked away again, at a loss for words.

CHAPTER 14

DOCTORS KEPT ANNA at Barnes Hospital three more days for observation and testing, during which time Luke moved into her house and stayed with the kids. It was a no brainer since his house was barely furnished and all the kids' stuff was there. When Anna came home, he stayed on in the guest room for a few days to make sure she was back up to speed and fully recovered—at least as fully as could be expected at this point.

They decided to tell the kids the following Saturday. They both wanted time to choose their words carefully, and they also wanted to plan some fun activity afterward that would help the kids to know everything would be okay for them. Luke had decided to take them to Hammer's Food and Fun, a local game and entertainment complex. They'd checked with Doctor Sousa and Anna was okay to go along, so they figured it might be her last chance to do anything like that.

The kids looked forward to Hammer's all week. Cassie and Mandy had never been, but Kyle had attended a friend's birthday party there once and regaled his sisters with tales of its "coolness." They were a little frustrated when Luke and Anna asked them to sit down in the Living Room for a family meeting before leaving, but that was more out of fear of being in trouble than impatience to get out and have fun.

Anna and Luke exchanged a look as they sat in chairs facing the three kids on the couch. Then Anna took a deep breath, looked at her babies, and smiled "We have something important to tell you."

"Are we in trouble?" Cassie asked, worriedly.

"No, sweet pea. Of course not. But..." It was hard for her. Luke smiled, lending his support. "You guys, mommy loves you very much. You know that, right?"

All three nodded and mumbled. It was always reassuring when they actually paid attention.

"Good. I'm glad. Because mommy has to tell you something hard."

"But we can still go, right?" Kyle said, clearly anxious to not have his day of fun averted.

"We're all going," Luke said.

Shoulders sank, bodies leaned back in chairs, and smiles returned as they all looked relieved.

"Mommy's sick," Anna finally managed.

"We can get you some aspirin, mom," Mandy offered, looking mildly concerned.

"Mommy doesn't have the flu," Luke explained.

"Chicken pox? Mumps? Measles?" Mandy loved to guess answers.

"If it is one of those she couldn't go, dummy," Kyle snapped.

Mandy stuck out her tongue at him.

"Mommy has cancer in her pancreas" Anna said, touching her chest gently.

Kyle looked at her, fear widening his face and mouth. Mandy looked like she was trying to believe but couldn't quite grasp it.

Cassie just nodded like it was no big deal. "What's a

pancreas?"

"It's an organ in your body, dummy," Kyle snapped.

"Kyle!" Luke scolded.

"It's for helping digest food, honey," Anna said, explaining as simply as she could.

Cassie nodded, sticking her tongue out at Kyle. "So, can they fix it?"

"It's a tumor! They can't fix that!" Mandy snapped, lashing out as her sister as her face showed her clearly wrestling with a cloud of emotions.

"Your Mom's doctor said it's the kind of tumor that they can't fix." Luke added, looking at Cassie.

Anna smiled, grateful for the help.

Kyle reacted as if he suddenly understood. "She's dying?"

Mandy looked horrified and Cassie started sniffling.

"But I need you, Mommy," Cassie said as the tears began.

Luke turned away, fighting tears as wet streams rolled down Anna's cheeks.

"I need you, too. All of you." She looked at Luke.

Did she mean that? he wondered.

"Mommy's on radiation and chemo," Luke explained, then looked at Cassie. "Medicines that are supposed to help."

"But there's a chance Mommy's not going to get better," Anna went on.

"You did this!" Kyle suddenly screamed and ran at Luke, pounding his fists into Luke's chest. Luke stood there and took it, shocked.

Anna stood and walked over close to them in front of the couch, holding Kyle's shoulders and looking him in the eyes. "No, honey. I have cancer. That's not your daddy's fault."

"Cancer?" Mandy repeated, knowing the word. She started crying. "Why, mom?"

Anna looked at Kyle, who pulled away, walking over to stand in the corner with his back turned.

Anna went over to hug Mandy. "We don't know why. It just happened. But mommy needs you all to be strong now, and help daddy."

"You left us! And everything went bad! It's all because of you!" Kyle shouted, whirling around and pointing at Luke.

Cassie and Mandy sobbed more loudly. Anna put an arm around Cassie, too, between them on the couch. "Kyle, don't say that. Don't ever think that. It's not true," she scolded.

Kyle looked away, tears forming on his cheeks. Luke stood there not knowing what to say or do. It was as horrible as either of them imagined, yet how else was it supposed to be? The kids understood only in limited ways. The doctors had told them that until age fourteen, most kids have no concept of death. But Kyle and Mandy were old enough to understand what they were being told, and they'd already lost three grandparents. The older two kids knew cancer, too, from Luke's mom. He had never felt so helpless.

"God can heal you," Mandy said.

Anna smiled and reached out to put a palm against her daughter's cheek. "I believe that too, honey, but sometimes he doesn't. We just want to be honest with you so we can pray and work through this together."

"God can do anything, mommy," Cassie said, trying to be helpful despite her confusion over what was going on.

Anna nodded. "Yes, He can. I love you guys. That's not going to change."

"We love you!" Mandy said and threw her arms around her mother. They held each other, and then Cassie joined the huddle.

Luke watched, keeping an eye on Kyle. "I'm so sorry. It's really hard to understand," he offered, knowing no words would suffice.

Kyle shook his head and stood. "You promised we could go to Hammer's. Let's go."

"We will, son, but your mom needed to talk to you first," Luke said. "Can you understand—"

Kyle glared at him, cutting him off, "We understand." He whirled and headed for the front door.

Anna hugged the girls again and then nodded to Luke. "It's okay. We have lots of time to talk later. Let's go."

"Are you sure you can, mom?" Mandy asked.

"Sure," Anna said. "And if I get too tired, I can sit for a while and watch you guys." Anna stood, to demonstrate she was okay, at least for now, and smiled. She was happy to get the kids' minds off what they'd just heard as soon as possible. At least for the moment.

"Yay!" Cassie said, cheering noticeably as Mandy stood and took her mother's hand and they all headed for the door.

THEY MADE IT to Hammer's Food and Fun by eleven and tried their best to be cheerful and keep the kids' minds off Anna's illness. Anna staked out a table near the all-you-can-eat buffet featuring fresh pizza, pasta, soup, salad and tasty desserts. "The Fairgrounds" entertainment complex included indoor Go-Karts, Bumper Cars, Glow-In-The-Dark Mini Golf, Mini Bowling, and a huge Game Room where you could redeem tickets for prizes. The kids were so filled with energy and excitement that heat radiated through her as a lightness filled her.

Kyle avoided Luke like the plague. Cassie and Mandy hung close to Anna, hugging her a lot. Even Cassie didn't seem as joyful as usual, and she was the one who could usually be distracted from bad news easily. The whole time, Luke kept a careful eye on Anna for any signs of pain or fatigue. He took charge of carrying all the daypacks and umbrellas, even the kids' when they didn't want them, and he assisted Cassie with her tray at the buffet as well as distributing gaming tokens, holding onto to tickets, and so on.

Anna managed to leave the table a couple of times and join Cassie in a round of Whack-A-Mole and a race car driving game during which you sat in a mock driver's seat with steering wheel and pedals. Luke expressed the worry she'd tire easily, but other than taking it easy, she remained alert and cheerful, showing endless patience.

They stayed at Hammer's for over three hours then headed back to Anna's, where Luke fixed dinner, while Anna napped. Afterward, he read to the girls and tucked them in bed. He even did the dishes. Anna was amazed. His cooking had definitely improved. She had thought he'd just learned how to make pies, but he'd obviously been working on other things as well. Was he actually becoming a renaissance man? When he finally joined her in the Living Room, as she sipped coffee in her favorite chair, he looked exhausted.

"I can't thank you enough for today. You were so helpful, and I can't believe you did all that," she said between sips.

Luke grunted. "At least you noticed. Kyle won't even speak to me." He'd hardly touched his coffee.

"You were making progress before. He'll come around," she said.

"He blames me for this, too. Another reason to hate me." Luke leaned back in his chair, eyes on the floor.

Anna knew Kyle was holding the cancer against Luke, too, but she didn't believe he hated him. Teenagers had such emotional bursts; she felt more than likely her son was just as confused as the rest of them about what to feel. "He doesn't hate you. He's just mad and hurt and confused, and he doesn't know who to really blame."

"Gee, that makes me feel better," Luke said and laughed.

"Better drink that before it gets cold," she said, motioning to his mug sitting on the coffee table untouched. Luke was too distracted to notice. "You're his easy scapegoat right now. He'll get over it. He won't like me much either tomorrow, when I make him rake the lawn. It's a mess since the snow melted."

"I used to hate doing that, when I was a kid, too." Luke said. "My dad always made me do it, too." He chuckled.

"I bet he'd love you to death, if you helped him with it," Anna said, not really thinking about what she was saying.

Luke reacted like a light had gone off. "Do you think so?"

"You're going to help him?" she asked, surprised by his reaction. "I was just kind of speculating." She took another sip of her coffee as she looked to him for an answer.

"It's a great idea, Anna. I would have been thrilled, too," Luke said, sounding excited.

"If you really want to—"

Luke jumped up and kissed her hard on the forehead. "You're the best, Anna. Thanks a lot," he said as he grabbed his keys and headed for the door, forgetting all about the coffee now.

"You're welcome," she said as the door closed behind him, and she wondered what she'd started.

BEING WITH ANNA again only reminded Luke why he'd never dated since the divorce. The girl he'd fallen head over heels for in college was his dream girl, the only one for him. And he still felt the same way about her all these years later that he had then. Just watching the expression on her face or in her eyes as she watched the kids play or listened to them regale her with tales of their gaming adventures made him fall in love all over again. She was always so attentive and caring, so energized by her passion for her family. *God, I was such an idiot to drive her away.* And now he'd never get the chance to win her back.

Luke had a business meeting until five, but as soon as he got home, he went straight out to the garage and loaded the rider mower he'd kept in the divorce onto a trailer to take over to Anna's. Kyle's eyes got big as Luke pulled up and hopped out, dropping two ramps from the back of the truck. He stared from beside the garage, holding a rake that looked like something Anna probably inherited from her father—a good forty years old with chipped and faded red paint and a few bent tines. Luke eyed the lawn which was covered with wet soggy leaves and definitely a mess. It would take Kyle hours to rake it with that thing. The grass had clearly been uncut since late Fall, and Luke assumed Anna probably had been pestering Kyle to mow it for a while.

He climbed the ramps to the mower, stopping to look at his son. "You gonna help me or just stare?"

"Why are you here?" Kyle snapped.

"Do you wanna use this or your grandpa's antique? 'Cause I can haul this back home," Luke replied.

Kyle immediately leaned the rake against the garage and hurried over to help his father.

"You just get up there and start her when I tell you, then back her down slowly," Luke instructed.

"Really? By myself?" Kyle asked. Luke had only let Kyle ride it with him when he was younger, but his son was too old now and there wasn't really room for him to drive it with Kyle on his lap. Not that the teenager would have agreed to that humiliation anyway. It was time for him to learn.

"Sure. You think you can handle it?" Luke said, keeping his smile to himself as he stared at Kyle.

Kyle nodded sharply and hurried up onto the trailer, sliding into the mower's seat.

"Okay then," Luke said. He straightened the ramps and checked that they were secure then stepped to one side. "Let's do it."

Kyle turned the key and the mower hummed to life, then he shifted it into reverse and slowly pushed the accelerator, causing it to jerk.

"You have to be steady," Luke said. "Slow but steady. Try again."

This time, Kyle managed to get the mower moving and hold his foot steady as he backed it down the ramp onto the drive slowly.

"All right, well done," Luke said, smiling. "You good to mow this sucker alone or you want help?"

"I got it," Kyle said, slipping the mower into gear and driving forward toward the lawn, as he turned the wheel to line it up for the first row.

Luke spotted Anna watching from the porch and smiled, waving. She hollered something but he couldn't hear. He watched Kyle get started, with a few rough moments before he got the hang of it. The mower stalled out once when Kyle tried to turn too sharply onto a large leaf pile. It didn't take Kyle long to figure it out, though.

Luke crossed the drive and followed the sidewalk, approaching the stoop where Anna was still watching. "What was that?"

"I asked if you want some lemonade," Anna said

"Really? Lemonade in January?" Luke grinned, not hiding his amusement.

"A riding mower to rake leaves?" Anna teased back.

Luke shrugged. "It breaks them up and sucks them into the bag and gets the job done. Plus, it's a hell of a lot more fun."

They both watched Kyle a minute as he successfully managed navigating the rider mower alone, Luke took a long, satisfied breath, suddenly feeling taller as he watched his son with pride. He seemed to be enjoying himself. He glanced over and saw a similar look of satisfaction on Anna's face, too.

Anna caught him staring and shrugged. "Cassie asked for the lemonade, since you asked. She loves it."

Luke laughed. "Ah, that explains it." They both watched Kyle a moment longer but then Anna leaned against the door and turned to go inside. "I think he's got it," Luke said then checking on Kyle one final time, he followed her inside.

CHAPTER 15

I N THE WEEKS AFTER, Luke frequently dropped by to check on Anna, lending a hand with driving the kids to and from school or other activities, picking up groceries, and even making sure the chores got done. In some cases, he took care of them himself, just to make sure they would be done the way he knew that Anna liked them. Even after all the changes she'd seen in him since Christmas, the fact that he still remembered such details really touched her. Since she'd scolded him about it, he'd never been late either, and more than once had shown up at a time when in the past, he'd always been working. He must have shuffled things around for them, and Anna knew the kids had noticed.

More than that, Luke somehow managed to keep the kids busy and their minds off her health. They both knew the kids hadn't forgotten, but they obviously weren't dwelling on it and didn't seem depressed or angry about it. Anna knew it didn't mean they cared any less about her. It was healthy for them to see that life goes on and live as if it did. They would have to do that when she was gone, and she was glad again to see that, like Luke, her kids were adapting well to the situation at hand. It gave her a greater sense of peace about the situation.

Kyle was starting to warm up to Luke, too. The rider mower-raking adventure seemed to have reminded him that his dad wasn't such a bad guy and could even be fun. Now, when

Luke was around, Kyle would greet him, and even engage in short conversations. Anna even walked in on Kyle trying to teach Luke how to play his new *Rock Star Seven* game that Luke had given him at Christmas. Luke was not exactly adapting to it readily, and Kyle seemed both amused and frustrated by this. Luke finally gave up after a particularly bad attempt at a guitar solo devolved into father and son laughter.

"I guess I was just never meant to be a rock star, huh?" Luke joked.

Anna was glad to see that situation working itself out. She wanted Kyle to grow up with a father, and she was confident now that Luke would have good influence and be a part of his life. She knew if they never reconciled, Kyle and Luke would both end up with a lot of regret, and thought Luke probably had enough regrets already without one more to worry about. Kyle was too young to see it clearly, but there were going to be lots of times ahead when having his father's guidance and support would be very important to him. As she thought about it, she started missing her own father, and tears formed in the corners of her eyes.

Midweek, she went back to Doctor Sousa for a checkup, and much was the same. She had been growing more and more tired and was less able to get through her days with the level of energy she'd grown accustomed to. The chemo and radiation were exhausting her body and mind, and she suffered frequent brain fog. She needed a couple of daily naps to have the strength to keep going, and shortness of breath became more frequent as well as the pains in her abdomen and vertebrae. Her hair was gone too, and though she refused to leave her room without putting on her wig, the two older kids had managed to catch glimpses, and she knew she'd soon have to explain it to Cassie as well. Even so, the chemo and radiation and didn't seem to be failing and Doctor Sousa had even said the tumor had showed only minor growth which was encouraging. To Anne, she wasn't doing as badly as she 'd expected to be, and though she continued praying for. Miracle and lighting her prayer candle nightly, she'd determined to treasure whatever moments she had while she still could.

On a Thursday, Luke picked the kids up from school, dropped by for her, and took them over to Brenda's for a barbecue. Although it was February, the winter had been so mild that Anna had heard the sound of baby finches chirping from the nest in the old oak outside the kitchen window that morning. She'd always loved having that tree there and watching the finches return every year delighted both her and the two girls. Cassie, in particular, loved to sit for hours just watching their every move. The tree itself was also a blessing because it provided good shade for the kitchen during the hottest hours of the afternoon, making it a pleasant backdrop for sitting at the table to read or do homework and other activities.

Because the weather was in the sixties, they gathered in the backyard where Brenda's husband, Dave, manned the grill. Dave was a tall, lanky, white engineer with dark thick glasses, who made up for his geeky look by being smart and funny and always great company. The mixed couple lived in a restored house near Forest Park, an area which had been revitalized when young families kept moving in. The house was taller and thinner than many modern ones with four levels, including the basement and a playroom on the top floor. The outside was solid brick, with tar shingles lining a roof which slanted on one side. The yard was smaller than Anna's and Luke's and had a tall privacy fence of wood slats. The children played together in various groups as they always did, while Anna sat at the picnic table with Brenda and Bekah keeping an eye on things and sharing news and gossip.

Brenda and Bekah had both observed more than once the changes in Luke. They'd also commented before on how impressed they were and how different he seemed. Today, they both said it was even more obvious Luke had really changed. Even Dave and John commented on it. He was the kind of husband Anna had always deserved and longed for, and they were happy that he'd come around when she really needed him. Of course, Anna reminded them that he wasn't her husband anymore. They had been divorced now three years. But while they all knew this, Anna found herself more and more thinking and interacting with Luke as if that wasn't the case. He was always there, helping out with the kids and house, checking on her. It was like a flashback to bygone days, which made it easy to forget their separation.

Anna also found herself more often thinking back on the past and their first apartment after graduation. It hadn't been the nicest part of town, because they didn't have a lot of money, and it was small and old, but they'd done their best and made the most of it. Their first Christmas together Luke had somehow scrounged up a small table-top tree with mini decorations because they didn't have space or money for a big one that year. He'd been so good back then at getting the door for her when she got out of the car or entered a building, offering her his arm like a chivalrous knight or gentleman. Roses would appear from time to time, sometimes with little notes and cards. When she would thank him for them, he would kiss her and tell her he always wanted her to know how special she was to him. Luke continued doing that until the business started to dominate his focus. It was one of the first things she'd noticed when things started to change between them.

Luke had also been good back then about making sure they always had a date night, even after Kyle was born. Luke called it their "special time," and they both treasured it, even when all it consisted of was a quick bite at McDonalds and a movie rental from Blockbuster. It was having time alone together and focusing their attention on each other that counted. It had kept them connected and close through so many times ahead. She wondered if Luke ever thought about those times. She knew he still regretted the way things had gone between them.

Lately, Anna had even found herself, on occasion, noticing how handsome and charming Luke still was. He'd taken up bringing her flowers once a week. Sometimes he would pick them in the neighbor's yard or at the park, and sometimes he bought them. But she always awakened from a nap to find them in a vase on the dresser, carefully placed where she would be sure to see them. Occasionally, there would be one of her favorite candies or a chocolate bar lying underneath—just a little something to make her feel special. Moments like that led her to wonder why things hadn't worked out differently for them. Maybe she hadn't tried hard enough to talk to him, when she was feeling so fed up. Maybe she'd given up on them too easily. It seemed so easy to do that these days. Divorces were a dime a dozen. She'd once loved him so deeply, and even now, she still had a special place in her heart for Luke and knew she always would. But after three years, had he started dating again? He hadn't mentioned anyone special. Still, he didn't owe her that. A lot could have changed, and she realized she was getting to know him again the same way he was getting to know her and the kids.

"You're awfully quiet," Bekah observed, smiling, as they all ate around her.

"Sorry," Anna said, "I was just remembering."

"Anything in particular?" Brenda asked.

"Many things," Anna responded, taking a bite of her hamburger. Dave was known for his superb burgers. He had a secret family seasoning mix that he mixed into the ground beef, and as the first bite hit her tongue, she her senses delighted in the savory flavors as always. She wished her burgers tasted this good.

"Anything you want to talk about?" Brenda asked again.

Anna smiled. "Yes, what the heck is Dave's secret? He's making the rest of us look bad."

"Uh uh, not telling!" Dave teased rubbing his index fingers together in a scolding manner.

Her friends laughed, and then Brenda said, "You know that's not what I meant."

Anna grunted. "Just looking back on my life, you know?"

Brenda and Bekah nodded. She knew they hated thinking

about what was happening to her, even though they all had no choice but to face it. Earlier that week, they'd pointed out that Anna had changed, too.

"You're smiling a lot more for one thing," Bekah had commented. "And you seem more relaxed, less hectic."

"Yes!" Brenda echoed.

"That's because Luke's been helping so much with the kids," Anna said dismissively.

"It's more than that," Brenda corrected. "It's like a burden has been lifted. The way you walk, your whole ambience is like it was when we first met you."

"It's so great," Bekah added.

Seeing their quiet sadness now, Dave tried to cheer them up. "Do you guys remember that time Luke rented the ski boat and tried to convince us he was an expert driver?"

They all laughed at the memory.

Bekah's husband John was shorter than Dave and Luke with a developing belly, but he had the round cheeks and face and warm smile common to Filipinos, making him the kind of guy who could make you join his laughter with just one smile. He was in insurance and one of those guys who told it like it is. "It was so obvious from the way he handled her that he had no idea what he was doing," John added, chuckling. "He almost led Dave and I right into the ramp rather than over it, remember?"

Dave laughed. "After it happened, he acted as if he had just meant to scare us."

They all laughed again as Luke shrugged, looking sheepish. "Hey, we all had a good time as I recall."

"Sure we did. We were happy to have survived it!" John said to another round of laughter.

"It was like our own version of Survivor!" John joked.

"More like Fear Factor!" Bekah countered to more laughter.

"You were always trying to impress us with some new skill, Luke," Brenda recalled.

"Just trying to keep you guys entertained," Luke said, smiling.

They had gotten up around five that day to drive together to the Lake of The Ozarks. Originally, the plan had just been swimming and floating in inner tubes, but when Luke saw the boat rental place on the way in, he couldn't resist. He'd always wanted to drive a ski boat. How hard could it be? They'd all liked the idea and chipped in. It had turned out to be much harder than any of them imagined. Luke hadn't even been able to get the motor started without Dave and John's help, and it took him several minutes to get the hang of pushing the accelerator at an appropriate pace without overdoing it. Dave had been dragged three times on skis before calling "uncle" and climbing back in the boat, but Luke insisted he'd get it and refused to give up the wheel. John tied next and had hardly gotten up on his skis, when he found himself losing control and falling. After the first few tries, everyone else refused to let Luke drive the boat.

The tantalizing smell of Dave's hamburgers floated over from the grill, and they all paused a moment to appreciate it.

Brenda noticed the younger kids getting curious and moving toward the grill. "Don't touch that!" She and Dave hurried off to run interference.

While John and Bekah were busy refilling their plates, Luke looked at Anna and said, "You know, I've been thinking about our 'special time.' Do you remember?"

Anna hid a smile. "Of course, I do. You were quite the romantic back then."

Luke shrugged. "If you call fast food and video rental romantic, then thanks."

"That was only a couple of times," Anna answered. "Most of the time, you took me to nicer places with candlelight or dancing."

Luke nodded. They both brightened at the memory. "Well, I was wondering if you might like to do that again sometime."

Anna looked at him puzzled. As fond as the memories were, she had never considered reliving those moments. Dating just wasn't in the cards for her. There was no future in it. "Are you asking me on a date?"

"Not a date, like we used to, maybe, but a night out, sure," Luke said. "You deserve to do that while you still feel good enough to go out. I thought you might enjoy it."

Anna was touched at his thoughtfulness. After all, hadn't she just been missing those times and remembering how much they meant to her? But she worried that there was something more to it for him, some longing to get back together. Could he be falling in love with her again? Or then again, maybe he had never stopped being in love. She didn't want to cause him any more pain than she already had, and she didn't want any more of her own either. "I don't know, Luke. Do you think that's such a good idea?"

Luke shrugged. "I'm not asking you to marry me or anything. I just wanted to enjoy a good night out. Something to remember, make you feel special, and romantic, and appreciated."

"Romantic?" She raised her eyebrows.

"I'm not trying to make you fall in love with me again, if that's what you're wondering," he explained. "But I know you don't get those opportunities anymore..." His voice trailed off.

"What? You don't think anyone wants to ask me out anymore?" Anna pretended to be offended.

Luke stuttered. "Not at all. I just meant—I..." The look on her face told him she was teasing, and he relaxed.

"Did you have something particular in mind?" she finally asked.

"How about if I surprise you?" he said, smiling, pleased that she seemed to be considering it.

She couldn't say no. The look on his face was too sweet and innocent. "Okay, Luke. That sounds really nice."

He leaned in and kissed her on the cheek as the others arrived back from their various distractions. Bekah and Brenda shot her a curious look, but Anna simply smiled and continued eating her burger.

CHAPTER 16

LUKE KEPT HER guessing for the next week about what he was planning. Whenever she would ask, he would just smile softly and tease, "You'll find out." She had to admit the curiosity was getting to her. He seemed to have put a lot of thought into it.

She awoke that Saturday from a midday nap to find a beautiful cocktail dress laid out on the bed. Beside it was a note telling her that a corsage was waiting on a shelf in the fridge. And when she walked in the kitchen to get it, she found the largest bouquet yet of mixed color roses waiting for her on the counter. He was sure going all out, and it left her a little nervous about his intentions.

Cassie called her to the door about five-thirty to find a dark limousine idling in their driveway. Anna, the kids and their babysitter watched curiously until the back door opened, and Luke climbed out in a suit and tie, looking as handsome as Anna ever remembered. With total chivalry, he strode up the sidewalk to the door, bending as she opened it to kiss her hand. Then he offered her his arm, telling the babysitter they might be out late, and led her out to the limo. Bright stars sparkled overhead in the dark, clean February sky, and the smell of pine needles and smoke from the neighbor's fireplace filled her nose, leaving her feeling warm and cozy.

As he opened the limo's back door, she asked again where they might be going. He smiled as he gently helped her inside, telling her to simply enjoy the ride. She'd know soon enough. For the entire drive Winter and snow-theme music played softly from speakers overhead as they enjoyed the rays from the city lights bouncing off snow drifts and lightly salted trees. The limousine driver exited the interstate just before the bridge to Illinois. Shortly thereafter, he pulled up in front of the Hyatt Regency in downtown near the Arch and the Mississippi River with great riverfront views.

Luke and Anna had spent a particularly memorable weekend there for their tenth anniversary. Anna smiled as the driver opened the door and Luke climbed out, offering her his hand. She took his arm, and he led across the cavernous lobby toward Ruth's Chris Steakhouse. Anna smiled as Luke stopped at the Maître'd's stand outside the dining room.

"Reservation for two, Morrison," he said to the Maitre'd, who nodded, grabbing two menus and leading them along past the pianist, who played "Girl From Ipanema" as they were led toward a table by the window. The soft tingling of silverware and glasses combined with the scents of fresh baked bread, pastas, and pies to excite her senses, the dim, red-tinted lighting and candles on every table lending the whole restaurant an aura ripe for romance.

Luke stepped quickly forward to pull back her chair for her, and after she'd sat down, scooted it back in, then moved to his own chair on the opposite side.

"You've really put a lot of thought into this, haven't you?" Anna commented.

Luke offered a soft smile and nodded. "I told you I wanted to give you a special night."

Anna's smile was less subtle. "Well, thank you. It takes me back to our tenth anniversary. Do you remember?" *Of course he remembers,* she chided herself.

"Of course, I do," he said. "Why do you think I brought you

here?"

They'd always considered it one of their best moments as a couple. A luscious hotel suite on the top floor with a king bed, Egyptian cotton sheets with high thread count, champagne and chocolates included had provided a stunning Arch view. They'd spent hours making love, talking, listening to music. No kids, no distractions, no interruptions. It had been one of the most romantic weekends they'd ever had. It hadn't come cheap, but even after, when the bill came, Luke never complained. He'd just smiled, kissed her, and handed his credit card to the desk clerk.

"Money well spent," he'd said at the time. Given Luke's tendency to micro analyze any expenses, Anna had been surprised and pleased about that. It told her it had meant as much to him as it had to her. It was really something special.

After they'd ordered, Anna looked at Luke. He was relaxed and quiet, totally focused on just being there with her in the moment. She caught a hunt of lavender and Amalfi lemon from his cologne, evoking more memories. It had been a long time since she'd gotten such attention from Luke, and she had to admit she liked it.

"Seems like an awful lot of work for just two friends going to dinner," she commented.

Luke swallowed hard, putting a fist to his lips to try and hide the hurt. "You know we'll always been more than friends, Anna, divorced or not. You're way more special to me than that."

She nodded, placing her hand gently atop his on the table. "I'm sorry. You're special to me, too, Luke." She'd said it off the cuff, not intending it as a dig.

"You were the one who taught me what real love is, the great love of my life," Luke went on. "And no matter what, that won't change."

"I'm glad we can still be friends after all that's happened," she said and squeezed his hand.

Luke squeezed hers back. "Me, too, Anna. There was a time not so long ago, I wouldn't have believed it."

She chuckled. "Me, too."

They spent the next two hours enjoying their meal and having quiet conversation as they recalled lots of fun times together, funny stories of their kids adventures, and their families and friends. From time to time, they stopped to look out the window at the great views, enjoying especially how the various tones of the setting sun cast shadows and highlights on the downtown skyline around them. It turned out to be a particularly clear night, with a spectacular sunset. The most romantic night Anna could remember in years, and she enjoyed every moment of it. Even if it was with her ex-husband and totally unexpected. She couldn't help herself. Despite any worries about his motives, everything was perfect—especially Luke.

After dinner, Luke had arranged a horse drawn carriage ride around the plaza surrounding the Arch. He'd pulled a chilled bottle of champagne from the limousine as they arrived and asked the waiter to keep it chilled until after dinner. He retrieved it for the carriage ride along with two plastic glasses and poured them each a glass as they rode along, staring up at the stars. The riverfront at night was always stunning, the raised shore looking out across the water to Illinois, interrupted only by a few islands, the masts of ships or the occasional flock of birds. They'd been there a number of times over the years, and Anna always found it moving to stare up at the stars and the moon through the Arch rising above their heads. It was so smooth and gentle in its design. They watched a few barges silently passing on the river, cars humming across the bridges, and even wondered about the source of the lights on the other side. There were still a few recognizable landmarks, like an old Peabody building, but many of the buildings had changed over the years. Today, there was also a faint glow from the casino complex to the north.

Later, asking the driver to stop so they could walk around a little, they sat on the top of the stairs leading down to the river, and just sipped champagne, taking it all in.

The truth was, even if it had been Luke's idea, Anna knew she couldn't have planned it better herself. It was a perfect evening, and she experienced a tinge of sadness when the carriage dropped them back in front of the hotel where the limousine waited again. It was dark now, tall industrial lights providing the only illumination. Luke took her hand and led her toward the limousine. But as they started back, she fell short of breath and felt a bit of pain.

She stopped, bending slightly.

Luke noticed immediately, tenderness in his eyes as he gently took her arm. "Are you okay, Anna?"

"I just need a moment," she answered. "I'll be okay."

But as the pain and shortness of breath lasted longer than before, she began questioning whether she could make it back to the limousine. She wasn't feeling well at all. She really needed to lie down.

Recognizing something was wrong, Luke handed the corked champagne bottle and glasses to the carriage driver, then bent down and picked her up. She draped her arm around his shoulders as he carried her the rest of the way to the limousine. As the chauffeur held the back door open, he leaned down to slide her onto the backseat as if it was no effort whatsoever. Anna smiled, despite the pain. He was amazing. She'd almost forgotten how wonderful he'd been before the troubled times. She knew she'd been very lucky the day they met, that God had blessed her, and despite all the troubles, she was so glad she'd had the chance to be reminded.

On the way home, Luke kept his arm around her as she leaned on his shoulder. He didn't say a word, just sat quietly, letting her rest. When the limousine pulled into her drive, he carried her to the door, setting her down only long enough to open the door, then carried her on inside and laid her on the bed.

"You really didn't have to carry me inside, Luke. I'm feeling much better now," she said, smiling.

"All part of the evening," Luke said.

"You clearly thought of everything," she joked. They both laughed.

For a moment, she thought he was actually going to lean down and kiss her, and she wasn't at all sure she would object. But then the babysitter, Caroline, appeared in the doorway.

"The kids all went to bed by ten," she said, clearly wondering if she could go. Caroline was seventeen but looked younger to Anna. She could hardly remember when she'd been that age. Suddenly, it hit her she would never get to see her own girls at that age and tears started to form in the corners of her eyes.

Luke pulled some bills from his wallet and handed them to the girl. "Thanks, Caroline. Do you need a ride?" he asked.

She shook her head. "My Dad is on his way. Good night, Mr. and Mrs. Morrison." She smiled and nodded.

"Good night," Anna said, as Caroline turned and headed toward the front door.

Luke looked at her, noticing the tears. He sat down beside her. "Are you okay?"

"Of course," she nodded, wiping at her eyes with a palm. "It just occurred to me that I won't get to see our girls at that age."

Luke's face fell. Clearly he was close to tears himself. He leaned over and kissed her cheek, hugging her. "I'm so sorry, Anna. I wish it was me instead."

The remark stunned her and she stared at him a moment before she could formulate a response. "Don't say that, Luke. It would be just as tragic if it were you."

"I'm glad you still think so," he said as he pulled away and looked down at her with soft, concerned eyes.

"Oh Luke, in spite of everything, I hope you know how much I have always cared for you," Anna said.

Clearly Luke was moved to hear that. He slowly leaned down, and she knew he was going to kiss her. She experienced a moment of panic but wasn't quick enough to pull away. Their lips met softly for the first time in over three years. He kissed her tenderly, eyes closed. For a moment, she thought he was going to hold it forever, but then he pulled gently away and stood again.

Seeing the surprise on her face, his smile changed to concern. "I'm sorry. I wasn't trying to take advantage. I got lost in the moment."

"It's okay," she said. "But I'm not sure we should be doing that."

Luke nodded, but his eyes narrowed with hurt. "Good night, Anna," he said, and before she could reply, he turned and hurried out the door.

For a moment, Anna wanted to call after him. Tell him she was sorry. He shouldn't have kissed her, but the night had still been wonderful for her, and she appreciated it. After all, she'd thought he was going to kiss her once before and hadn't been sure she didn't want him to.

Before she could say anything, she heard the front door shut, and she realized he was gone. She turned on her side and winced with pain. Now wasn't the time to be falling in love all over again. It was a distraction neither of them needed. Their attention had to be on the children—preparing them for the future and Anna's pending departure. Anything else was unimportant.

Yet, as she lay there awaiting sleep, she found Luke's face filling her mind and an unbidden smile coming to her lips.

LUKE HADN'T PLANNED on kissing Anna. In fact, the kiss

had taken him as much by surprise as it had her. It had totally been the moment. But the uncertainty of her reaction still hurt more than he cared to admit.

The whole idea that night had been to make Anna feel beautiful and special again. But Luke hadn't counted on the effect revisiting one of their old romantic haunts would have on him. It had brought everything back. For a moment, he'd almost forgotten they'd ever divorced. Forgot the cancer. Forgot everything except being with the love of his life, and as he drove home, he wondered if it had all been a huge mistake.

That moment when their lips met—soft, moist, warm, his heart pounding. Or when he'd taken her hand to help her into the carriage—the fluttering of a hummingbird pulse tingling his hand as their skin touched. He shook off the memory. Anna was dying. Now was not the time. As much as he hated the cancer that was stealing her from him and the kids, he couldn't change it, and deeper emotional involvement between them as a couple would only make things harder. They had to focus on their kids. They had to prepare for life after Anna. That's why she'd invited him back into her life.

As he drove, rain fell and tears filled his eyes. *God, why are you taking Anna from us? We still need her?* It seemed immeasurably cruel and senseless. She was so young, had so much left to give. The kids needed her more than him and always would, no matter how hard he worked to repair their relationship. He realized now he needed her too, more than he'd wanted to admit the past three years.

When he got home, he poured himself a Scotch and sat by the fire, reliving memories, including those made earlier that night. *I love you, Anna Morrison. I'm sorry, so sorry I messed it all up.*

It was after midnight before he drifted off to sleep in the recliner and stayed there all night.

CHAPTER 17

L UKE ARRIVED AT the office before seven to catch up on paperwork. It had rained non-stop since ten minutes after he'd dropped Anna off the night before. It seemed like nature echoing what had happened in Luke's dreams. The rain only added to the already potent humidity which encased everything and everyone it touched. To make matters worse, it added a dreary ambience, which Luke found depressing. It was hard to be cheerful or motivated when your dreams were saying daily over and over again. But on a day like this, you wanted to stay at home with a good book or DVD and wait it out under a blanket. Luke knew if he didn't stay busy, he'd just be thinking about Anna and cancer, and those were the last two things he wanted to be thinking about right now.

Since he'd started spending time again with Anna and the kids, he'd been more relaxed and easier going than usual, laughing and joking with his employees as he walked through the business suite or across the factory floor. He had always been a great boss and treated them like family, but he had grown even more well-liked and respected over the past few months. But today he was quiet and brooding. His employees noticed at once that something had changed when he offered none of the typical "hellos" as he walked right by them on the way to his office.

His secretary, Elise, had stacked meticulously organized

stacks on his desk of checks to be signed, forms to be endorsed, and reports to be read. This kept his mind off Anna for a couple of hours, but when the paperwork ran out, he sat in his office trying to understand why he'd kissed her. She'd already told him more than once that she didn't want to be pursued. Not quite directly, but it was clearly implied. Yet their time together brought back a flood of memories and feelings, and caught in the moment, he had kissed her. Totally on impulse. Because he wanted to.

Again, he flashed back to the moment when their lips met—so soft, gentle, magical. It sent shivers down his spine and a surge of joy through his body that he hadn't felt since their first kiss years before. He shouldn't have been surprised that she rejected him, but the sting of it lingered. They had been getting along well for the past few months.

She had once been so passionate about him that he could barely walk in the door without her jumping into his arms and drowning him in kisses. He'd pretended to be embarrassed about it at the time, but inside, he'd loved every minute. Of course, once the kids got old enough to remember, she had toned down some of that passion, at least in front of them. Making out that way in front of your kids was just weird. Certainly, they had not hidden their affection entirely, but they had always tried to demonstrate it in appropriate ways. They wanted their kids to grow up and fall in love and find what they had, of course. They just wanted them to understand that everything had its place, and some things were private.

Luke understood all that and went along with it, though secretly he'd wished Anna would forget every once in a while. She never did. Still, after the kids went to bed, and they were alone, she was back to her passionate drowning. He loved that about her, the unbridled lover who can't help herself. It made the anticipation of being alone with her so exciting. You never knew quite what to expect, but you knew it was going to be wonderful. He'd always regretted that they'd somehow lost that passion along the way. And being drawn to her again now, he wondered if she had missed it, too.

Anna was the only girl he'd ever dated more than once, and from the beginning, her love and respect for him had taught him so much about himself. He had never felt lovable until he'd met Anna, and he had never imagined someone so beautiful could be so excited about him. She had taught him how to be loved and how to love.

Sitting in his office, he found it hard to believe this room had once had so much pull. These days, he came here because he needed to keep things going, but as soon as he could get away, he was out the door. A year ago, he'd practically lived here ten hours a day. All he knew was that twice in his life, Anna had changed him. Twice in his life, she'd helped him become a better man, and he couldn't bear to imagine life without her. He'd already spent three miserable years trying and failing.

Yet they couldn't escape the cancer. The doctors had tried everything. The clock was ticking, and she was going to a place where he couldn't just drive by and sneak a peek if he missed her. He couldn't call just to hear her voice and make up some excuse. She was leaving his life for good, but she would never leave his heart or his memory.

No, he decided, he couldn't help what had happened. It was natural. He was as much in love today as he'd always been with the girl of his dreams. Was that really so hard for her to appreciate? If she was scared, he was scared more. He was the one who had to figure out how to go on without her.

Too distracted to work, he took an early lunch and drove over to his dad's condo. He hadn't visited in three weeks, and he knew his dad ate lunch alone. Maybe Lee could use the company. Luke sure could use some. As he crossed the property from the parking lot, he admired the way the groundskeepers kept everything looking so beautiful. Each building was surrounded by trees, shrubs, and flower beds—all beautifully trimmed. There were plenty of benches to sit on and read or watch the birds. Luke had been hesitant when they first considered moving his father to a retirement community, but if their dad had to live in one, Luke felt at peace knowing it was a place like this.

When he answered the door, Lee took one look at Luke and asked, "What happened?" He stepped aside so Luke could enter, and then shut the door behind him. "Come on in and sit down, son. Tell me all about it."

"Nothing happened, Dad. Can't a son just visit his father anymore?" Luke said testily.

"I can see it on your face and hear it in your voice, Luke. I've known you thirty-six years, remember?" Lee said as they sat across from each other at the kitchen table. His eyes never left Luke's as his brow creased, his eyes narrowing.

"I was just trying to give her a romantic evening, make her feel special," Luke said. He mumbled a bit, so Lee had to lean forward to catch everything he said.

"You took her on a date?" Lee asked.

"Not a date date, dad, but a night out, as friends," Luke explained.

"Oh right. Married, divorced, friends. That's how it goes these days." Lee said, teasing.

"We're doing our best," Luke said.

"So, what happened? Did you spill something on her? Get in a car accident?" Lee asked.

"I kissed her," Luke blurted out.

His father didn't look at all surprised. Instead, he relaxed noticeably and grinned. "How was it?"

Luke grimaced, absentmindedly reaching up with his left hand to rub the back of his stiff neck. "It was awkward. And then she rejected me."

"Must have lost your touch," Lee teased.

"Dad, this really isn't something I find funny," Luke said, pinching his lips together as he stiffened in the chair and rubbed his neck harder.

Lee stopped grinning and leaned forward in his chair. "So, you kissed her, Luke. You'll both live. She might change her mind and decide she liked it. Women are weird like that." Lee grunted but managed to swallow the amusement Luke could see lingered in his eyes. "But they rarely do it overnight."

Luke didn't know what he'd expected but certainly part of it had been more sympathy, an ally. Instead, his dad was casual, unperturbed, as if Anna's reaction was what he'd expected. He regretted coming over. Maybe he should have called Ray or Grace. "You know, I came here for a little support, and I don't know why I bothered," he said, grabbing his keys and heading for the door.

"I thought you came to me because I always tell the truth," his father replied. "Always have, always will. Don't get mad at me because the truth is hard for you."

Luke grabbed the door and pulled it open.

"Aren't you going to stay for lunch?" Lee called.

Luke ignored him and walked out, slamming the door behind him.

He drove back to the office still thinking about Anna. He still loved her, but he couldn't keep hurting like this. He had to keep his emotions in check so he could take care of the kids and his business. He had too many responsibilities to allow himself to get sidetracked. If she didn't want him anymore, he would have to move on.

There was only one problem: *I don't know how.*

BEKAH AND BRENDA arrived at Anna's with lunch from Saint Louis Bread Company. As they sat around her kitchen table, Anna told them about her date with Luke. They seemed both moved and amazed by how romantic and detailed he'd been.

"I can't believe he thought of all that," Bekah said as she took a bite of her bread bowl soup.

"I wish my husband were that romantic," Brenda added.

Both laughed knowingly and nodded.

"But it was crazy for him to kiss me like that," Anna said, shaking her head. The Smokehouse Turkey sandwich in front of her remained untouched.

"Why?" Bekah asked. "It was such a romantic evening. We all know Luke's always loved you. He wasn't the one who wanted the divorce. What's so surprising?"

"Besides," Brenda added, "it probably felt natural after the history you have together." Her friends exchanged such a casual look that Anna had to fight to hide her annoyance.

"But he promised me his intentions were friendly only," Anna said.

"People always promise that," Brenda said with a dismissive wave. "Don't you remember high school?"

"Right?" Bekah agreed. "You have to go with your own instincts. You can't trust what they say, but see what they do, especially men." Again, they laughed.

Anna knew they were right. And if she were in their shoes talking to one of them, she might find it amusing as well. She shouldn't have been that surprised by Luke's planning or the kiss. He had called it a "date," after all.

Deep down what bothered her the most was that she hadn't pulled away. Instead, when Luke had leaned in to kiss her, she'd let it happen. Could it be she was still in love with him, too, after all that had happened? That was crazy! She'd divorced him, moved on. Besides, she was dying. Getting romantic had to be the worst idea in the world. It was definitely the last thing on her mind. She didn't want to hurt Luke or herself any more than she already had, and what about the kids? They were confused enough! The last thing they needed was confusion about their parents' relationship.

"Was it a good kiss, at least?" Bekah asked and Brenda chuckled.

Anna shot them a look, then slowly, smiled. "It was nice and gentle, tender."

"Ah, it was good," Brenda said, winking as she took another bite of her Fandango salad.

Anna surrendered, sighing. "Okay, it was, but I didn't expect that."

Bekah grinned. "The big question is what are you going to do about it?"

Anna shook her head. "Nothing. We're divorced. The kids have finally gotten used to that. I'm glad Luke's back in their lives, because I've been able to see that he's capable of taking care of them the way they'll need when I'm not there. But falling in love again... It would be unfair to Luke, to the kids... to me."

"Life is never fair, Anna. You have to figure out how to make the most of what you get," Bekah said. "You used to be so in love with Luke, we were all jealous of you. It's not a shock that you're feeling some of those old feelings again."

"Exactly," Brenda echoed. "You got divorced because he lost touch with this side of himself. Now that he's found it again, why shouldn't you enjoy it?"

"No. I have cancer," Anna said, frustrated again that they didn't understand what she was saying. "I didn't invite him back in our lives for romance. We both need to focus on preparing him and the kids for when I'm gone and rebuilding that relationship. I don't have time left to fall in love. There's not going to be a happy ending."

"So you've given up on hope? You know that for sure?" Brenda said.

"I have to prepare for the worst," Anna countered. "And romance is the last thing I can handle right now."

"Okay, you guys make fun of me, but those books I read can teach you something," Bekah said as she finished her soup.

Anna and Brenda exchanged a look, making gagging faces. Bekah loved losing herself in cheesy romance novels, mostly Harlequin. But anything that had lots of kissing, hot sex, swooning, and happily ever after.

"Come on, Bekah," Brenda said.

"I'm serious, you guys," Bekah went on. "Forget the sex. Those books say a lot about life. They don't always have happy endings. And reading them, I learned that sometimes just spending whatever time you have with someone you love is a precious gift. Even if it ends, you have to grab it while you can."

"You learned that from cheesy romance novels?" Brenda teased.

"And Nicholas Sparks," Bekah added. "All I'm saying is do what makes you happy. You never know how many days you have but make them count."

Brenda nodded, liking the sentiment. "Mmmmm." Then she offered a mischievous grin. "Complete bullshit."

"Hey" Bekah protested then realized Brenda was teasing her.

Her friends chuckled again, but Anna was lost in thought. They sat in silence, letting her sort things out in her mind. Bekah had a point. True love was a precious gift, and even if she'd known when they met that things would turn out as they did, Anna couldn't be sure she wouldn't have done the same thing. They'd had some amazing times together she wouldn't have wanted to miss. Who would want to go back and miss her entire life? There was a lot there she valued.

"I don't know what I should do," she finally said. "I know it really hurt him the way I reacted. Maybe he won't even try again."

She was already feeling sick daily and struggling to make it through entire days. She didn't need anything else to drain her energy. She had to focus all she had on getting through. It just couldn't be. It was too late for that now. The more she thought about it, the more strongly she felt. She'd had a wonderful love with Luke once, but they'd lost it. She still cared for him, and would always treasure their history together, but it was too late for love. She had to make sure Luke and the kids would be okay without her. She couldn't be distracted by anything else right now. No matter what.

That was her only mission now.

CHAPTER 18

WHEN LUKE ARRIVED at Anna's two days later after a late season early March snowstorm, he was determined to act as if nothing had happened. Other than greeting her at the door, he didn't pay her much attention. Anna watched as he had a tea party with Cassie in the Living Room, but didn't say anything when he didn't offer to get her beverages or to fix lunch like he'd been doing of late.

Luke had decided he wouldn't bring up what had happened between them. He had blown it with her, and he accepted that despite his hopes, he had blown it for good. He'd gotten swept up in the feel of her body against his as he carried her that night—overcome by the touch of her skin, the smell of her hair, her perfume. It brought back so many old feelings and memories. He may have always loved her, but her response had made it clear those days were in the past. With what was happening to her now, Anna had no wish to revisit the past, and Luke would respect that.

When the tea party ended, he went to work on reading with Mandy, who was really into learning more words these days. The book was a funny mystery she had brought home from school with amusing characters and events. She read the girl characters, doing her best to make distinctive funny voices for each, while Luke read the male characters and did the same. As they read together, he stopped patiently to explain each unfamiliar word she asked about. She also insisted that he read any character who didn't seem nice. Mandy had never liked the villains. It scared her to read those parts, almost as if somehow their evilness would invade her heart. Luke had found this attitude something precious he hoped she would never lose.

He noticed that Anna was falling behind in her housework. A stack of newspapers had fallen over in the hall beside the door, and dishes waited to be loaded into the dishwasher on one side of the kitchen sink. He also spotted dust gathering on some of the shelves. He had been helping out some, but he just didn't feel like it today. But Anna observed him eyeing the dust and went to get her duster.

Luke and Mandy finished the book as Kyle came down the hall. "Want to help me with my guitar solos again?" Luke asked, referring to the video game.

Kyle shrugged. "Sure, Dad." There were other instruments which could be played at the same time, so Kyle sat behind the drum kit and offered Luke the guitar controller. The driving rock beat began as Kyle initiated the game, and they started playing along.

When Anna returned to dust, they were laughing and smiling. Luke even tried out his rock moves, sliding around and grinding his hips while he played. At one point, he even fell to his knees and leaned the upper part of his body back, shaking with intensity like rock stars on TV.

Kyle guffawed. "You look ridiculous, Dad."

"Not bad for an old guy, huh?" Luke said, grinning. He gyrated some more and suddenly froze, grabbing his back and moaning in pain. That made Kyle chuckle harder.

Moments later, the song ended, and they slapped each other high fives. "That was great," Kyle said. "You've actually improved."

"I have a great teacher," Luke said. Kyle smiled appreciatively. "When I was a kid, we never had games this cool."

"When you were a kid, did they even have television?" Kyle teased.

Luke made a face and lent his voice a tremor, "Where's my cane, son? Can you find my cane and glasses?" He bent over, holding his hand against his lower back as if he was in pain.

Kyle pointed to the top of Luke's ear. "What about your hearing aid?"

"Eh?" Luke said, cupping his ear as if he were hard of hearing. They both devolved into a fit of laughter again.

"I'm so glad we can play this together, Kyle. It means a lot to me," Luke said afterward, standing normally again.

"Yeah, Dad. It's kinda fun," Kyle agreed.

Kyle hadn't joked with him like this in a very long time, and Luke really enjoyed it. He'd longed to restore a relationship of such give and take with Kyle, and now it seemed that his efforts were paying off. He could almost cry. "I love you, son," Luke said.

Kyle's face changed. Clearly he hadn't expected this.

"I guess I need to say that more often, huh?" Luke went on.

Kyle looked at him, as if trying to read whether he meant it or not. Luke smiled warmly, hoping it would confirm that he did, but Kyle suddenly looked away.

"Well, I sure know how to ruin the mood, huh?" Luke joked, trying to break the tension.

Kyle whirled around, angry now. "Why did you leave us, Dad? Why did you abandon us?"

"It wasn't intentional, son," Luke choked out. "I was starting a new business, and I got my priorities messed up. I am so sorry."

"Aren't we important to you? More important than some business?" Kyle asked.

"Of course you are, son." Luke nodded.

"Then why didn't you act like it?" Kyle stared at him, demanding a better explanation.

Luke didn't have one. He struggled for the right words. For a moment, he wanted to run away the way he had when Anna scolded him. Hearing Kyle yelling at him, made his chest tighten and ache. Especially when they'd just been laughing and enjoying each other. But he was determined to face this. He had to if Kyle was ever going to forgive him. "Sometimes fathers mess up, son. Sometimes we don't do the right thing."

"Don't tell me you love me! If you loved me, you wouldn't have missed three years of my life!" Kyle screamed.

"That's not fair. I wasn't completely absent—" Luke began but Kyle cut him off.

"How many of my soccer games did you come to the last three years? What about my school plays?" Kyle demanded.

Luke had missed all of them. He fought back tears. "I should have been there, Kyle. I'm sorry."

"You suck as a father!" Kyle shouted.

Luke heard Cassie sniffling and knew the girls had heard every word. "You're right, I've been lousy, but I'm trying to change that."

"Well, that really makes up for it," Kyle said, throwing down the drum kit and stomping off down the hallway.

Luke leaned back on the couch, devastated. Just when he'd thought they were making progress. He'd known there was still pent-up anger and hurt, but he hadn't realized how much. He sat there, stunned, his heart and head throbbing, then caught Mandy staring at him. He smiled at her as if all was well.

She sighed. "You hurt us, Dad." Then looked away.

Luke was stunned. Mandy always held things in. She had never been so direct.

Anna watched him from the corner, duster in hand, but hadn't said a word. He looked at her, his eyes pleading, "Thanks for your support," he said.

"What did you want me to say, Luke? He needed to tell you that," Anna said going back to her dusting.

"He could have done it a little more quietly," Luke suggested.

"He has to let it out somehow," Anna said. "It's healthy for them to talk it through, confront the problem."

"Well, I'm doing my best to fix it," Luke said, turning away. He wasn't angry with her. He was embarrassed that she and the girls had witnessed that. Mandy and Cassie remained frozen at the table, not wanting to break their silence, watching him and Anna.

"I know you are," Anna replied.

"All I know is I'm doing everything I can to show you all I've changed, to help you, to love you, to support you, and it's really hard to do that when I keep getting beaten up for old mistakes," Luke said.

Anna carried on dusting. "Sometimes you need to tell people how they hurt you to heal," she finally added.

He knew she was right, but it still stung hearing it. And trying to be a good father and lead the family was hard when you were constantly being told your inadequacies and cut down in front of everyone else. Kyle had so much built up in him. In time, it would heal, but Luke wondered how long that would take.

He took a deep breath then stood, seeing his daughter's sadness. "At some point, you all need to forgive me. I really look forward to that, so we can move on together." Tears formed at the corners of his eyes and his lungs suddenly needed air. "Right now, I have never felt more alone." He turned, grabbing his coat off the back of a chair, and disappeared out the door, shutting it behind him.

"I SHOULDN'T HAVE lost it," Luke said staring at his feet, crestfallen in Grace's kitchen an hour later.

"What? Blow up at your kids for being jerks?" Grace said, looking at her husband, Karl, who chuckled.

"It happens," Karl said with a shrug. "Sometimes it's good for them."

From the other room, they heard yelling as the kids got into some sort of altercation and Karl hurried off to deal with it, leaving Grace and Luke alone.

"It is good for them," Grace said. "They need to know you're human, that you hurt, too."

"But they also need you to listen, to validate their feelings," Karl said.

Grace shot him an amused look. "Wow. You actually did hear our therapist."

Karl grinned. "Just because I don't say much doesn't mean my ears don't work. Anyway, this is about Luke." He nodded toward Luke, who sat bent over at the table, face in his hands.

"I lost it and I left, Grace," Luke said. "It's going to reinforce their fear that I'll leave them again like I did before."

"Not if you go back."

Luke sighed, wishing he believed her.

"Luke," she scolded, waiting until his eyes met hers to continue, "families fight, and you can't be with them twenty-four hours a day no matter what happens. But as long as you keep coming back, they'll get over the fear of you leaving just because you disagree. You can change the pattern by creating a new one."

"I'm trying."

"Exactly. So give it some time to work."

The next day, Luke mustered up his nerve and headed over to Anna's determined to show her and the kids both that he would be there no matter what. When he arrived, he found the kids outside in the snow. Mandy and Cassie were having some sort of tea party on a show table and two benches they'd packed together, while Kyle was touching up the snowman.

Luke parked on the street and took a deep breath before climbing out and following the cleared path leading up the drive.

As he approached, the girls looked over and he smiled and waved. "How's the tea?"

"We're not having tea," Mandy said with a frown, and Luke immediately assumed she was still pissed at him for the day before.

But before he could form a response, Cassie added, "It's hot chocolate, silly. We have to keep warm, you know?"

Luke pursed his lips. "Mmmm. Hot chocolate sounds really good. Can I have some?"

Cassie brightened but Mandy eyed him warily.

"Sure," Cassie said with genuine enthusiasm, and Luke trudged across the snow packed lawn toward them. As he did, he glanced over to where Kyle busily touched up the snowman as if he hadn't heard a thing.

Luke made his way over beside the girls, but when he made to sit on the bench, Mandy waved a palm to stop him. "No, don't smash it." She turned and motioned toward a snow mound adjacent to the table. "You can sit there."

Luke frowned. "It doesn't look very comfortable."

"He can use my bench," Cassie offered.

"He's too heavy," Mandy warned. "He'll smash it."

"Well, maybe I can help make it stronger," Luke suggested.

Cassie went to work preparing Luke a mug of invisible hot chocolate. "Have this first," she said, finishing stirring with a small plastic spoon, before lifting it by the handle and holding it out toward him.

'Thanks," Luke said, accepting it carefully. "Can I stand for now?" He twisted the mug so his fingers could grasp the handle and looked at Mandy, who shrugged.

Luke smiled, taking it as consent, and raised the plastic mug to take a sip.

"Careful!" Cassie hollered in warning. "It's very hot."

"Oh, okay," Luke said and slowed his arm, then took a careful sip. "Mmmmmmm. This is terrific. Did you make it with milk or water?"

"Snow, silly," Cassie said with a giggle. "And milk, like mama."

"Mmmmm, delicious," Luke said taking another sip. Then he noticed Mandy's face change suddenly and he heard the THWAAP as the snowball struck his neck on the left side. "Hey!"

He turned to find Kyle grinning from beside the snowman where he'd prepared several snowballs and was lifting another. "What's the matter?" Kyle taunted. "Too hard?"

"Oh, I guess I deserved that from yesterday, huh?" Luke said, then looked at Mandy. "I'm sorry I left like that."

THWAAP. Another snowball struck him center chest.

"You know, if you don't watch it, I might strike back," Luke warned, narrowing his eyes at his son.

"I dare ya!" Kyle teased, teeth gritted as he finished another snowball and raised his arm for another throw. This time, he went to throw it harder and slipped, causing his aim to drift and the snowball hit Cassie on the arm.

"Ow!" she cried out, then glared at Kyle. "You stop that right now, meanie!"

THWAAP. A snowball flew from beside Luke and struck Kyle on the leg. Luke glanced over to see Mandy grinning as she prepared another snowball.

"Well, I can see where this is going," Luke said. He set the mug down on the table and quickly knelt to make his own snowballs as both girls rolled their own. The temperature was in the mid-twenties but there was no breeze, so it wasn't unpleasant with the coats and layers Luke had on, but it remained cold enough to keep the snow from melting quickly. The powder was crunchy, having fallen a few days past, but still soft and pliable, and Luke used his gloves to pack it tightly into a ball.

"Three against one?" Kyle teased. "Too chicken to take me on alone?"

"You hit Cassie," Mandy called back.

"That's right," Luke agreed. "They have a right to defend themselves."

With that, Luke and the two girls hurled snowballs full might at Kyle who ducked behind the snowman then threw one of his own, right at Luke. Luke dodged just in time and it landed on the table, knocking over the hot chocolate mugs.

"This means war," Cassie said through gritted teeth as she rolled another snowball.

Mandy and Cassie threw snowballs, Mandy's striking Luke full on in the chest as Cassie's landed short. Then Luke threw his, feinting just before he released it so that Kyle dodged toward its trajectory and slid around as he tried to correct. It wound up striking him square on the butt. Cassie and Mandy erupted in laughter.

Kyle frowned. "Okay, fine. War it is!" He fell to his knees and began packing more balls, then firing them off as quick as he could.

Cassie, Mandy, and Luke returned fire as fast as they could, while still trying to dodge or duck under his onslaught. Soon, they were all four laughing and soaked, and Luke couldn't remember the last time he'd had so much fun with his kids.

ANNA HEARD LAUGHTER and glanced out her kitchen window to see Luke and the kids covered in snow, having a blast pelting each other with snowballs. It made her smile. He'd come back. *Good call*, she thought.

Half an hour later, they all sat around her kitchen table as she served them hot cocoa with mini-marshmallows and fresh baked sugar cookies.

"Ahhhh," Luke said as he finished his mug and reached for another cookie. "Now *this* is perfect."

Anna chuckled. "You all look exhausted."

Luke grunted and leaned back against the chair. "Never felt better."

The girls giggled and when his dad looked at him, Kyle couldn't help but join them.

Luke tipped his head toward his son. "Kyle started it."

"He did!" Cassie agreed.

"But we held our own," Luke said with faux machismo and lifted his palms toward the girls who both high fived him, one on each side.

"I'm glad you had fun," Anna said. "Didn't expect to see you today."

"I had to come back," Luke said. "I shouldn't have left yesterday." Then he looked at Kyle. "But, you know, I'm human. Words can hurt. Still, I want you guys to know I'm not going anywhere. I'm gonna keep coming back."

"Yay," Cassie said, clapping her hands together, her fingers stained with hot chocolate and frosting.

Luke locked eyes with Kyle. "Even if I have to fight my way in here with snowballs every day."

They all laughed at that.

"It would be awesome to have snow every day," Cassie said.

"I used to think so when I was your age," Anna said, tousling her youngest's hair. "But trust me, it's really nice to have spring."

"And fall," Mandy added.

"Yes, that too," Anna agreed.

"All the pretty leaves, the birds chirping," Mandy said.

Anna nodded. "Walks in the park, later sunsets."

"Mowing the lawn, allergies," Kyle jumped in, his face making it clear his list was things he didn't like.

"Heat, humidity," Luke said with a nod, joining his son. "Winter rules," he declared. "Sledding, snowmen—"

"Hot cocoa," Cassie chirped.

"And cookies!" Mandy said as they all laughed again.

"Every season has it's blessings," Anna said. "You'd miss all of them if we didn't have them."

"I've heard rumors," Luke said.

It was the most normal time they'd spent as a family in ages, and Anna found herself surprised at how much she was enjoying it. The warmth radiating off the oven and the cocoa pot, the smell of the fresh baked cookies, the laughter of her children and Luke, and the general contentment it created. It was a great memory they'd carry with them, and for Anna, making great memories was her number one goal in the time as she had left.

"You don't have work today then?" Anna said, looking at Luke.

"I'm the boss," Luke replied. "I took the morning off."

She smiled. "Okay then."

"If you don't watch it, I might take the afternoon, too." His face was faux threatening but Cassie looked delighted and then Luke grinned.

"Hmmm, I don't know if we can take much more of you," Anna teased. "Besides, you'll probably need a change of clothes."

Luke glanced down at his dirt-stained jeans and flannel shirt. "They can be washed." The kids looked just as messy with their hair disheveled and traces of dirt and grass from lying or sliding in the snow-packed yard staining their clothes.

"Yeah, but the girls wanted to go to the mall to spend some Christmas money," Anna said.

"So?" Luke said with a shrug.

Anna frowned. "You want to go like that?"

"Why not?" Luke teased then flexed his arms and made fists.

Kyle grinned. "Yeah, mom, what's the big deal?"

Kyle ganging up on her with Luke? It was unheard of.

Luke nodded at Kyle, then said, "We're men." He growled and grunted, and Kyle echoed him.

"Yeah, men," Kyle agreed.

Anna rolled her eyes and joined her daughters in laughing. "You two can come, but only if you keep your distance," she added.

Luke sighed. "Such a mom thing to say."

Kyle guffawed and high fived Luke.

Anna waited until Luke looked up and their eyes met then gently scolded, "You're supposed to be a good influence, remember?"

Luke screwed up his face, then looked at Kyle. "Someone

could use clobbering with a snowball."

"Yeah!" Kyle jumped to his feet and headed for the door.

"Don't you dare!" Anna warned.

Luke laughed and shook his head at Kyle, who stopped and turned back toward the table.

"More cookies!" Luke said and pounded the table. "More sugar!"

Kyle and Cassie joined in, grinning ear to ear. "More cookies! More sugar!"

Mandy quickly followed. "More cookies! More sugar!"

"Oh my God, I've created my own monsters," Anna said with mock horror, then she poured more cocoa and carried over another tray of cookies.

CHAPTER 19

FOR THE NEXT few weeks, Luke's life became all about his family. He dedicated himself to his children and Anna, taking every day off from work at three p.m. so he could arrive at her house when the kids arrived from school and staying until early evening to help with homework, play with them, and eat dinner together as a family. For Luke, it was a chance to prove something to the children and to himself. And he wasn't about to waste the opportunity. For Anna and the kids, he hoped it provided a chance to get to know him not as he was in the past, but as the new man he wanted to be, tried to be, and was determined to be now.

A few days after the snowball fight, he helped Mandy with a science project involving a relief map of South America, then a week later worked with Cassie on collecting bugs for her own science assignment. To his surprise, Luke came to him on a Friday for help with photographing stars. So, they studied the manual to Anna's digital camera and how to set long exposures, then set up a tripod on the back deck aimed up at the night sky. Luke set the timer for six hours, and then disabled the motion sensor lights for the night. When everything was set, they went inside for the last batch of cookies and more cocoa.

In mid-March, as the weather warmed a bit, Luke helped Kyle with prepping the yard equipment and going over what needed to be done. "You're the man of the house now, and with your mom sick, someone has to look after things," Luke told him. "I'll help, but the girls aren't ready for this responsibility, so we really need you to step up. Think you can handle it?"

Luke expected pushback, but instead Kyle beamed with pride at being given real responsibility. "Yeah, I've got it."

Together, they drained and changed the oil on the lawnmower, then cleaned the blades, and Luke made sure Kyle knew how to start it without flooding the engine every time. They made a brief circuit going over the flowers and trimming that would need to be done as well as tilling the soil for the garden to get it ready for fresh planting. The ground was still too hard and most of the plants still wet and partially frozen for them to do much, but Luke made sure Kyle had the basic idea. The rest he could teach him later.

Lastly, Luke went over the sprinkler and hoses and how to set them up, where they'd work best, and so on—all without turning them on. "We'll go over it again when the pipes can't freeze, but at least you have a mental picture of what needs to be done."

"Yep," Kyle agreed.

When they finished, Kyle actually returned his handshake enthusiastically, standing straight and determined as they headed back into the house.

"What was all that about?" Anna asked as she set a defrosted lasagna on the counter beside the warming over, and Kyle headed for his game console.

"Just challenging him to take charge of some things and help you out," Luke said.

Anna looked somewhere between amused and doubtful. "And he agreed?"

Luke shrugged. "I get the feeling he likes the feeling of being treated like a man. I know I did at his age."

"Time will tell," Anna said, her mouth wrinkling in that not quite convinced but hopeful way.

"Yep," Luke said in his best Kyle imitation, and they both laughed.

That night, they ate Anna's lasagna and had family movie night, watching the latest Pixar film accompanied by generous servings of microwave popcorn. Then Luke helped put the girls to bed before heading home.

"How'd your checkup go?" he asked as his fingers touched the knob on the front door.

Anna smiled. "Surprisingly well."

"Oh yeah?" A tinge of hope rose in him like a warm wave as she said it.

She nodded. "Doctor Sousa said I'm 'surprisingly stable,' his words. Like everything has stayed steady for the past two months."

"What does that mean?" Luke asked, eyes locked on hers, craving good news.

It was her turn to shrug. "Just that I'm no worse, but no better. It's not a bad thing. He said we need to keep watching it and hope for the best."

"So, you could be getting better?" Luke asked.

Anna offered a soft knowing look, patting his arm, then shook her head. "He definitely didn't say that. But sometimes cancer slows for unknown reasons. It just means I have more good days than bad right now, and I'll take what I can get."

"Absolutely," Luke said and before she could object, grabbed her and pulled her into an embrace, gently stroking her hair. "I'm so glad, Anna. Really happy." He leaned back so their eyes met again before pulling away.

"Me too," she agreed and smiled. "Thank you."

Luke raised his eyebrows in question.

"For everything," she continued. "You've been really great

these past few months, and don't think I haven't noticed."

Luke felt a sudden flush. "I'm doing what I should have been doing the last few years. Doesn't erase my mistakes, but if it makes a difference, I'm really glad."

"It does," she assured him, then surprised him by reaching out a palm to gently touch his cheek before lowering it again.

He smiled at her and nodded. "Get good sleep. Good night."

"Good night," she said as he opened the door and had to resist hard not to skip and hum his way down the drive to his car.

The following Saturday was Mandy's birthday, and instead of the party with her friends Luke had expected, they celebrated as a family with dinner at her favorite restaurant—Spaghetti Factory—downtown then a trip after to the famed Crown Candy Counter on St. Louis Avenue in a rough, rundown part of the city. Mandy had the Johnny Rabbit special banana shake, her favorite, while Kyle went with chocolate and Cassie had cherry. Luke and Anna split a Vanilla—Anna eating from the tall glass shake glass and Luke settling for the leftovers that accompanied each shake in a metal milkshake maker. It had half as much as the glass did, but when he finished that, he devoured Cassie's and some of Mandy's as well. The kids always said "no" when he asked, thinking they'd have plenty of room but even Kyle struggled to finish everything on his own, the shakes being so filling.

Afterward, they drove down to the Arch and took a ride up its tight, curved elevator cars to the top to enjoy the stunning nighttime views of the city before returning to the car and heading back to Anna's. Though they'd been there before, the kids reacted like the first time, gazing with amazement at the constellations in an unusually clear sky, and commenting on the patterns of pretty city lights coming from downtown and the surrounding buildings. They stayed at the top as long as allowed before climbing back into elevator pods for their descent. By the time they pulled into the driveway, the girls were yawning, and Luke knew Kyle wouldn't be far behind. As Anna and Luke helped the girls to their beds, Kyle plopped down in front of his game console and quickly became engaged.

Twenty minutes later, the girls tucked in and drifting off, Anna and Luke shared decaf in the kitchen.

"I'd say that was a successful birthday," Luke said.

"Yep," Anna agreed. "We nailed it." They high fived and chuckled, then each sipped their coffee again.

Remembering the date, Luke watched Anna until she noticed his look and frowned. "You're staring."

"You're pretty. Don't lots of men stare?"

She grunted. "Aren't you exhausted yet? You're hitting on me?"

Luke grinned. "Well, I've never stopped being crazy about you, but no, actually, I was thinking about something else."

"What is it?" she asked.

"Your birthday," he admitted, having realized it was two weeks away.

"What about it?"

"Have you decided how you want to celebrate?"

She guffawed. "Oh, Luke, at my age birthdays are hardly a big deal."

"Celebrate 'em while you got 'em, my dad always says," Luke replied.

Anna chuckled "That sounds like Lee. How is he? I miss our chats."

"He comes over," Luke said, then wondered if his dad had been staying away from Anna's for some reason—maybe to let his son have time to rebuild.

"Yeah, every couple months, but it's been since before Christmas," Anna said. "I think he wanted to 'give us time' to figure things out."

Luke sighed. "That's dad. But I'll get him over here." He brightened and said, "Maybe for your birthday party?"

Anna shook her head. "I don't want a party."

"Even if I surprised you?"

Her eyes found his and her face took on a somber look. "Please don't. It's too much, really."

"So maybe a quiet celebration with the kids?"

"Or a few cards at breakfast and a slice of the cake they always throw together."

"Oh my God, remember the rocket cake?" Luke chuckled at the memory

"Oh my God, it looked so much more like..." Anna's voice trailed off, not wanting to say it.

"Yeah, a penis," Luke finished for her. "They even put that chocolate chip at the tip."

Anna chortled. "And they were so oblivious."

"I think Kyle might see it now," Luke said. "Where are the pictures?"

Anna shook her head. "You're not going to ask him."

Luke shrugged. "I'd kind of like to see his reaction."

"No! Luke Morrison!" she replied in that motherly half-scolding tone and then Luke arched a brow to let her know he was teasing and they both laughed again.

"Kyle was so disappointed. Almost as if he expected real flames to shoot out of the bottom."

"And then there's the famous igloo cake."

Luke chortled. "I think they were covering. It just looked like a giant mound of frosting."

"Oh, there was cake in there, but they definitely overdid the butter cream," Anna agreed.

"Something I never dreamed I'd ever say: 'too much butter cream.'" Luke laughed and Anna joined him.

When they both reached for their coffee, Luke said, "But look, if there's somewhere you'd like to eat or somewhere I can bring home takeout from…"

Anna nodded. "I'll think about it. Thanks."

Luke cocked his head and raised his palms. "You know, assuming I'm invited."

Anna grinned and punched his arm. "Of course you're invited."

Luke swallowed the rest of his coffee and shrugged as he set the mug on the counter. "I missed a couple years. Just checking."

"Yeah," she said with a sigh and for a moment they lost themselves in memories of the hard times.

Luke sighed and straightened from the spot he'd been leaning against the counter. "Well, sorry to be a downer. I should let you rest."

She reached out and touched his arm. "Thanks for today. Mandy was so happy."

"Yeah, I think she even liked the new sweaters and the books."

Anna grunted. "Birthdays do get less exciting the older they get. She'll be fine. All the kids have been a lot happier now that you're around more."

"Really?" Luke hadn't expected to hear that, and he was surprised how much it pleased him, a sliver of warmth rising through his body at the thought.

Anna nodded. "Yes, of course." And then their eyes met again. "We all have."

Luke stared at her a moment and their eyes locked. He could

have sworn he saw real joy there before she broke the gaze and breathed again.

"Well, good night. Drive safe," Anna said as he headed for the door, and she followed.

"I'll ask you again about the birthday, so get to thinking," he said and stopped beside the front door as Anna stopped beside Kyle, watching his intense focus on the game and pondering how and when to interrupt him.

"Night," she said as he opened the door.

"Goodnight," he said, his hand on the door as he stepped out, shut it behind him, and headed for his car.

"The kids have been a lot happier now that you're around more. We all have." The words echoed through his head over and over as he walked down the drive and climbed in his Subaru. As he closed the door, he realized he hadn't even registered the chill of the night air, nor did he remember anything from closing the door and walking to the car. He'd gone completely on automatic, totally enraptured by the words. *"The kids have been a lot happier now that you're around more. We all have."*

And at that moment, Luke was sure he hadn't been happier in years.

ANNA KNEW THAT look. She'd seen it so many times before. She'd seen it again in Luke's eyes when he asked if there was something special, she wanted to do for her birthday. He was falling for her again. Or maybe he'd never unfallen. He'd asked her the question, and she'd seen in his eyes exactly what he wanted to hear. And in those words, he'd said right before, too: *"I've never stopped being crazy about you."* It had scared her then, and it scared her now.

She was sick. Period. That wasn't going to change. Sure, she was having a good spell, a lull in her illness, but it wasn't remission. The doctor hadn't said anything about that, and he would have told her. No, Anna had known from the moment she'd been first diagnosed that her days were limited. The cancer would kill her eventually. Even though she hoped that would be year as from now. Falling in love and dating with all the uncertainty seemed like asking for more pain. The last thing any of them needed.

"I've never stopped being crazy about you." The problem was when he'd said it, it had excited her too. A warmth shot up her limbs, a tingling of her skin. Words she'd never dreamed she'd hear from Luke again, never imagined she'd want to, and yet he'd said them, and she'd liked it! What had Bekah said? *"…do what makes you happy. You never know how many days you have but make them count."*

Oh my God, Anna, this is crazy! She shook her head back and forth as if she could shake off the craziness of her feelings, but when she stopped, they hadn't changed. She still loved Luke. Always had. That had never been the problem. She'd left him to protect herself and their kids. To ensure they had the life they deserved. And it had been one of the hardest decisions she'd ever made. But she'd done it.

Asking him back in had been almost as hard. She'd put it off for months, hoping for a miracle, or something. And then she'd realized she was being foolish. This wasn't just about her. It was about her kids. The three beings she'd loved more than anything on earth, more than herself. She had to give Luke another chance to make it right; to try again to be the man she's always hoped and prayed he could be. Because like it or not, when cancer won, he was all the kids would have,

So, she'd called him, and she'd prayed. And Luke had stepped up far better than she'd ever expected. The kids had slowly let down their guards; lowering the walls they'd put up after feeling abandoned and hurt. It was exactly what she'd hoped would happen if Luke came back. And every day he tried harder, and things got better. Kyle even smiled and joked with him now. And they'd worked so well together in the yard. No, her plan had worked perfectly, beyond her wildest hopes.

Except for one thing.

She'd never counted on Luke reviving long dead feelings in her for him.

"I don't have time to fall in love," she said aloud, then hurried to the door leading to the living room and peeked out, hoping Kyle hadn't overheard.

He hadn't. He was still lost in his game.

She sighed in relief. But what was she going to do about these crazy feelings. It wasn't fair to her, and it wasn't fair to Luke. It wasn't fair to the kids to get their hopes up again, when she knew they'd be devastated after she was finally gone. It could happen any time, after all. Every day was borrowed time.

She had feelings for Luke. She'd denied it for so long, hoping she'd one day believe it. Hoping it would one day be true. But now she realized, two years later, she still loved the man deeply. Well, so what? She was an adult. Just because you have feelings doesn't mean you have to act on them. So what if this was the only man she'd ever truly loved; the man who'd swept her off her feet in college. The man who'd been her lover and best friend for thirteen years and started a family with her.

All that was great. Great memories for sure. And she wouldn't trade the kids for anything. Not in a million years. So falling in love again—that was something she couldn't do. It was too late now. No, whatever Luke had in mind, she would resist. She would refuse. It would be better for everyone.

So why couldn't she just stop hearing those words: "*...do what makes you happy. You never know how many days you have but make them count.*" And "*I've never stopped being crazy about you.*"

CHAPTER 20

ANNA MET HER friends for lunch at St. Louis Bread Company on Tuesday while the kids were in school. Bekah and Brenda hugged her at the door, then insisted on her waiting at the table, while they took care of the order. Anna's nose warmed at the cornucopia of baking bread, spices, warm soups, and coffees filling the air as they crossed the room. Brenda led them to a booth in the back. Anna asked for broccoli and cheese soup in a bread bowl, then sat down to wait.

This Breadco, as locals called it, was located in Affton in a strip mall called Grasso Plaza off Valcour and South Rock Hill near the U.S. Post Office, Dollar General, and a Club Fitness. It was the closest location the chain had to Anna's home and had always been one of her favorite places. For many St. Louisans, St. Louis Breadco was a mainstay—known for its great bread baked daily, soups, coffee, and free Wi-Fi. A great place to hang and relax alone or with friends and their locations were always busy. Because it had been founded locally, the St. Louis branches continued under the company's original branding, even after stores throughout the country had been rebranded Panera. Anna especially loved the bread bowl soup which came in a hollowed-out loaf, providing fresh bread and soup as a tasty combo.

Today, the restaurant's patrons were a mix of workers from

nearby stores and offices, college students from schools like Webster University, and housewives like Anna. Several students worked alone at laptops, sipping tea and soda or cappuccino or even one of the Frappuccino's Breadco was famous for. Students and housewives snacked on sweet rolls, bagels, or warm bread, while workers enjoyed soup, salads, or sandwiches with their beverages. It was quick, easy, and always fresh and delicious.

Brenda and Bekah joined her after ten minutes in line with a square brown pager and three Frappuccino's, sliding into the booth on the opposite side. Both immediately put on warm, friendly smiles.

"How ya doing?" Bekah asked with the exaggerated cheer of a high school pep squad member.

"You look great," Brenda added.

"Guys, I appreciate the effort, but I didn't ask you to lunch to be pandered to, okay?" Anna said, hiding her irritation. "You're my best friends. I called you so I can be myself, and I need you to do the same."

Brenda and Bekah's faces immediately changed to guilty looks, their eyes looking away.

Bekah sighed. "We're sorry, hon. We're just worried about you."

Brenda nodded. "Yeah, we were afraid you had more bad news. You know we love you."

Anna chuckled. "I love you, too. Having cancer doesn't mean I'm breakable, though. It's good to see you."

"Does this mean there's no news?" Brenda asked.

"No," Anna said, with a slight shake of her head.

Her friends leaned forward, elbows on the table.

"Well, tell us," Bekah urged.

That's when the pager vibrated, lending a slight shake to the table as it buzzed and bounced on the surface.

"While we're eating," Anna said, nodding toward the pager and stifling a laugh.

"You're cruel, Anna," Bekah said as her friends stood, Brenda grabbing the pager, and headed for the counter again.

In a few moments, when they'd returned and all settled in with their food, the women's eyes returned to probing Anna for the news she'd promised in between bites.

"Okay," Anna said after a few minutes enjoying her soup, "Luke gave me *that* look."

"Which look?" Brenda asked as she swallowed a bite of lettuce and avocado drenched in dressing from her Green Goddess Cobb salad with chicken. Her eyes closed as she savored it and waited for Anna's response.

"He told me 'I've never stopped being crazy about you,'" she quoted.

"He did?" Brenda's jaw dropped as Bekah narrowly avoided spitting out a big bite from her Deli Turkey sandwich.

"When? What happened?" Bekah asked.

"We took the kids to the Arch to watch the sunset, see the lights," Anna recalled. "Afterward, when the girls were tucked in, we had some decaf and started talking. Recalling memories. And he said it." Anna sighed and took another sip from her soup, reaching down after to tear off a bit of the bread bowl. She dipped that in the soup and then savored the mix of sourdough and cheesy broccoli as it hit her tongue and she swallowed.

"Oh my God, just like that?" Bekah said.

"Well, we always suspected he was still in love with you," Brenda added, Bekah agreeing with a nod.

"You did? I didn't. It's been three years," Anna said.

"He's always been crazy about you," Bekah said. "That wasn't why you divorced him."

Anna frowned. "It was. I thought he loved work more than

his family. He was never home."

"That wasn't because he didn't love you," Brenda corrected. "It was because he lost his priorities."

"He did always insist he was doing it to take care of you," Bekah agreed.

Anna clenched her jaw as she pointed an index finger across the table. "You two are happy about this. Aren't you?"

Brenda raised her palms. "We're not sad."

Bekah ate another bite of sandwich and took a sip from her Frappuccino before answering, "We want you to be happy, hon. You deserve it."

"And you've always been in love with him," Brenda said.

"What?!" Anna protested.

"Come on," Brenda said. "Remember that guy Paul from your church? How many times did he ask you out?"

"At least a dozen, right?" Bekah added.

"We were barely separated," Anna said. "I wasn't ready. I was focused on the kids."

Brenda raised an eyebrow.

"Or that NTB guy, was he a mechanic?" Bekah asked.

"Greg," Brenda recalled and they both grinned.

"He was short, chubby, and slimy," Anna said. "Not my type at all."

"You didn't have to marry him," Bekah said. "Just get out of the house and stop moping."

"Exactly," Brenda agreed.

Anna sighed. "I don't date just to get out of the house. I want someone I can build a life with."

"And you're supposed to know that from one or two encounters without getting to know them?" Brenda asked.

"Maybe he's good in bed," Bekah teased and they both laughed.

Anna glared and went back to her soup for a bit, ignoring them.

"Sweetie, we know one-night stands are not your thing," Brenda said. "We were just kidding. The point is you have to try. Finding someone to share your life takes time and effort."

"Right. Not just sitting around waiting," Bekah agreed.

"I wasn't even looking," Anna said.

"Yeah, because you're still in love with Luke," Bekah agreed.

Anna scoffed, ripping another piece of sourdough off her bread bowl and stuffing it in her mouth, but her mind was racing. Could they be right? She had always cared for Luke. And lack of love wasn't why she'd divorced him. But they were ignoring the obvious problem: she was dying. As much as they and Luke might hope for a miracle, Anna's days were numbered, and that made it hardly the time to launch into a serious relationship. Even it was with her ex.

To their credit, Bekah and Brenda continued silently enjoying their meal, occasionally chatting about the weather or their kids to give Anna the space she needed to think.

She thought about the kiss. She had felt the same old magic, no matter how much she wanted to ignore it. Even now she could feel the tingle of their lips meeting and the warm wet touch of his breath on her face. Luke had always been a great kisser, at least to her. And she had to admit that having him around again had brought her a comfort and happiness she hadn't felt in several years. But what he wanted—she didn't know if she could give it. They had the kids' feelings to consider, not to mention their own. Pain lay ahead, no matter what path they took. And hadn't they all had enough of that? Why add the potential for more when some was already unavoidable?

I've never stopped being crazy about you—Luke's voice kept echoing over and over in her mind. Her stomach fluttered, and why did the restaurant suddenly feel so hot? Had they turned up the temperature? Was the heat malfunctioning? She put her elbows on the table and buried her face in her palms.

"You okay?" Bekah asked, her voice gentle but filled with concern.

Anna looked up to find both of her friends staring at her with worried looks.

"I don't know what to do," she admitted.

"Anna, you have limited time," Brenda said, reaching across the table to place a palm on Anna's arm. "What do you want? You should do that. No matter what. Because you deserve to be happy while you can."

"Absolutely," Bekah agreed.

"Whatever makes you happy for the moment, do it," Brenda urged. "While you still have time."

"But the cancer—" Anna objected.

"Screw the cancer!" Bekah snapped.

"You win or it wins," Brenda continued. "What's it gonna be? You can die like a champion who lived the life she wanted, or you can hole up and wait to die. Who do you want to be?"

"Exactly!" Bekah agreed.

Anna's body felt so tight she could hardly breathe. *I've never stopped being crazy about you. I've never stopped being crazy about you.* She sighed and slid her spoon back into the soup. "Can I please finish my lunch first?"

The laugher they all shared broke the tension and they finished the meal discussing their kids and Spring plans without any of the pressure or tension that had consumed their lunch time before. Anna knew she had a decision to make, but she was glad she didn't have to make it today.

LUKE HADN'T STOPPED thinking about the conversation with Anna that Saturday for the past two days. And Tuesday morning he could hardly work. Could it be he'd been the only one to feel those old feelings? Had she really fallen out of love with him? Or was it really all about the cancer?

A knife stabbed at his heart every time he thought of that, but despite the episodes he'd witnessed, Anna remained so vibrant in his memories. He'd always been the most alive when he was be her side. And he couldn't picture his life without that. The past three years apart had been hardest because he didn't have her there for strength, support, and inspiration like he always had.

Being honest, he just couldn't believe Anna's time could really be over at thirty-three. She was too young. God wouldn't let that happen. Wouldn't take away the most wonderful gift He'd ever given Luke and their kids. Luke had always been taught that God was a loving, fair God. No, there was nothing fair about that. It would be cruel, heartless. How could they go on without her?

Her words echoed over and over through his mind: *"The kids have been a lot happier now that you're around more. We all have."* And he could have sworn when he'd told her he'd never stopped loving her, he caught a familiar look in her eyes and she'd shivered. She used to do that when they spent romantic time together, could the past three years have changed it from excitement and love to loathing? He just couldn't believe that.

As he struggled to get through paperwork at the office, a weather report came over the radio. KMOX was predicting heavy rain and winds starting over night. Originally, they'd been predicting less than an inch, but now they anticipated three to seven in some places, which meant the possibility of flash flooding. That meant he needed to leave early for work. And then he thought of Anna. She'd mentioned her driveway was prone to flooding in heavy rains. What if she couldn't get the car out to go to chemo and radiation? Did she have sandbags and would she even be strong enough to carry them if she did? Did Kyle even know how, let alone have the focus to do it right?

His chair scraped against the carpet as he suddenly slid back and stood from his desk, whirling to grab the coat from the coat tree behind his desk. "I'm taking the afternoon off," he called to Elise as he headed for the door.

"What about that meeting with sales at three?" she asked as he passed her desk in the front office.

Luke grunted. "Find a hole and reschedule it for tomorrow. There's something I need to do."

"Okay," Elise replied in the sing-song tone she'd always used when he presented her with a challenge. She was fantastic, always getting done whatever he asked without complaint. And the truth was, she'd been doing a lot of adjusting to his schedule the past few months as he sought more time with Anna and the kids and hadn't questioned it once. Luke made a mental note to give her a raise and a special bonus.

As he pulled his Subaru out into traffic and headed for Home Depot to buy bags of salt, he realized not a single person at work had complained or questioned his frequent absences of late. He hadn't explained himself either, yet they just took it in stride. In fact, Elise looked almost happy every time he left early to spend more time at home. He knew she'd been worrying about him after the divorce, offering the occasional subtle hint of an invite to dinner with her family or suggesting a bar or gathering the employees were having that he was welcome to join. Luke had always declined them, and he regretted it. He had treated his employees like family as a matter of policy, but now he realized he didn't really know them, and that needed to change. Other than the annual summer picnic and the Christmas party, they rarely spent time with him. His employees had his back, and he owed them more. Right then, Luke made a vow to start changing that as well.

Luke parked the Subaru in his usual spot by the curb and started unloading the sandbags he'd purchased. He'd bought enough to store at both his and Anna's houses in case there were too many and she didn't have the room.

Stacking two bags outside the garage, he broke the seal on the third and set to work. Placing sandbags was tedious but it was important to know where the water flowed so he examined the drive and found signs of drainage trails. He decided to start there. He could always move them later, after checking with Anna. At least lining the drive should help a lot. Luke made a mental note to at least teach Kyle the concept, even if he wasn't sure yet about trusting him to handle it entirely on his own. Teenagers weren't known for either their patience or attention to detail, and neither road salt nor car repair was cheap enough he wanted to let his son take charge of it just yet.

As he worked, he glanced toward the house from time to time. He assumed Anna was home, since he could see the hood of her car through the garage windows. But the couple times he thought about knocking, he remembered their last conversation and lost his nerve. He'd be there for her and the kids no matter what, but the kids wouldn't be home from school for at least three hours, and he had no desire to relive the same rejection over and over again.

After half an hour, he'd finished the driveway. That was when the door cracked open, and Anna appeared. She was wearing well-worn Levi's with faded blue denim and a red and white flannel long-sleeved shirt tucked in at the waist. Her feet were bare, and her hair was still wet from showering.

"Luke? I thought I heard someone out here," she said. "I was taking a shower. What are you doing?"

"Getting things ready for the storm," Luke said as he took her in. She had no make-up on, and her hair was uncombed. But all Luke could think was he'd never seen anyone more beautiful in his whole life. She literally took his breath away.

"It's just supposed to be an inch or less," Anna replied, "but thank you."

He shook his head, trying to catch his breath and gather his words before she noticed he was staring. "They've changed the prediction to several inches," he finally managed. "Looks like it could make for a real mess. Let's hope it doesn't ruin your birthday."

"I told you I don't need all that," she said as she came down the steps to the stoop and stood beside him. The scent of the orange ginger aroma therapy shampoo she loved was as breathtaking as her beauty. He hadn't smelled it in such a long time, and it brought back a flood of memories with it. Her face wrinkled as she shot him a questioning gaze. "Are you all right?"

Suddenly, he couldn't help himself, Luke leaned forward and kissed her right there. It only lasted a few seconds, and it was soft and gentle, but when he pulled away, she had the bulging eyes, flaring nostrils, and wrinkled brow he recognized from many past fights. "Why'd you have to do that?" she demanded.

Luke stepped back, shocked. "I don't know. It just felt right to me."

"Well, it isn't," she said, angrily. "You should know better than to take advantage."

Luke reacted, getting irritated. "I wasn't trying to take advantage. I got lost in the moment. I haven't smelled that shampoo in a long time. So many memories."

"Well, that doesn't give you the right to just…take advantage," she scolded, then shook her head.

"I know, I'm so sorry," Luke said and meant it. "And about Saturday night, too. I will always love you, but I have no right to expect anything more than your friendship. I'm so grateful you let me back in with the kids—" Stumbling for the right words, he turned away. "I'm sorry. I'm like a confused teenager around you, for some reason. I just can't seem to get anything right."

With that, he started toward the steps, intending to go back and store the salt and shovel in the garage before heading for home. But as he moved his foot to take a step, Anna rushed forward, blocking his way, and before he knew what was happening, she'd tilted her head and *she* was kissing him! He didn't know whether to kiss her back or to just stand there. But then she grabbed the top of his coat where the zipper met his neck and pulled him against her, dragging them both back through the door into the house.

The kiss was filled with passion and longing, and soon he couldn't help but kiss back. He felt her tongue dancing with his and automatically his arms went around her. It lasted at least a minute or two—or seemed like it—and when she finally pulled away to catch her breath, he asked, "What are you doing?"

"Do you want to talk about or just let it happen?" she asked. With that, she yanked him against her and their lips met again. Her palms rubbed against his chest, gently caressing, and he felt a pressure and excitement down below he'd long suppressed, wondering if he'd ever need it again.

Then she was taking his hand and leading him toward the hallway that led to the bedrooms.

"Anna, I—"

She put a finger to his lips and shook her head. "I want you. I know what I'm doing, okay? I've been thinking about this ever since we talked."

They moved together, her pulling his hand, both walking quickly past family photos in the hallway and a few prairie paintings she'd acquired at local festivals. And then they were in her bedroom, the door swinging shut, and she was pulling off his coat. It was like a dream—a moment he'd envisioned but never actually expected would ever happen again. And yet, it all felt totally natural and normal. Like it always had with her. They were two people meant for each other, who knew each other better than anyone else in the world, and that included each other's bodies.

He reached for her clothes too, and they quickly undressed each other, and then they were on the bed together, and she rolled atop him, her breath against his face.

"I love you, too, Luke," she said. "I always have."

And then they made love as if nothing that had happened between them the past three years mattered anymore.

CHAPTER 21

LUKE AWOKE WITH his arms wrapped around the love of his life. He felt like he was floating on a cloud of joy. He almost thought it was a dream until she stirred, and said, "What time is it?"

He glanced over at the clock on the dresser behind her and said, "Three fifteen."

He'd never seen Anna's eyes fly open so fast. She sat up like and shot and reached for her clothes. "Oh my God, get dressed."

"It was that bad?" Luke frowned, hurt by the critique. He might be rusty, but he thought their lovemaking was pretty good and from the verbal clues Anna had given, he'd figured it was good for her as well.

"Not that!" Anna scolded, and she hurriedly dressed. "That was wonderful. But the kids will be home any minute."

Luke took a deep breath, relieved. "Oh. That. What's the big deal? We're their parents?"

"Their *divorced* parents," Anna replied, shaking her head. "Get up and get dressed!"

"Are we hiding from them?" Luke asked as he pulled back the top sheet and leaned over to retrieve his clothes off the floor on his side of the bed.

"Luke!" Anna's face creased as she waved her arms. "Hurry!"

"I'm putting them on," Luke said as he slid into his boxers. "Just not sure what the hurry is."

"We just made *love*," Anna said, as if it should be obvious.

"Yes, and it was wonderful," Luke said.

Anna sighed. "That doesn't mean I want our kids to find out. Things are confusing enough for them already."

Hearing her say it stung. He winced as he slid on his Levis. "Thanks a lot for that."

"Luke," Anna said as she checked the clock again, "the last thing either of us wants is to hurt our children any more than we already have, right?"

"Of course." Luke reached for his t-shirt and sweater and began untangling them.

Anna nodded. "They don't need to know about things that will cause more questions than answers."

"We love each other," Luke said. "What's to question?"

"A lot, Luke. We've been separated for three years, okay? We need to take this slow and be careful until we're sure what's happening between us."

Luke slid on his t-shirt and stood, turning so his eyes met hers. "I've never been more sure of anything in my life. I love you."

"I love you," Anna replied and Luke's heart fluttered as he slid into his sweater. "We will always love each other. That was never the problem. But that doesn't mean we should rush back into being a couple."

"Why not?" Luke looked at her as if she'd lost her mind.

"Because we're not," Anna said. "Not yet. And we may never be. Time is running out."

"I've loved you since I was nineteen years old, Anna," Luke said, feeling like he'd discovered a whole new world. He couldn't believe the time together had gone by so quickly. "It never changed. Even when we were fighting. When you left me. And not when you asked me for a divorce. I hated losing you, and I can't imagine losing you again, but whatever time we have, I want it to be together. I want to know you knew how much I love you." He took a long, deep breath, euphoria sweeping through him as he said it.

"I know," Anna said, looking down as her shoulders sank and her voice came out almost a whisper. "Sometimes that's not enough. I don't know if I can do this."

Luke sat on the bed and pulled on his socks. "Do what?" Love me? Be with me?" He tried but couldn't conceal the anger in his voice.

They both heard the sound of hydraulic brakes and a loud engine outside and Anna hurried to the window, peeking through the curtain. "They're here. I'll tell them you were salting the drive and we had some coffee. Try and hurry out there before they get inside. I'll go greet them." She hurried out, leaving him alone.

Luke sighed, putting his face in his hands. The scent of Anna's soap and perfume was in his skin. God, making love to her again had been amazing. They knew each other so well, slipped back so easily into the easy rhythms with their bodies. He heard the kids' and Anna talking outside and reached for his shoes. *Damn it.* He'd thought their making love was a sign she'd come around; changed her mind about being with him. But what she'd said had left him feeling so confused. Had it meant the same to her it did for him? What did this mean?

By the time he'd grabbed his coat and gloves and made his way down the hallway to the kitchen, Anna and the kids were already inside, and she was helping Cassie with her coat.

"Daddy!" Cassie yelled, cheerfully.

"Hi, Dad," Mandy added.

"Hey," Luke said as both girls hurried over for quick hugs. "Thanks for the coffee, Anna. I have to go treat my own drive, okay? Kyle, next time we'll do it together."

Kyle nodded from the couch, where he'd already settled with a glass of soda and was flipping on his game console.

Luke hurried to the door and slipped out without further word, hurrying toward the drive. He opened the garage and stowed two bags of salt and the snow shovel safely inside, then closed it and headed for the Subaru and home.

RAIN STARTED FALLING at midnight that night and continued for most of the next two days. Winds reached forty miles per hour the first night but grew milder as it continued. Luke found himself stuck at home, working remotely on logistical problems like shipping and delivery delays, workers cut off from factories or offices, and so on. The whole time, he struggled to stay focused, his thoughts constantly returning to the situation between him and Anna.

Despite her concerns about the kids, which he shared, what had happened between them had been amazing, and he knew Anna well enough to feel confident she'd felt it, too. After all, she'd kissed him back. Sure, he'd taken her by surprise the first kiss, acting on impulse. But she had pushed against him, kissed him, the second time, and she was the one who'd led him inside to the bedroom. He'd simply gone along. If he'd felt resistance at any point, he'd have absolutely stopped right then. No, Anna had wanted him as much as he'd wanted her. Of that, he was certain.

But when he tried to call her the next morning after the storm hit, he got voicemail twice. Once on her home phone and the second time on her cell. If the kids were home, that was strange, as one of them would usually pick up. Had she told them to let it ring? Why would she do that? Anna wouldn't have gone out in this. Unless she'd made a sudden trip to stay with friends or family out of town, but why leave the night of a storm. Who lived close enough she wouldn't risk being stranded?

He cursed himself for being paranoid and answered a call from a supplier in Oklahoma City, turning his focus back to his work. *You're just being paranoid, Luke,* his inner voice chided, even as he listened to Bob Johnson explaining how screwed up their deliveries were with the ice storm that had shut down the city.

"It's okay, Bob," Luke reassured him, when the man paused long enough for a response. "It's everywhere, really. Do what you can, and we'll send out apologies and coupons to customers when the storm clears. Smooth it over."

Bob took a deep breath. "I'm just worried about BSG and ST Kirk. They've had delays all month for one reason or another."

"How much stock do you still have?"

"Some, but our shipment is also delayed."

Luke grunted. "That will be cleared up as soon as possible." He checked a spreadsheet on his laptop. "Your truck is stuck in Lawton. It'll be there as soon as the roads are clear."

"Good."

"Go ahead and offer ST Kirk and BSG ten percent extra for the trouble. Can you manage that?"

"We've got enough, sure," Bob replied.

"Okay," Luke said. "I'll add that amount to your next shipment for free to make up for it, okay?"

After listening to Bob sing his praises for a couple minutes, Luke hung up, customer satisfied and returned to his brooding.

Anna wouldn't have gone anywhere. She hadn't been driving much lately, due to her illness, and she'd always been a planner. Spontaneous long-distance trips were so unlike her. No, they had to be there.

An idea hit him, and he asked Siri for the number to AT&T and called to check if there'd been an outage in Webster Groves. When the rep said there hadn't been, he did the same with Verizon. Nope. Anna's phones worked. Why wasn't she answering?

He stood and hurried to the window, checking the streets. There had been flooding in places with bad drainage, and a few streets had been closed. Then the rain started up heavy again, like cats and dogs, and he could barely see his driveway from the house. He could try and drive over to check on his family but a number of residential and small side roads involved would send him past new developments which had been causing flooding the city was still wrestling with developers to fix, so he worried he could run into flooding and wind up stuck and waiting on AAA.

With a deep sigh, Luke sunk into the couch and tried Anna's numbers again for what seemed like the tenth time in three hours. *Come on, Anna. Answer it.*

Again, the phone rang and rang.

ANNA STARED AT the alerts on her cell phone telling her she had several voice mails and groaned. Eight inches had fallen over the past three days, meaning school delays and flash flooding in some areas. For Anna, that meant streets around her neighborhood, and so she and the kids had stayed at home, a fire in the fireplace, and she'd done her best to keep them occupied.

Luke, of course, hadn't been over, though he kept calling, and Anna knew they needed to talk, but she wasn't going to do it over the phone with kids listening in, so Luke could wait. In a day or two, when everything had cleared up, he'd be back at her door anyway. They'd make time to talk then. For now, he could wait. She hadn't listened to his messages for the same reason. The kids might overhear, and anyway, she knew what he would say. That too could wait until the right time.

It wasn't that she was mad at him. She wasn't mad at herself either. They had a history, and she'd always treasured that. Luke had been making a real effort, and the caring and kindness and dedication he'd shown to her and the kids touched her deeply. So did his obvious love for her, the romantic gestures, even making love. Other than a slight awkwardness from nerves, they'd fallen back into it like no time had passed as far as she was concerned. It had been special, and she didn't regret it. But that didn't mean she thought it should keep happening. The last thing she needed was more pressure, more worries, and more complications in her life. Becoming a couple again, over even lovers, would be very complicated. Dying seemed complicated enough.

She'd wanted to kiss him. Not at first. At first, she'd pushed him away, scolded him, but then all those urges and questions flooded her, and she gave in to the moment. The heat of his breath on her body, the musky smell of his sweat mixed with cologne, the feel of his muscled arms—that great ass and soft, hairy chest—all of it still excited and turned her on, even after all they'd been through. The problem was for her and Luke there couldn't be just a moment. She'd opened the proverbial can of worms, and unfortunately, this particular can would be very hard to close again. The last thing she wanted was to hurt her family all over again. With whatever time left, she wanted to make good memories for them, not bad ones.

That night, when the kids had settled into bed, Anna closed the door to her room and dialed Bekah.

"Hey, you," Bekah answered. Anna could hear her smile. "How are you guys getting along with the snow?"

"We're okay," Anna said. "Kyle has taken charge of the sandbags."

"Really?"

Anna chuckled. "Yeah. No yelling involved."

"That's awesome," Bekah said. "What's motivating him?"

"I think it's the time with Luke," Anna said, "but I'm really not sure." She smiled. "I do love watching him be a little man, though."

Bekah laughed. "Yeah, I'll bet that's fun to see."

"It's probably because I'm sick," Anna said.

"Well, let him show his appreciation for you while he can. It'll mean so much more to him later."

Anna nodded, then realized that wouldn't translate over the cell phone and said, "I know." Her mind was back on Luke and the words came out almost like a sigh, with a touch of sadness.

"Okay, I know you. What's the real reason you called?"

Anna took a deep breath, her skin itchy. What would Bekah say? Was this good or bad?

"Come on, tell me," Bekah urged. "You know I always have your back."

Anna closed her eyes and grunted, then forced the words out, "Something happened with Luke."

"Oh no, did he lose it again?"

"No, not at all," Anna said, choking back a laugh. "We made love."

"What?!" She could picture Bekah leaning forward on her bed or a chair, phone pressed tightly to her ear. "Tell me everything." And so Anna did, Bekah listening without comment or interruption until she'd finished. "Wow, so hot," Bekah said. "I wish John and I still had that kind of passion more than once a month."

"Really? It just happened."

"Yeah, but you were thinking about it. You basically

admitted that at Breadco."

Anna scoffed. "At Breadco I was leaning toward never letting anything happen."

"So why did it?"

Anna sighed as she got up and went over to the window to light her candle. "I hate when you guys cut to the chase."

Bekah laughed. "There's nothing wrong with it. You were married and you still love each other. It's not like either of you are dating other people. No cheating factor. Just old lovers reconnecting. The question is what do you want to do about it?"

Anna groaned as she laid back down on her bed, her face in her hands. "That's the one question I don't have an answer for."

CHAPTER 22

ANNA STILL HADN'T found the answer when Luke came over the next night and helped Kyle reshuffle the sandbags to address leaks and holes. Ironically, the flood waters drained quickly and were almost gone by the following weekend, the weather transitioning from the 40s to the 50s and 60s, making for the first Spring-like weekend of the year. Luke also played catch up at work because of logistical issues the storm caused, so he didn't make it over as often that week, and when he did, the kids kept him occupied. Anna felt relief, tough she knew they'd have to talk soon enough.

Despite Anna's insistence that she didn't want a big fuss, Luke's family gathered in her backyard for a barbecue that Friday night, two days before her birthday. Lee, Luke, and Ray traded off on grill duties while Grace and Julia handled everything else, and Karl supervised the kids. Anna had never been one who liked being waited on when there was work to be done. It went against her upbringing, but no one would let her do a thing. They insisted she just relax and enjoy herself, so she surrendered to the inevitable and did her best. And she had to admit to herself later, she really did enjoy it.

Lee made his famous barbecue ribs, with Ray and Luke ably assisting, while Julie and Grace had prepared an assortment of side dishes from Brazilian feijoada to green bean casserole, pickled beets, a veggie tray with spicy ranch dip, corn on the cob, several varieties of chips, and several desserts in addition to ice cream and cake. Anna couldn't remember the last time she'd eaten so much, and watching the kids all laughing and playing was truly a delight.

Anna had been surprised when Mandy opted to celebrate her birthday with the family rather than a big party with her friends. It was the first time she'd ever chosen that, and Anna suspected it was because, of all the kids, Mandy was the one most worried about her mother's illness. Mandy had always been the sensitive child, quiet and reflective, and Anna suspected she'd downplayed her birthday as a way of making things easier on her mother, even though Anna had never dreamed of asking her to do so. Even with all her cousins and siblings around playing actively, Mandy took time at Anna's party to come over and check on her mom. Julia and Grace had brought out a deck lounge chair with flowery cushions and insisted Anna plant herself there in the middle of the yard to watch the activity.

"It's your day," Julia said. "Let us take care of everything."

When Anna objected, Grace playfully smacked her hand and pointed with mock sternness. "Your throne awaits. We got this."

So occasionally, Mandy would wander over during a break in play and ask Anna if she needed a refill of her drink or wanted something to snack on.

"I'm okay, honey, really," Anna would always reply.

At least once, Mandy took her red pilot cup for a refill anyway. "Gotta stay hydrated, Mom, like Doctor Sousa says," she gently admonished. Then she brushed her hand through Anna's hair, patted her arm, and smiled before running back to join her siblings and cousins for more play.

Although Anna had always hated the thought of her kids fretting over her, she found the whole thing charming and choked down any objections. This was what birthdays were all about, Luke had reminded her more than once. And she couldn't be certain how many more opportunities like this she'd have for her family to make hers a special day.

Watching Mandy acting this way, she found herself imagining what a wonderful mother her daughter would one day be and choked up. *I won't be there to see it. To meet my grandkids. To experience so many landmark moments.* That was true with all her kids, and though she'd thought about that before, suddenly it hit home in a whole new way. Her chest tightened and tears welled in her eyes.

"Hey! What's this?" Grace said, jarring Anna from her thoughts as she stood over her with a concerned look. "We thought the party was going well."

"We're doing this to make you happy, not sad," Julia added, her mouth turning down into a sad frown.

Anna quickly wiped at her eyes and smiled. "It is. I'm sorry. Just thinking about the future and having a moment."

"Awwww, sweetie," Grace said and put a hand on her arm as Julia reached over to tousle Anna's hair.

"It'll be okay," Julia said.

Anna reached her hands up to clasp theirs. "I know it will. Thanks."

At that moment, a huge argument broke out amongst the kids, and everyone rushed over to referee, while Anna stayed in her chair, fighting to suppress smiles and laughter that suddenly came upon her. Some things she might not miss as much, but they made her feel alive, and that was a great feeling as long as she could have it.

THE FOLLOWING NIGHT, the kids went over to friends' houses in late afternoon, and Luke surprised Anna with a night out at her favorite Italian eatery—Charlie Gitto's on the Hill, the Italian neighborhood of St. Louis. At first, she tried to object. They hadn't sorted through their feelings or relationship status yet, so a date didn't feel appropriate.

But Luke dismissed her objections with a wave. "It's a special night out for your birthday," he insisted. "You don't have to call it a date. Just two friends enjoying a fancy dinner. But I called in a favor for these reservations. They're looking forward to seeing you."

"They'll probably embarrass me with cake and singing," Anna groused.

"If they do, it's because they love you," Luke said. "Enjoy that while you can. Everyone wants you to feel special, and you are."

He was so charming about it that she surrendered with no more complaints and hurried to her room to get ready.

Situated in its own two story, brick storefront in the midst of a block on Shaw Avenue, Charlie Gitto's was classic in every sense from the brick exterior and interior walls to the bar with its embossed front and dark polished wood surface to the lighting, tables, and chairs. Even the food was pure classic and very delicious. This was one of the oldest and best on the Hill and also one of the pricier. Anna had first come here for dinner with a friend and her parents as a teenager and she'd loved it ever since. Luke and Anna hadn't been in several years and only twice since the kids were born, instead preferring faster, cheaper options mostly out of necessity. But the night started at five and Luke told her, "We've got all the time in the world."

They both dressed up—Luke in a tie and sport coat and Anna in a rose-colored dress her mother had made for her a year before the accident. Arriving at the restaurant a few minutes after five to warm greetings from the Maitre' d and staff, they started by ordering a bottle of the house red wine, which was terrific, and then casually browsed the menu. Anna decided on Linguini with fresh clams while Luke opted for Gnocchi Bolognese. Anna ordered a baked potato with plenty of sour cream, chives, and diced bacon as a side while Luke chose the Chef's vegetable which was mixed peas, carrots, and broccoli. Then they settled down to wait.

The waiter arrived shortly thereafter with the bottle of wine and poured a sample for Luke to approve, then lit two candles in the center of the table. Luke swirled the wine in the glass and sniffed it, before taking a small sip. "Perfect," he said, after which the waiter filled both glasses and retreated to the kitchen.

The dinner salads with house dressing that followed were as generous as they were delicious, and Anna was glad Luke had encouraged her to eat a light lunch. Tonight, she was going to test her stomach's limits, and it would be well worth it. Across the table, she admired Luke in his suit. His hair had been perfectly combed, his face clean shaven, and he'd put on just the right hint of the aftershave she'd loved and gifted him every Christmas while they were married. He looked every bit the dapper gentleman, and she could see him gently assessing her similarly. Mandy had helped her curl her hair and fasten it up in a bun, and she'd showered and put on her best perfume, feeling more like a lady than she had in ages.

As they ate, Luke peppered her with questions about what she'd been up to the past couple of years—from her volunteering at the kids' schools and the local library to her adventures with Brenda and Bekah. He was quite attentive and looked interested, responding appropriately with various follow ups or remarks, even throwing in a few witty quips or anecdotes from time to time. It took Anna back once again to the old days and the charming man she'd fallen for in college and later married. The only mention he made of himself or his work was when she asked direct questions, and even then, he was succinct but open, not rushing or being evasive as he'd often been in the past.

By the time the main courses arrived, Anna felt lightheaded and tingly. Was she actually falling for him again or had she had too much wine? An inner voice fired off warnings: *this is a bad idea. It can only lead to more hurt. Guard your heart, Anna!* But she was so caught up in the moment, she let them quickly pass and focused on her food and charming companion.

They finished dinner about seven-thirty with amazing desserts, and then headed back to Anna's to await the arrival of the kids. Cassie was due at eight-thirty while Mandy and Kyle would arrive closer to nine. Luke had arranged rides with other parents. As they arrived and Luke suggested they finish the wine bottle they'd brought from the restaurant, Anna sank onto the couch.

"It's been a long time since we finished a bottle together," Luke said.

"Yes," Anna agreed. "Probably because it's dangerous when you have kids to tend to."

"We ate enough tonight, I bet we'll barely feel it," Luke said, half-serious, and Anna couldn't disagree. She felt a bit like one of the stuffed birds her father had collected as hunting trophies and used to decorate his study.

"Just half a glass for me," she finally said, and Luke disappeared into the kitchen to retrieve fresh glasses.

"You're having fun, right?" Luke asked as he returned and handed her a glass, then settled onto the couch beside her.

"Yes," Anna said with a nod then sipped her wine. "It was a charming night, a great birthday gift."

Luke swallowed his own sip and smiled. "I'm glad."

"You really are a new man," Anna said, watching him and marveling.

Luke shrugged. "Same man. But wiser and older."

"Improved with age," Anna joked.

Luke raised his glass. "We both have."

"If the kids weren't due any minute, I'd think you were trying to seduce me," Anna said.

Luke cocked a brow and offered a mysterious look. "Would it work?"

She opened her mouth with a look of mock offense. "What

kind of girl do you think I am?"

"A lady," he responded immediately and with utter charm.

"Don't you forget it," she said, mock scolding and drank more wine.

Luke raised his palms in surrender. "I'm a pure gentleman," he said, "who simply wants you to have a memorable birthday."

"Well, that it has been," she said and leaned back against the sofa, feeling content. Then she noticed Luke was staring at her. "What?" she finally asked.

"You're so beautiful," he said.

"You look handsome yourself," she replied. His eyes stayed locked on hers in a look she recognized, having seen it before on numerous occasions. He was thinking about kissing her. And then to her surprise, she found herself pondering the idea and liking it. *It's got to be the wine.*

Luke scooted closer and slid his arm gently around her and she leaned her head over to rest on his shoulder. "Thank you," she said.

She giggled and glanced over to see him watching her intently, his face dead serious. Her nose caught a hint of the rosemary and sage in his cologne. He smelled as good as he looked, and before she could stop herself or even consider consequences, she'd leaned toward him and their lips met in a warm, wet, magical kiss. It was soft, not forced but natural, with just the right amount of passion, and they held it for a bit before the door rattled and the lock clicked.

They hurriedly pulled away, and Cassie appeared, grinning ear-to-ear.

"How was your play date?" Anna asked, quickly switching to mom mode. Cassie had spent the evening with her best friend Henna's family.

"So awesome!" Cassie almost sang. "Her dad made homemade pizza and it was amazing!"

"Really?" Anna said.

"What was on it?" Luke asked with genuine interest as Anna scooted over to make room for Cassie between them on the couch.

Cassie plopped down between them and began rattling off a list of toppings, while her parents asked her about the rest of her evening. She and Henna had played with the other girl's American Girls dolls and had a tea party before dinner, then played a My Little Pony game on PlayStation for a while after.

When she'd finished, Cassie's face took on a mischievous look and she rubbed her hands together. "Cake."

She was referring to the leftovers of Anna's birthday cake in the fridge.

"How can you still be hungry?" Anna asked.

Cassie shrugged. "It's cake."

Luke laughed and tousled her hair. "Only if you promise to go straight to bed after."

Cassie held up crossed fingers and Luke stood, chuckling. "Come on."

Anna called after them as they headed for the kitchen, "A small piece. We don't want her stomach upset."

The door opened and Mandy bounced in, all grins, like her sister.

Anna had just started asking her about it, when Kyle appeared and glanced in the kitchen. "We're having cake? Cool!"

He and Mandy hurried for the kitchen as Anna stood, carrying her wine glass and went to join them.

The pain hit her as she reached the kitchen doorway. Suddenly, her face changed, and she dropped the wine glass, stumbling back against the doorframe. She bent over, grabbing her abdomen and moaning.

"Anna?" Luke asked, getting to his feet and hurrying toward her

"Mommy?" Mandy cried.

Suddenly Anna vomited. And then, Anna collapsed. She fell back hard against the edge of the couch, then banged her head on the floor, as Luke raced over, trying to catch her. He didn't get there in time. He rolled her carefully onto her back, listening for breathing. "Get the phone, honey!" he said to Mandy, as the girls looked on horrified. "Hurry!"

Mandy ran off to get the phone as Luke put a pillow under Anna's head

"Mommy?" Cassie said, crying.

"Mommy's fine, honey. She's just sick," Luke said, trying to sound reassuring. Mandy ran back with the cordless phone and Luke dialed 911.

CHAPTER 23

LUKE LOADED THE kids in his Subaru and followed the ambulance to the hospital. Thirty minutes before he and Anna had been having one of the most romantic nights they'd ever had in years. A night he'd planned, knowing she might resist any relationship, but yet again, she'd showed signs she cared for him as much as he cared for her. Now, here he was racing to the hospital with distraught kids, fighting to control the fear she might not survive the night.

It was hard to wrap his mind around it. As he pulled into Barnes Hospital's Emergency Room parking, he took a deep breath and tried to steady himself. *You have to keep it together for the kids, Luke.*

Twenty-five minutes later, Anna awakened, unsure of where she was. Doctor Sousa examined her, reassured her, then came out to the waiting room to tell Luke and the kids that she was stabilized.

"She seemed fine and then just collapsed, Doc," Luke said. He couldn't shake the feeling that it was his fault; that he'd pushed her too hard. "We thought she was doing fine..."

Sousa nodded and put a hand on Luke's arm. "That's cancer. You go through periods of remission where things look better, patients feel better, and then one day it just comes back with a bang."

"So it's back?"

Sousa nodded. "It never went away, and it never will. It hibernated for a bit. You have to come to terms with that."

"I'm trying, but we're not ready to lose her," Luke said, looking away, his throat and chest tightening at the thought.

"I know," Sousa squeezed Luke's arm then lowered his hand. "We'll want to keep her here for now, and we need to run some tests. Hopefully, she'll have an upswing and be able to go home again in a few days." He smiled over Luke's shoulder at the kids, who were watching anxiously from down the hall in a waiting area too far to hear what the doctor had said. Luke knew it was up to him to break the news, and he dreaded it.

The doctor lowered his voice again, "But you need to prepare yourself. There will be a time when she won't get better. I hope this isn't it, but that day will come, and you need to be ready."

Luke shook his head adamantly. "I don't know how I could ever be ready for that."

Sousa put a hand on Luke's shoulder a moment, before excusing himself and walking over to the nurse's station to fill out Anna's chart and talk with the nurses.

Luke took a deep breath and rejoined the kids, trying his best to explain in terms they'd understand. It was the first time the kids had seen their mother in the hospital. They'd been with them that day at the Emergency Room, but never came into the treatment room. He wished he could think of something to say to reassure them, but the looks of concern on all their faces, reminded him that words weren't sufficient in such moments. As soon as she saw Anna, Cassie began to cry. Mandy was sniffling. Kyle just grew silent.

In fifteen minutes, a nurse came to take them in to see Anna. Anna did her best to sit up and greet them warmly and look like she was fine as they entered her room, but with the IVs and tubes running to her arms and chest, and her hair a mess, it was a tough feat to accomplish. "Hey, guys. I missed you!" She motioned for them to come hold her hands. The kids shuffled over reluctantly.

"Are you okay, Mom?" Mandy asked through the sniffles.

"I'll be fine, Mandy. I just fainted is all," Anna said. But when her eyes met Luke's, they acknowledged the seriousness of it. "I just need some rest. The doctor said I'll be home in a couple days. Can you guys be real good for Daddy for me?" The girls nodded as Kyle looked at Luke. "I'm sure your dad won't mind staying at our house for a couple of days," Anna prompted, smiling at Luke.

"Of course," Luke smiled at them. "It'll be like an adventure.

Kyle glared at Luke as if he blamed him for everything, then barked, "An adventure at our house, big wooo!"

Luke and Anna exchanged a look.

"It's all in how you look at it," Anna said cheerfully. "Your father will be doing all the cooking."

They all exchanged looks of apprehension. "It'll be fine as long as he makes pies," Mandy said.

Anna and Luke laughed.

"Mmmmmm. Pie for breakfast. I like it," Cassie said, brightening, as she wiped away her tears.

"I think you'll find I've learned to make a few other things, too," Luke said, trying to distract them again when a nurse appeared and checked Anna's IV. He had been practicing with a new cookbook he'd bought, and he thought the dishes he'd made had turned out pretty good.

"I love you guys," Anna said.

"We love you, too, mommy," they all said together, each hugging her as best they could. Luke lifted Cassie up so she could do it right.

On the drive home, the kids were quiet. Luke hoped he could do this. He knew the kids had grown comfortable with their parents getting along again, but this time Anna was sick again in a way they could see. And Luke still felt intimidated by the thought of handling all the questions and emotions all alone. *Time to learn*, he told himself, fearing that all too soon he would be doing it daily. He tried not to think about that. He didn't want the kids to see him crying. They needed his strength right now. He flipped on the radio, turning the dial looking for festive music.

Kyle pushed his hand away. "No, Dad, let me choose it." He shot Luke another glare as he fiddled with the dials, and Luke turned his attention back to driving and mentally preparing himself for the next two days.

By the time they arrived at Anna's, it was well past midnight, and Luke carried a sleeping Cassie in from the car as Mandy led the way to the girls' room. By the time he'd tucked them in and went to check on Kyle, he found the door locked, and Kyle refused to answer him. In that moment, it felt like all the progress he'd made with his son over the past few months had been erased.

The look Kyle had given him at the hospital haunted his thoughts as he lay awake, struggling to find sleep. *Anna, please, we still need you,* he pleaded silently then offered prayers for healing and strength as his eyes finally fluttered and darkness overtook him.

"YOUR WHITE CELL count is low," Doctor Sousa told Anna, dashing her hopes of going home in the next few days, so Luke took vacation days and stayed at her house to shepherd the kids, who were all still noticeably upset about their mother.

Kyle remained openly hostile, ignoring Luke unless he had to and then only responding with short, sharp answers. Mandy was withdrawn and somber, while Cassie wavered back and forth from a giggly little girl to sad and tearful. Luke suddenly realized how much the kids had gotten their hopes up during Anna's recent remission.

"How's Mom?" Mandy asked each time he returned to the waiting room after visiting her room. Though Luke had offered to get Grace or Ray to babysit, the kids always insisted on coming with him, even if they weren't allowed to visit her room. They kept hoping the hospital would relent, but it wasn't looking good so far, and each time he watched them becoming more and more discouraged.

"She's doing okay," Luke said, trying to sound encouraging. "The doctor says another day or two."

But after hearing that every time for several days but seeing no changes, Mandy would sigh and Kyle glare, while Cassie just looked down at her feet.

"She's coming home soon," Luke reassured them. "I promise." And then he immediately regretted making such promises. The looks on their sad little faces tore his heart apart, but cancer was unpredictable. What would happen when he turned out to be wrong?

"We need her," Mandy replied, looking totally crestfallen.

"I know," he said, his heart breaking.

At home, he did his best to keep them busy, figuring sitting around was the worst thing they could do right now.

Monday after school, he took the kids to a movie and out for pizza at Racanelli's, the family's favorite local New York style eatery.

After pizza, instead of heading for the hospital, he took them over to Grace's to hang with their cousins. In part, he hoped it would cheer them up, but secondly, he really needed some adult conversation and a plain old break.

While Charlie supervised the kids in the living room, Luke and Grace had coffee and cinnamon rolls in the kitchen.

"Is this mom's recipe?" Luke asked as he savored his first

bite of the tangy, sweet, cinnamon delight he recognized so well from his childhood.

"Of course," Grace scoffed. "As if you even need to ask."

Luke grinned. "Busting your chops never gets old. They're terrific. Brings back memories."

Grace growled like a jungle cat then grinned. "Yeah, I know. You look exhausted."

Luke cringed, his forehead crinkling as he rubbed at is temples with his index and middle fingers. "Does it show? Kyle and Mandy are really angry at what's happening to their mother. Cassie's just sad. And I don't know what to tell any of them."

"Well, maybe you should get counseling, someone who can help?" Grace asked.

Luke waved a palm dismissively before returning to rubbing his temples. "She's gonna get better. She has to. We can't lose her."

"You don't get to decide that, Luke," Grace said, brow furrowed as her eyes locked on him. "I wish you could. I really do. But you remember what happened with Mom. You have to prepare yourself and them."

"I just got her back, Grace," Luke said, almost pleading. Tears welled up in his eyes and he took another sip of coffee, trying to fight them off.

Grace reached over and rested her hand softly on his left arm across the table. "It sucks. I know. But she's been in the hospital what—three or four times since Christmas? That doesn't sound like a person who's getting better. You have to help the kids face it."

"I'm still trying to figure out how to face it myself," Luke confessed.

"Yeah," Grace said, then just waited while he wiped at the tears.

From the other room, he heard Charlie and the kids laughing

and playing. Charlie had managed to organize some sort of trivia game and they were yelling out answers and teasing and taunting each other with enthusiasm and laughter like he hadn't heard from them in several weeks.

"Charlie's like a miracle worker," Luke said with admiration.

Grace guffawed. "He's an overgrown man-child, but he's my man-child. He knows what they need right now."

Luke nodded. "Can he do miracles? 'Cause that's what I need?"

When Grace didn't answer, he looked over to find her turning away, fighting her own tears, and they sat there in silence together, listening to Charlie and the kids, no words necessary or adequate enough, and cried.

"It must be hard to get through each day, knowing you're dying," Grace finally said. "It would be killing me, leaving the kids behind. I don't know how she does it. If I were her, I'd feel real lucky to have you. I'm sure she does in her own way."

"That's why I'm doing all I can to make it as easy for her as possible. I just want her to be happy, you know?" *Even if it is without me,* his inner voice added and his heart ached at that thought.

"How was the big date?" Grace asked, leaning back in her chair and shooting him a look that said she knew they needed a change of subject.

Luke's face told her the answer without him saying a word.

"That bad, huh? Man, with all you put into, I would have been swept off my feet."

"I kissed her," Luke explained.

"Next time, a little mouthwash first might go a long way," she teased and grinned, enjoying his scowl.

"Very funny. I don't think she feels that way about me anymore," Luke explained.

"I wouldn't be so confident you know what any woman is

thinking or feeling, Luke," Grace reminded him. "We like to keep you guys on your toes. Emotions are funny things, big brother. She loved you a lot once. Don't be so sure she couldn't do it again."

Hearing it from Grace got him thinking again. He didn't dare to hope. He didn't want to get his heart broken, but she was right about men and women, and Luke knew he'd long ago lost his ability to read Anna's mind. He still had all these feelings he couldn't seem to shake. Something had revived in him that he'd shut away after the divorce, and he couldn't seem to lock it away again. They'd kissed three times now, and Anna had initiated at least one of them. Then there was the making love. But even after that, he could still sense the uncertainty she felt, the conflict inside. She might still love him, and she must be feeling lonely, but that didn't mean she still wanted or needed him him like he needed her.

Luke ached to be wanted and loved like that again. To get back what he'd lost. It had once made life worth living. He used to be such an optimist, until his mistakes and life had beaten him down. With the cancer acting like a billboard calling out that he'd lost it for good, he doubted he'd ever be optimistic about anything again.

The next morning, after sending the kids off to school, Luke headed for the hospital hoping to talk with Anna, but found himself instead heading right for the chapel, where he fell to his knees at the altar.

He prayed like he'd never prayed before. Asking for forgiveness for his failings and bad decisions. Praying for strength for his kids and himself. But mostly he pleaded for God to have mercy on Anna. "I love her, God, though I'll never deserve her. And if it's not your will for us to be together, I'll find a way to live with that, but please, don't make my kids grow up without their mother. Please. If you can part the Red Sea, you can heal cancer. Please. Heal her. Not for me. For Kyle, Mandy, and Cassie. They need her, Lord."

The words continued to flow out for almost fifteen minutes.

Pleading, bargaining, begging—he did all of it, even telling God he'd welcome the cancer upon himself if Anna could just be spared. He'd be happy to walk away and disappear if that's what God required. But please, let Anna live. He'd never felt so desperate, so scared, so utterly despairing. But he'd been told his whole life God was merciful and wanted the best for us, and he refused to believe the best for his kids could ever involve living without Anna.

When he was almost done, his phone buzzed in his pocket, and he retrieved it to find a message from Elise with the headline in caps: CRISIS AT WORK. He finished his prayer quickly, reciting the Lord's Prayer, then hurried to his car. His chat with Anna would have to wait. He'd done what was most important. He had to go put out fires at work, then he'd come back later.

He made the promise as he snapped his seatbelt in place and started the engine, then he continued praying as he drove toward the office by rote, his mind totally focused on Anna's healing.

CHAPTER 24

ANNA LAY IN her hospital bed two days later, frustrated and lonely. Luke had come by every day since they brought her in, but only stayed for an hour because the hospital was picky about allowing the kids to come up to her room. She knew the kids probably kept him very busy, but still, she was here alone, sick, and she missed him.

Wow. She thought. I miss him. I actually need him. Before now, she hadn't even realized. Luke had somehow again become the person she needed most at times like this, and he wasn't around, because she'd hurt and confused him, again. She sighed, leaning back against the pillow, not knowing what to do.

Anna's room at Des Peres Hospital occupied a corner on the second floor in an area that had been renovated five years ago to convert double rooms to single rooms and add private bathrooms. The room was small, but private and on a quiet wing—factors which only served to deepen her sense of isolation and loneliness. After a few minutes, a nurse named Sarah came and told her Lee was waiting outside. She asked the nurse to wait a few minutes while she got herself together. So, the nurse nodded and brought her a brush and some makeup.

"Do you need some help?" Sarah asked.

Anna shook her head. "No, thank you. Please tell him I'll be ready shortly."

The nurse smiled. "Of course."

Anna had always liked Luke's parents. They had been very supportive from the time they started dating. Luke's mother Glenda's death had been sad for her. She'd grown close to Glenda, who was almost like a second mother to her. Luke's father, Lee, had also been great about spending time with the kids, even when Luke wasn't very good at it. But she hadn't expected Lee to come to the hospital. It touched her that he'd done that.

She got herself ready and waited. No one came. She checked the clock, and it had been ten minutes since Sarah left. She waited again, puzzled. Maybe Lee was talking with the nurses? He'd always been a charmer with the ladies. After about fifteen minutes, just as she was considering ringing the call button to inquire, she heard a knock at the door.

"Come in," she said.

Lee entered, smiling, and came over the bed. "Hi, gorgeous. How are you feeling?"

Anna took his proffered hand, and he leaned in to kiss the back of hers. The scent of Old Spice reminded her of her grandfather. "Fine, Dad. It's good to see you."

"You, too." He stood there, his warm hands wrapped around hers and leaned in to kiss her on the cheek. His hands were big and calloused from years of hard work, but his touch was so gentle, it projected kindness.

"It is a little unexpected," she added.

"Unexpected?" He gave her a slightly wounded look. "Do you think I stopped caring about you just because you divorced my son?"

"Of course not. You've always been there for me and the children, and I love you for it," she said, clasping his hand in hers.

The smile came back to his face and he patted her hand. "He's doing better now."

He meant Luke, and she nodded. "Yes, he is."

"The kids came over last night for a cookout, and they seemed to be having a grand time," Lee added.

Anna took a breath and relaxed. She had been hearing good reports from others as well and it put her at ease. It was hard to be away from the kids, but she knew this was good for them and Luke. Still, she wondered why Lee was here. She was sure it was about more than checking on her. She knew he worried about her, and he'd always been kind, but when she in the hospital, he usually waited to come by the house when she got home. *Oh my God. Do they think this is it for me?* "So, what brings you here, Lee?"

"Thought you could use some company," he said with a shrug. "Hospitals aren't exactly the funnest places to be." He motioned to the standard electronic panel which outfitted every room so it could be used in case of cardiac arrest to monitor the patient. In Anna's case, it made her feel worse about being there, almost as if she was somehow made weaker and more critical by its presence.

Anna sighed. "You're right about that. But I should be going home in a few days." The doctors hadn't said that, but she felt better, and she was determined to get well enough to leave as soon as possible.

"Good. I'm glad to hear it," Lee replied as he opened the curtains wider to reveal a view of the trees and landscaped lawns outside, an attempt to improve the ambience. "What did the tests show?"

"The tumors have gotten bigger. I'm afraid there'll be a lot more bad days than good from now on," she said.

Lee's face showed his concern as he sat down in the rolling desk chair he'd pulled over next to her bed. "I'm sorry, dear. It's a terrible thing to be going through at your young age."

Fighting back tears, Anna simply nodded.

Lee sat there allowing her to compose herself for a moment,

then said, "He loves you, you know." He meant Luke.

Anna nodded. "Yes, I know."

"He'd do about anything for you and those kids," Lee added.

"Well, I used to have my doubts, but he's obviously making the effort to change, and it's good to see that," Anne replied.

"We men sometimes have a problem with our priorities," Lee said, "but I knew we'd raised him right. He just needed a good knock in the head to get himself on track again."

Anna chuckled. "Is that what happened? You knocked him in the head."

Lee smiled. "Didn't have to. He came around on his own. But I was about ready to."

They both laughed. Anna squeezed his hand. "You've always been so great to us."

"You've always been a gift to our family," he replied. She waited for him to get around to his reason for coming. Finally, he let go of her hand, and said, "He's trying real hard, honey. He's really made me proud these past six months. He's like the man he should have been, the man he once was again."

Anna nodded. "He's been great."

"You're the great love of his life, you know. There was never any other for him. You were the first and only."

Anna knew that Like had been unsuccessful with girls when he was younger. She'd heard that many times. She also knew that although he'd dated some in college, it was never more than a couple of dates, until he met her. What they had was special, and they'd both known it from the moment they met.

"He'd do anything for you, including put himself in this bed instead of you, I have no doubt." Lee said. "It was terrible for him, when you left."

"To be honest, I wondered if he'd even notice," Anna confessed.

"He was a mess. It broke his heart."

"I tried and tried, Dad. I just couldn't let the kids deal with that anymore," she said, the sadness apparent on her face.

"I never blamed you. I knew how bad he was, saw it happening. I should have said something to him. I've always regretted that." Lee sighed, his eyes wet and dull as the eggs of his eyes and lips drooped.

"It wasn't your fault." Anna was touched by his concern.

"I know, but he's my son, and a father should be there to set his son straight when he gets off course," Lee explained.

Anna's eyelids felt gummy, suddenly missing her parents. "You're right about that. I want that for Kyle, too."

Lee grunted. "They seem to be making amends now. They were laughing and teasing each other like buddies last night."

"It's amazing, isn't it? Luke's really winning them over." Anna nodded, smiling as she pictured them together.

"What about you, Anna?" His brow furrowed as his eyes found hers.

Anna knew that finally he was getting to his reason for coming. "What do you mean?"

"Is he winning you over?"

"He's convinced me he's a changed man, if that's what you mean, Dad." She admitted, but from his eyes, she knew he meant more. "We're divorced now. I only have a little time left. I can't risk putting my kids through anything again. We had some beautiful times together, but it's too late now."

Lee hmmmmed and patted her hand again. "It's never been my way to interfere. Especially not in my kids' marriages, but Luke never stopped loving you."

"I love him, too, Dad. A part of me always will, but I'm getting weaker every day," Anna said.

"All the more reason." Lee replied. Anna looked away, not

sure how to convince him. "You tell me to stop if I'm out of bounds."

She shook her head. "It's okay."

Lee pulled his hand back and thought a moment. "What I'm trying to say, Anna, is we all have limited days, but not all of us get notice of when our limit is coming up. You have to decide how you want to live those days. Your children are happier than I've seen them in two years. And I think you are, too."

Anna was shocked that he could read her so well. She had been happy lately, and she knew Luke's change was a big part of it. Ever since her conversation with Bekah and Brenda, she'd been thinking about their date. Old feelings kept coming back to her. She knew she still cared for him deeply. She just didn't want any more pain in their lives. It would already be hard enough to say goodbye. "You make it hard to say no, don't you?" She finally said, looking at Lee.

He shrugged. "Glenda always hated that about me."

Anna laughed, taking his hand again and squeezing it. "I don't know if I can, Dad. You know I care about him." Lee nodded. "But he has made things so wonderful lately. None of us have been happier in a long time."

Lee smiled at the admission. "Well, I just stopped by to make sure you were okay." Clearly, the discussion was over. He let go of her hand and kissed her cheek. "I'll stop by in a couple of days, when you're up and around, okay?"

Anna nodded, smiling. "That would be great. The kids love their grandpa." At the last comment, Lee beamed. He blew her a kiss and was gone.

Anna sat up in bed, thinking through what he'd said. Could they really find love again so late? It seemed almost silly. But she had to admit Luke had made her very happy lately. Her own friends had told her how much she'd changed. She felt different, too, and it felt good to her. She liked what she had become. It was like she'd been teleported back to a place in her past where her life was almost perfect, and she had everything she'd always wanted. Somehow, they'd both become better people through the reconnection with each other. She wouldn't trade that for anything.

Even when he'd kissed her, she'd only been angry because it was so unexpected and because she was afraid. She'd enjoyed it, in spite of any reservations. She hadn't been able to get it out of her mind—the smell of his cologne, the touch of his lips. Even the resentment she'd felt against Luke for so long was almost forgotten. She no longer felt a jab in her heart when she saw his face or heard his voice. She was happy to see him these days.

How would the kids feel about them being together again? They had just started getting used to Luke being a part of their lives again. She didn't want to disrupt that. They'd cried so much, when she and Luke had separated. It was overwhelming to think about. She sighed and laid back on the pillow to rest.

TWO DAYS LATER, the first of April, Anna was in the middle of a visit from Bekah and Brenda when Dr. Sousa arrived. The women stood on either side of the bed as he entered, having been updating Anna on the latest antics of their husbands and children. They stopped laughing as soon as they saw him.

"Well, you're in good spirits," he said with a smile of his own. "That's good to see."

Anna nodded. "These two always keep me entertained."

"Laughter *is* the best medicine," Brenda joked.

"I actually agree," the doctor said. "I wish it was easier to prescribe in fact." His white was amazingly spotless and crisp for late afternoon and the stethoscope slung around his neck hung perfectly centered—more like decoration than a functional tool.

The ladies chuckled as Bekah and Brenda moved back, turning toward the door.

"We'll leave you two alone," Bekah said.

Anna raised a hand to stop them. "No, you can stay." She looked at the doctor. "These ladies are like sisters. They're family."

Dr. Sousa nodded.

"We're also big crybabies so we hope you have some good news," Brenda teased.

Bekah and Anna chortled and Dr. Sousa joined them.

"Actually, I might," he said, looking at Anna.

She stopped laughing and locked eyes on his. "What is it? Can I go home?"

"Not today, but your white cell count is up," he said. "I'd consider that promising."

Bekah and Brenda grinned and hurried back to the sides of the bed, reaching out to clasp Anna's hands as they all exchanged happy looks.

"So tomorrow then?" Anna said hopefully.

Dr. Sousa chuckled. "More likely a few days, but we'll do the best we can, okay? What matters is your body's still fighting, and that's encouraging."

Anna nodded. "Thank you so much."

Dr. Sousa patted her leg then excused himself and headed out the door for his next patient.

"Wow! Such good news," Bekah said.

Anna sighed. "For now."

"Are you gonna call Luke?" Brenda asked.

Anna shook her head. "I'll tell him tomorrow. I want to make sure it's not a fluke first."

Brenda and Bekah squeezed her hands again, eyes filled with sympathy.

"You know we're praying for you," Brenda said.

"And I appreciate every word," Anna said.

Bekah held up crossed fingers. "I'm keeping these fingers crossed until it's verified, just in case."

The ladies laughed again.

Anna said, "Now tell me more about John and the car. The muffler actually fell off on the street?"

Bekah grunted. "The first time he backed it out. He'd barely left the driveway."

"Oh my God!" Brenda said as they all broke into laughter again.

CHAPTER 25

LUKE WATCHED AS Kyle grabbed his second slice of pizza and began shoving it down his throat like it might evaporate any moment, tomato sauce and grease dripping down onto his t-shirt, jeans, and the tablecloth.

"Would you please use a fork as I asked you to?" Luke scolded for the third time. "And slow down. It's not going to disappear."

Kyle glared at him and let out a loud belch as his sisters dissolved into giggles on either side of him, and Luke sighed in disgust.

It was the end of one of the longest weeks of Luke's life. With Anna in the hospital, he'd limited his working hours to the middle of the day when the kids were at school. For convenience, he'd chosen to stay with them at Anna's house, but despite his efforts at kindness and understanding, neither Mandy nor Kyle seemed to have cooled their anger toward him. Instead, he'd experienced one rebellion after another, with snide glares and sarcastic comments filling the moments in between. He was exhausted, and his patience almost used up.

It was bad enough the kids had ganged up to demand pizza tonight, rejecting the leftovers from several pretty decent meals he'd managed to recreate from his cooking class, but their constant passive aggressiveness and rudeness left him feeling like an outsider all over again, despite what he'd thought had been months of progress.

He stared at the two large Racanelli's boxes and open 2-Liters of Coke and 7-Up spread across the center of the table. Each of them had paper plates and plastic utensils and drank from red pilot cups he'd dredged up from picnic supplies in Anna's pantry. He just didn't have the energy for more dishes tonight.

As Kyle reached for a third slice, Luke dropped his fork, letting it noisily clang against his plate and swung his arm out to grab Kyle's wrist. "Enough! If you can't have the respect to even acknowledge me, let alone eat with the manners you know your mother would insist upon, you're done."

Kyle yanked his hand away. "Don't touch me!" But as he hurriedly reached for a third slice again, Luke grabbed his wrist and held it fast—inches above the pizza.

"Don't talk to me in that tone!" he scolded. "I understand you're angry with me, even though I'm not sure why. But I am still your father, and I deserve your respect."

"This is abuse! I'll call social services!" Kyle threatened.

Luke called his bluff. "Go ahead. And then you and your sisters will be taken from this home and put in foster care. I'm sure that'll be a lot better."

Cassie started sobbing as Mandy stared at him, jaw dropped open in shock.

"You're mean! What kind of father would say that to his kids?!" she shouted.

"A father who loves his kids so much he's fed up with their cruelty and disrespect to him when all he's trying to do it be there to help and support them while their mother's sick!" Luke snapped back.

Now tears flowed down Mandy's face as Luke turned and pulled Cassie into an embrace. "I'm sorry, sweetie. You've been wonderful, but Mandy and Kyle need to cut it out. Daddy's had enough." He dabbed at Cassie's tears as she sobbed on his lap, then glared at Mandy and Kyle across the table to either side.

"Why should we be nice when it's all your fault?" Kyle demanded.

"You'll probably just run off anyway, like you did before," Mandy added.

"I'm here, aren't I? Trying every day for the past several months to show you I love you and I want to be here," Luke said, locking eyes with hers. "I'm not going anywhere."

Mandy looked down and sobbed, her mouth downturned as she refused to meet his eyes.

Luke paused to reach for Cassie's red pilot cup and refill it with 7-Up before he turned his attention to Kyle. "What are you talking about? What's my fault?"

Cassie sniffled as she wrapped her hands around the cup and took a long sip of the bubbling soda.

"Everything," Kyle said. "You destroyed our family, abandoned us, stressed mom out 'til she got sick…everything!" Kyle yelled, his face red with anger, but his eyes darting away.

"Kyle, I love your mother. I always have, I always will," Luke said, choosing his words carefully. "And it's tearing me apart that she's sick, but cancer isn't caused by stress. It's caused by lots of things, but not that."

"Stress can speed it up," Kyle said, "we read about it in science class."

While he searched his mind for what he knew about the topic, Luke made a mental note to call the school and find out why they were teaching cancer, especially to a kid whose mother was in treatment. "Okay, yes, it can, but that doesn't mean I caused it. It's not the same thing."

"You made it worse. You made her sicker!" Kyle replied.

Mandy nodded. "If you'd stayed with us, maybe she'd be better."

It was all he could do to breathe and stay upright in his chair—their accusations struck him like a tornado, leaving him feeling numb all over, his limbs suddenly weak, his heart somewhere between hurt and disbelief. Tears welled at the corners of his eyes as he struggled for words—something, anything to say. "Is that what you guys think? Really?" he finally managed then took a deep breath, trying to hold it together. "My God, you guys, if I could trade places with her, if I could do anything to take cancer from your mom, I'd do it an instant. I would never want her to suffer this way. Or all of you."

"Is Mommy gonna die, daddy?" Cassie asked, sniffling again.

Luke winced, tears streaking down his cheeks now. "I hope not, baby. I pray so hard for a miracle."

"We need her," Kyle said. "We don't need you." He loudly scooted out his chair from the table and stomped off down the hall toward his room.

Mandy wiped at her tears with a sleeve and shook her head. "We still need her, dad." And then she stood too and ran off crying.

Luke sat there, devastated, his heart pounding, tears flowing freely, and hugged Cassie to him again as he whispered, "I'm so sorry, baby. I'm so so sorry."

"I know, daddy," Cassie said. "I love you."

And Luke buried his face in his hair as they sobbed together.

THAT NIGHT, AFTER the kids were in bed, Luke called Grace and told her the whole story. "Give me a good reason not to just get in the car and keep driving," he groused as he sprawled out on Anna's bed, his head propped on a pillow. He hadn't even found the energy to change into sleep attire yet.

"Well, for one, they're your kids and they need you, whether they're admitting it or not," Grace said. "For another, driving away will prove their point. Do you really want to give them the satisfaction?"

"Thanks for being so damn dead on accurate when I need sympathy," Luke snapped.

Grace laughed. "Welcome to parenthood, Luke. My kids can be mean little bastards too, sometimes. Goes with the job. Ungrateful, mean, disobedient, disrespectful… Really they're struggling to understand and deal with the overpowering emotions of the fact their mother is dying. They're too young for such a heavy, emotional thing, and so they take it out on whoever's close and you make an easy scapegoat."

Once again, she'd nailed it, only this time she sounded like a psychiatrist. "Did you go into therapy when I wasn't looking?"

Grace chortled. "Ha! That's a much friendlier response than what I usually get from Charlie when I talk like that."

"Well, no one wants their wife psychoanalyzing them," Luke said.

"I wasn't psychoanalyzing you," Grace countered. "I'm psychoanalyzing your kids, and besides, it's your own fault for getting your priorities so out of whack for a few years."

Luke winced, grabbing the second pillow from beside his head and burying his face in it with a groan. "Whose side are you on anyway?"

"Everyone's. It's a complicated situation, but I love you, and so do your kids, and they'll get over it," Grace said. "But not if you run away. So, get some sleep, have some coffee, and brace yourself for another day."

"I think I'm gonna start calling Ray instead," Luke snapped.

Grace sighed. "Hey, tough love, remember what dad used to say?"

"There's a reason I'm talking to you, not him," Luke said.

"He's softened over the years, especially since Mom died. Maybe you should talk to him."

"I think I've been beat up enough for one day, thanks, Grace," Luke said.

"You're welcome. Sweet dreams," Grace replied and hung up.

Luke stared out the window at the Big Dipper and then caught a glimpse of Orion. It was one of those rare nights when you could see the full constellation—even the pelt of the dead animal the great hunter held aloft. Luke related more to the pelt than the Hunter tonight. "Can I borrow that bow?" he joked, then sighed and forced himself to stand.

He walked to the door and opened it a crack, listening to be sure the kids weren't still awake, then closed it softly and reached for the shorts and t-shirt he'd left that morning on the chair beside Anna's vanity. The vanity was antique oak with intricately carved patterns of leaves and vines circling up and around the oval mirror. It had three drawers to each side, and Anna had inherited it from her grandmother. She'd once told him stories of the childhood memories it evoked—sitting there as a child while he grandmother gently stroked her hair with a brush and talked about falling in love with her grandfather, or the times she'd helped her he grandmother with makeup or curlers as she got older and arthritis attacked her hands—all the things grandmas and granddaughters loved to share with each other.

Luke hadn't inherited any furniture from his grandparents, but he did have some of his grandfather's tools and a couple nice hats—all of which evoked similar memories. His grandfather, that's who he wished he could talk with. Grandpa Glen may have had a tough exterior but inside he was a real softie, at least to his grand kids, and he'd given great advice and attention to each one over the year as when he was still around. He'd died almost ten years ago now, and Luke often thought of him and missed him. He wondered if his father and his siblings had ever treated Grandpa Glen so cruelly when they were upset about something? Probably not. When he'd died, Lee had taken pleasure in tossing the switch his father used to use on them as children in a fire.

"No point keeping that thing around to torture another generation," Lee had joked. Not that his father was cruel. But it had been a different age. Spanking was regarded differently now. Then it was the primary recourse for disciplining children, and Grandpa Glen might be a softie with his grandchildren, but Lee had recalled him taking no "bullshit" off his own kids when they were children. "You were lucky. He's nice to you," Lee teased as the switch burned. But his eyes were filled with pain at losing his father, and Luke had always known the two loved each other as deeply as Lee loved his own kids.

Maybe he should seek his dad's advice, he thought. Then he yawned and stretched his arms, sitting back down on the bed. "Not until I get some sleep," he mumbled, before pulling back the covers and crawling under them.

Just then, he heard a soft knock at the door, and it began gently creeping open. After a few seconds, Cassie appeared. "Daddy, I can't sleep."

"What's the matter, honey?" Luke asked, motioning her over with a pat on the bed beside him.

Cassie came in, turning to close the door gently behind her, then sat on the bed. "I had a bad dream."

"Oh, sweetie," Luke said and gave her a gentle hug. "Do you want to talk about it?"

Cassie took a deep breath and shook her head. "No, but can I sleep here with you?"

Luke's heart did a little leap in his chest, and he smiled. "Of course, baby girl." He pulled the covers back and patted the bed again.

Cassie was sliding under the sheets when she glanced over at the window to see the unlit candle. "Daddy!"

"What?!" Luke sat up, looking toward the window, his brow

furrowed. *Dear God, don't let her be seeing a ghost now.*

"Mommy's candle," Cassie said, her own brow creasing, her voice filled with serious concern. "You forgot to light it. She can't get better if we don't light it."

Luke could feel his throat tightening as he fought back tears. The hope in her voice almost destroyed him. *God help me,* he thought. The faith of a child. *"Mommy's not going to get better,"* he'd almost blurted out, but then realized—that's what he wanted too. A miracle for Anna. He took a quick deep breath, recovering and said, "Oh honey, I did forget. Do you want to help me light it?"

Cassie nodded, her lips curving upward into a smile.

Luke pulled back the covers further and stood. Cassie took his hand and led him toward the window, pointing to the box of matches waiting on Anna's dresser as they drew near to the candle. Luke handed her the box and slid it open. "You light, I'll lift."

Cassie delicately took a match and lit it, holding it with both hands as Luke lifted her high enough to reach the candle and light the wick. They both watched it flickering a moment as Cassie shook out the match, and then he lowered her again.

"Now, it's time for some sleep," Cassie said, sounding so much like her mother Luke felt a mixture of pain and amusement.

"Okay," he said and let her lead him back to bed, then he climbed back into his spot and she followed. He ticked them both in then and rolled over to kiss her on the forehead, then shut out the beside lamp.

"Good night, Daddy," she said sweetly and then closed her eyes and quickly went to sleep.

Luke watched her for a moment, just listening to her breathe. It had been a while since one of his kids slept in the same bed and the experience brought back fond memories. He stifled a yawn as his own tiredness surged again. After a few moments of shifting to find the right position, he glanced over at the flickering candle and said a silent prayer, then settled in beside her and fell quickly to sleep.

THE FOLLOWING MONDAY, ten days after Anna had collapsed in paid and been admitted, Luke was alone with Anna in her room for a visit, when Dr. Sousa stopped by. Luke and Anna had been discussing the struggles with the kids, which had started out serious with both concerned, and somehow devolved into silly laughter as they realized their kids' behavior was probably just as normal as their parental befuddlement.

"It's good to see you two laughing," the doctor said as he entered and crossed the bright white room to stand beside Anna's bed, opposite Luke.

"We were just discussing the pitfalls of parenting," Anna said. "Especially preteens."

"Dear God," Dr. Sousa said, "well then, this news might not be so welcome."

Both Luke and Anna stopped laughing, exchanging worried looks, as Anna locked eyes with her doctor and took a deep breath. Her eyes searched his face for some clue of what he might say next, but he looked calm and relaxed, which probably had come from years of dealing with patients but did nothing to reassure her. He obviously had gone home and come back for evening rounds as his clothes looked crisp and ironed and his hair and face were perfectly groomed.

Anna braced herself. Whatever he had to say, she needed to hear it. She wasn't one of those patients who wanted their doctor to pussyfoot around the seriousness of her condition. She could handle it, whatever it was. "Good news or bad, I need you to tell me," Anna said. She reached out and clasped

Luke's hand in hers. "We're ready."

"Ready as we can be," Luke agreed.

Dr. Sousa nodded. "Okay, how do you feel about going home tomorrow?"

Both Anna and Luke broke into smiles, their bodies relaxing as if they'd each been freed from a vise and could breathe again.

"Are you serious?" Anna asked, smiling.

"You had us scared there, doc," Luke added.

Dr. Sousa laughed. "Well, given the topic at hand, I thought you might actually prefer to stay a few more days. Just to get some rest. I have two teenagers at home myself."

They all laughed.

"Hmmmm," Anna said, rubbing her chin with her middle and index finger like she was considering it. "That is tempting." She shot Luke a mischievous look. "But I'll take it. When?"

Dr. Sousa's face turned serious again. "I sometimes wish I could book a night or two. There is one caveat you may not like."

Anna pursed her lips, her brow creasing as Luke squeezed her hand. "Just tell me."

"I'm concerned about your mobility," Dr. Sousa continued. "And you're not getting enough rest. You need to take it easy. The long and short of it is I'm sending you home, but I want you to use a wheelchair."

"A wheelchair?" Luke's face pinched up as if he'd felt a stabbing pain. "We'll have to get a ramp."

The doctor nodded. "I've already checked with your insurance. You can rent a wheelchair friendly van and ramp temporarily for as long as you need them."

"Fully covered?" Luke asked.

"Seventy-five percent," Dr. Sousa said.

"So, I'll have stay in the wheelchair full time?" Anna asked.

Dr. Sousa shook his head. "You can sleep in your bed. And use the shower, provided you are able to stand that long. And I do recommend installing a seat and handlebars. Refitting a bathroom is also covered by some insurance."

Luke nodded. "Whatever we need to do, sure."

Dr. Sousa looked at Anna again. "I want you to use it for the first week or two, at least until we see how you do; make sure you're steady on your feet. Abdominal pain, vomiting, and the weakness remain a concern, so we want you to take it easy for a bit, give your body time to recover."

"Okay," Anna agreed with no hesitation. She nodded to Luke as she squeezed his hand then let go, focusing on the doctor again.

"What do we tell the kids?" Luke wondered aloud.

"The truth," Anna said.

Dr. Sousa nodded. "I'd tell them their mom needs it right now, but you hope she'll be better soon."

"Of course," Anna said, then looked at Luke again. "We won't lie to them. They need to know what's going on."

Luke sighed. "Okay."

Dr. Sousa's eyes narrowed, filled with concern. "One of the stages of grieving can be rebellious behavior and blaming others. If that's anything like what you're experiencing, I can tell you it heals with time. Especially once they feel comfortable about what's going on."

"Well, they're not grieving," Luke said. "Their mom's not dead. And how are they supposed to ever feel comfortable about her dying?"

"They won't," Dr. Sousa agreed. "But they will learn to cope."

"They'll be glad I'm still here, Luke," Anna said.

Luke's face softened, and Anna thought she saw tears welling. "Of course they will. So am I."

"That's why we're going to be honest," Anna said, turning to place her hand atop his again. To her surprise, she wasn't feeling emotional about the new development. Instead, she felt determined. She had to start preparing her family for her death, while she still could. Luke might not be strong, but she would be. That's what mothers did.

Dr. Sousa nodded again. "They'll follow your lead. If you are comfortable with what's happening—to the degree anyone can be—they'll feel safer and adjust."

Anna sighed, still looking at Luke. "But we need to start talking to them about what's going to happen…after."

Luke winced, shaking his head. "They can't handle your sickness as it is. That will just scare them."

"They're already scared," Anna said.

"Yes, they are," Dr. Sousa. "And studies say kids their age struggle to understand the permanence of death. But they are getting used to momma being sick. And they'll know something's wrong whether you try to hide it or not."

"Exactly," Anna agreed. "Better we are open and honest and help them through." She patted Luke's hand. "It'll be okay."

"No," Luke countered. "Nothing about losing you will ever be okay. But I guess we'll figure it out."

Dr. Sousa grunted. "That's the best anyone can hope for."

CHAPTER 26

GETTING ANNA HOME was easy. Explaining the wheelchair to the kids was not.

After the ambulance dropped her off, Luke had rolled her in through the garage, having rigged up a temporary shorter ramp there while they awaited the arrival of the rental, and set her up in the front hall beside the family room. The kids had greeted her arrival with great excitement immediately tempered by the sight of two paramedics helping her into the wheelchair and rolling her up the drive.

"I'm okay," Anna had assured them as soon as she arrived inside. "Really. The doctor just wants me to take it easy for a few days." Anna smiled and stretched her arms wide, urging the kids to give her hugs.

All three reluctantly gave in, and once they had she continued, "I missed you guys."

"Oh mama, you're still sick," Cassie whined.

"I'm much better," Anna said with enthusiasm then tempered her voice to add, "But yes, honey, mama's sick. And I'm not going to get much better. We'll talk about what that means later. For now, can we be glad I'm home again with you?"

Cassie clapped her hands, smiling, and raced to hug Anna

again. "YAY!"

When Cassie pulled away again, Anna looked at Mandy and Kyle. "You two are too quiet. I'm fine, okay?"

Mandy nodded as Kyle replied, "We heard you." But their faces told the story. The sight of their mother in a wheelchair scared them, as Luke had expected. The seriousness of her condition was on full display and the kids looked as disheartened by it as Luke himself.

"I love you," Anna said, holding open her arms for a hug. Mandy swept toward her for an embrace, and then Kyle. Anne held them each tightly for a few moments before releasing them. Then she smiled as she locked eyes with them.

"We missed your cooking," Mandy offered, seemingly making an effort to be more cheerful.

"Yeah, dad's meatloaf sucks!" Kyle said.

"It's like a brick," Cassie observed.

"Hey!" Luke mocked scolded as Anna laughed. "It wasn't that bad."

"Bad enough to clog the disposal," Kyle countered. "Wanna see pictures?" He smirked at Anna, who shook her head.

"No, thanks, I'll take your word for it." She shot Luke a look of understanding and empathy. "I'm sure your dad did his best."

"Maybe he should go back to cooking school for that one," Mandy teased.

Luke threw his hands in the air. "They can't cover everything in two days. And you guys complained when I started repeating the menu."

Anna chuckled. "Really? Hmmmm. They never complain when I make Kraft Mac-N-Cheese twice in a row."

"I thought this would be healthier," Luke argued, then relaxed when he saw she was teasing.

"Only if our teeth were rocks," Kyle said and rolled his eyes.

"Okay, enough picking on your dad," Anna said. "I'm really glad he was here to look after you guys while I was away. He deserves all our thanks."

"Thanks, daddy," Cassie offered eagerly, then ran to hug Luke, who seemed to cheer up.

"Thanks, dad," Mandy echoed giving him a hug that so short it seemed more symbolic than heartfelt.

Kyle just gave Luke a thumbs up and turned, flipping off his game console and heading for his room. Shortly thereafter, the girls went out to play in the backyard leaving them alone.

Anna turned her wheelchair to face Luke, who was preparing lunch. He saw her turning, and hurried over to her, but she was too quick. "Let me help you!"

"You've done enough already," she said.

Misinterpreting her words, he nodded, turning away. "I was just trying to help you."

"No, Luke. I'm sorry. That came out wrong. I was talking about our date."

Luke looked at her, hesitant to think about it. "Before the hospital? I'm sorry, I just wanted you to have one special night but clearly it was too much—"

She grabbed his hand, holding it with both of hers. "Oh Luke, you've made me happy for a lot more than just one night." His eyes showed his surprise. "You've been simply wonderful through all of this, for all of us. And I haven't said enough about how much it means to me, about how grateful I am."

Luke watched her, seeming to be at a loss for words, so she continued, "I was so angry with you for abandoning us. It hurt the kids a lot. They needed their father. But even worse, you abandoned me. You were supposed to be my best friend. You were my lover, my knight in shining armor. It was like you took me to this fairy tale life, then ran off for some other damsel in distress, when it got too routine."

"There was no other damsel," Luke assured her.

"Your business was the damsel. In some ways that made it even harder. Imagine a business being more important, more interesting than me. It was like the passion we'd had for so long had been given to an institution. How do you think that felt?" She paused, trying to find the right words.

"It must have been awful for you. I can't say enough how ashamed I am," Luke said, tearing up and turning back to the counter to continue making sandwiches as he struggled to control his emotions.

"It happens to a lot of marriages, Luke. A lot of relationships are damaged by bungled priorities. But not very many people figure it out and do something about it," Anna continued. "The way you've changed amazes me. I never imagined it was possible. And I never knew until now how wrong I was to lose faith in you."

"You gave me a second chance, I didn't deserve," Luke said. "I'm the one who's grateful."

"No, Luke. You've made us all so happy again, and I know it's because you've always loved us. You just lost your way for a time. I punished you for it. I resented you for it. But here you are, fighting to prove that you want to be a part of our lives. Showing all of us, how much you care." Using both hands, she rolled her wheelchair over beside him at the counter.

"I'm sorry I forgot that for those three years," Luke said sadly.

"You've more than made up for it the past six months," she said, smiling.

Luke smiled, too, clearly surprised at all she'd said, but he turned and returned her smile, before he began tearing lettuce for a salad and dropping it in a wooden bowl. "It means a lot to me to hear you say this." Their eyes met and for a moment there was a flash of the old chemistry they'd felt when it was magic between them. Suddenly, Luke looked away as if he'd done something wrong. "I'm sorry if you didn't want to kiss me, Anna, but I've always loved you, and I always will."

Anna sighed, tears forming in her eyes. She'd had a lot of time to think over the past week, and she knew what she had to do. She had to admit what was happening between them. "So have I, Luke. I love you, too, and I always have," Anna repeated, leaning forward in her wheelchair toward him.

Luke's lips formed a smile bright enough to rival the sun. He looked like he was ready to jump through the roof with joy. She leaned forward as he bent down, and their lips met again. It was magical, and they both held the kiss, clearly not wanting it to end.

When they finally pulled away, they turned to see Kyle staring at them from the doorway. Before either of them could say a word, he turned and ran back to his room.

"I never thought this would happen again," Luke said.

"I wasn't sure I wanted it to," Anna confessed. "But I have so little time to feel this way again. How can I deny what's been happening between us?"

"I can't even think about living without you again," Luke said sadly. They kissed again, even longer. Neither wanting it to end.

Finally, Anna pulled away, squeezing his hand tightly. "I better go talk to Kyle."

Luke cut her off. "No. I'll go."

She nodded as he released her hand. Their eyes met like a silent kiss, and then he turned and hurried after Kyle.

LUKE'S HEART RACED as he moved away from Anna, feeling almost like he was in a dream. What had just happened between them lingered like a miracle he'd never thought he'd see. He pushed back thoughts about the cancer. He couldn't think about losing her right now. He had to make every moment count this time around, even if it meant leaving the business. He'd wanted this since the moment she left him. He'd almost given up. Yet somehow, he'd found a way to win her back. As he stopped outside Kyle's room, he whispered a quiet prayer that God would help him win back his children, too.

He knocked on Kyle's bedroom door. Silence followed for a moment. He knocked again, and it opened. Kyle's lips pressed tight into a grimace as his shoulders sank at the sight of Luke.

Luke reused to give in. "Can I come in?" he asked.

Kyle shrugged, not saying a word. He stepped back into the room and sagged onto his bed as Luke followed. It was a typical preteen boy's room—posters of pretty models and rock bands, none of whose names Luke recognized, clothes and belongings thrown around into various piles. It looked a lot like Luke's room had at that age.

"What do you want?" Kyle demanded with a heavy sigh.

Luke grabbed the chair from the desk and pulled it over next to the bed, sitting down. "Can we talk about what you just saw?"

"You kissed mom. Big deal."

"Well, it is a big deal," Luke admitted and felt good saying it. "It wasn't something any of us expected, but your mom and I have rediscovered something we'd lost these past few months. I love her very much." Before Kyle could roll his eyes, he added, "I love all of you very much."

Kyle fiddled with his iPhone, not even making eye contact, his only response the lifting of a single eyebrow and the slackening of his mouth.

Luke pressed on, "You can hate me, or you can forgive me,

Kyle. Either way, I'm going to be here doing the best I can to love you."

Kyle just kept fiddling with buttons on the small device.

Luke finally stood, returning the chair to the desk, and walked out, closing the door behind him. He had no doubt Kyle heard him, but he didn't know what kind of effect his words had had on him. He'd long ago learned his actions would be more important anyway.

He returned to the kitchen to find Anna with the salad bowl in her lap, finishing preparing the lettuce. She looked up and smiled. "How did it go?"

"He's still determined to hate me," Luke replied.

"You know most of that is the normal nightmare of having a teenager," she offered.

"Is that supposed to cheer me up?" Luke asked, smiling.

"No, but you've been making progress with him. I hope you know that."

"It seems like for every step forward, there's another step back," Luke replied.

"And that's just the nature of being a parent," Anna said.

They both chuckled, knowing she was right.

Finally, she took his hand again. "About us...we have to take it one day at a time."

Luke nodded. "That's all we can do."

"It's all I can handle," she responded.

"Okay," he said, nodding. "I understand."

And without a word, he stepped up beside her wheelchair, her arm touching his thigh, and began helping her with the salad.

AFTER THAT DAY, Luke and Anna almost returned to the way things had been before the divorce. Luke didn't move back in, but the family ate their meals together every night, and Luke was there fairly to tuck the kids in and help Anna around the house.

At the end of the month, Cassie's birthday party was a great joy. Anna had recovered enough to enjoy herself, and Luke and Brenda took care of all the hosting duties, leaving her free to completely focus on having fun. When her health continued to decline, Luke cut his hours back at the office. His new Vice president had really grown into the position, and the whole staff knew how sick Anna was and insisted they could take care of things so Luke could focus on his family. Kyle continued to warm up to him. Though they still had some rough moments from time to time, they settled back into a healthy pattern of father and son interaction. The tension eased for all of them, and things began seeming more normal again.

When Anna was feeling good, the family did things together. They took her to the Butterfly House. It resembled a visit to a rainforest filled with beautiful insects fluttering around them. There were plants from South and Central America, and they watched with delight as new butterflies hatched from their cocoons. Luke wheeled her around in the wheelchair without complaint, and Kyle pitched in from time to time, sometimes with Mandy's help. They made a game of sorts of it. The children were clearly thrilled to be a family again and growing more and more confident that it wouldn't fall apart again. The sicker Anna got, the more Luke saw the strain in Kyle and Mandy. Cassie seemed eternally hopeful that it was the kind of sickness that would get better. Mommy just needed rest and medicine and she'd be all better again soon enough. The older two still struggled to understand it, but clearly they understood enough to dread the future.

The family went to church together for the first time in two years the following Sunday. Anna worshipped from her wheelchair, but Luke couldn't see any diminishment to her joyful participation. He had thought her strength would wane, but somehow, she seemed more alive than ever during the service. Their voices lifted in harmony with their hearts to praise the God who had blessed them so much.

For the next two weeks, things continued getting better and better. As they both got used to being a couple again, it became easier to forget that they'd ever been apart. Anna told him again and again how happy she was. Sometimes, she even forgot about the cancer, she confessed, even though the breathing issues and pain continued. Luke felt as happy as she did. He always came home for the night by five fifteen every night, and he continued taking at least half a day off every week to be at home with the family. Life was what he had always dreamed of again.

CHAPTER 27

A MONTH PASSED, April changed to May, and Luke almost felt like he'd resumed living his old life. Anna stayed in the wheelchair for three weeks before she began weaning her way out of it, only using it on occasions that required extended walking or standing. They'd replaced the manual one with an electric, thanks to insurance, so she was able to use it at the grocery store, for shopping, and so on. Luke knew she hated the appearance of being weak or sick, especially around the kids, but the kids seemed to have taken it in stride, even competing over who got to "push mom" on occasions when they all went out together with Anna in the chair.

That Saturday, they attended Mandy's school play and Cassie's concert together and had a blast. And the next week, Bekah and John invited everyone over to celebrate their son Josh's graduation form middle school to high school with a backyard barbecue. The first gathering of friends they'd been to in months.

As John worked the grill, Brenda and Bekah handled the other preparations. Anna complained that she felt useless in the chair.

"Are you kidding? Having our best gal pal here makes us so happy," Brenda argued. "That's not useless."

"Not at all," Bekah agreed.

"Can I at least do something—set out silverware or make a salad?" Anna suggested.

"It's already done," Bekah replied. "We appreciate how you're feeling. We really do, but we got this."

"Yep. We just want you to relax and have fun," Brenda said. "It's okay to just enjoy being our guest, sweetie." She patted Anna's shoulder, and both shot her fond smiles.

"I'm not good at that," Anna admitted to Luke when her friends headed back inside to bring out more serving bowls and plates for the table.

"That's because ever since we met your life has been dedicated to taking care of everyone else, starting with me," Luke said. "It's your permanent mode, but right now we just want to take care of you."

"I don't want to be taken care of," Anna said.

"Yes, but it's how we show our love," Luke replied. "Maybe you can try to just appreciate it for that. You are very loved." He squeezed her shoulder and smiled, wandering over to the grill to chat with John and Dave.

Anna angled her wheelchair away from the table and watched the children play. The boys were tossing around a baseball in a triangle as the girls played on a swing set across the yard. Suddenly, Kyle sent a toss toward Josh that curved, causing John to strain to catch it. He slipped and it rolled on past, coming to a stop beside Anna's wheelchair. Josh loped over with a mischievous grin to retrieve it.

"How you doing, Auntie Anna?" he asked, cheerfully. He'd really gone through a growth spurt the past few months, and Anna found herself marveling at how much he'd grown to resemble both of his parents, almost a perfect mix. He had Bekah's soft eyes and flat nose, but his father's cheekbones and darker skin—pure handsomeness, and from what Kyle had said, Josh had been getting plenty of attention from their female classmates.

"Feeling useless," Anna admitted.

Josh frowned, his brow creasing. "Nah, you could never be that. It's good to see you. Mom and Dad were just talking about how excited they are you can join us again, and I like having you here."

Anna chortled. "You sound a lot like them."

Josh scowled. "Hey, I'm the guest of honor, be nice."

They both laughed.

"Do you need anything?" Josh asked as he juggled the ball in his mitt a moment.

"No, hon, you can get back to the boys, I'm fine," Anna assured him.

Josh brushed back a lock of hair that had slipped to dangle over his forehead. "Auntie Anna, I'm sorry you're sick. I know you've had a rough time. But it's really good to see you and Uncle Luke together, and Kyle is really proud."

Anna grunted. "He is? He never tells us anything."

Josh winked. "Yeah, well, don't tell him I told you. He talks about it all the time—how happy they all are to be a family again."

"I'm glad," Anna said.

John grinned. "Me too."

"Hey, dumb ass, we're all waiting!" Kyle called from across the yard.

Josh gave the ball one last toss and waved at the boys. "Coming." Then he turned back to Anna and said, "You want to toss with us? Seriously. Have some fun. It's a party."

Anna shook her head. "Nah, I'm not very good, but thank you."

"Okay," Josh said with a shrug, then quickly bent to hug her before running off to rejoin the other boys.

Anna watched him go, sagging a bit in her chair.

Luke spotted her and came over. "You okay?"

"A little tired maybe but fine, why?" Anna asked.

"You just sunk down in the wheelchair," Luke replied. "For a moment, I thought you might faint again."

Anna deliberately pushed herself back up straight in the chair. "I'm fine, Luke. Really."

"I'm sure we could find a place for you to rest inside if you need—"

"Stop! I said I'm fine," Anna insisted. "Really."

Luke nodded, backing off slightly but for the rest of the afternoon he kept a constant eye on her, a gesture that only furthered her sense of sadness and being an outsider who contributed nothing to help her friends.

OVER THE NEXT month, life returned to mostly normal for them. Anna began using the wheelchair less and less, and to Luke it seemed she was getting back to her old self. She and Luke started doing things together like they used to—grocery shopping, yard work, even coordinating carpooling. He even joined her now in preparing family meals, a gesture she delighted in. Kyle and Mandy even started asking Luke if he'd teach them some recipes he'd learned. It was the family life he'd lost returning to him like the restoration of Job in the Bible and he felt so thankful every moment.

In early June, they attended the wedding of one of Anna's cousins, their first outing in public at a family event since they'd reunited. The wedding was held at Kirk of The Hills, a large, white, traditional Presbyterian church in Creve Coeur, a suburb north of the I-64 central corridor. The carpet was red, the pews dark stained wood, the walls inside as white as the outside, as the family made their way to their seats. Along the way, several family and close friends called out greetings, Anna and one or more of the kids stopping to chat or hug or giggle for a few minutes before continuing on. Luke did his best to put on a smile, but he couldn't help wondering what was going through people's minds at the sight of him. These were her side of the family, after all, and though no one had said anything negative to him that didn't mean they wouldn't, and the last thing he wanted was Anna or one of the kids to have to deal with negativity.

To his complete surprise, people seemed genuinely happy to see him. After the ceremony, several greeted him in the aisle with warm smiles, and at the reception, both in line and later at a table with Anna and the kids, a steady stream came by to say they were glad to see them together again and wish them well. Luke was exhausted from smiling back and his was pretty sure if he hadn't brought hand sanitizer, he'd be going home with COVID or something just as bad.

Anna had a great time at the wedding, chatting and laughing much of the time, enjoying the food and the fellowship. The kids also enjoyed visiting with cousins and friends old and new. Luke and Anna sat together watching them, Luke half-expecting Anna to want to leave any time and go home for a nap, but instead, she surprised him and asked him to dance.

"You want to dance?" he repeated.

"Did I stutter?" she teased.

"No, I thought you'd be tired," he replied as she stood and offered her hand.

"I've got a little life in me yet, Luke Morrison," she said with a sparkle in her eyes as he accepted the hand and stood, and she led him onto the dance floor.

As he took her in his arms, hand in hers, and swung her around to "I've Got You Under My Skin," a Frank Sinatra classic, he marveled at how resilient she was. She'd had good and bad days since they'd gotten back together officially. This was a particularly good day, the day before not so much.

"I'm not even sure if I can go," Anna had complained.

"We'll find a way," Luke said, knowing how badly she wanted to be there.

To his relief, she'd woken up spritely and energetic and been that way the entire day so far. It was a remarkable blessing seeing her like that, and Luke hoped they'd have more days like that than the former.

"Old Blue Eyes," Anna whispered in his ear as they danced. "Such a charmer."

"The song's certainly a classic," Luke agreed as he hummed along.

The DJ was playing a classics set for older attendees, and when they'd finished the Sinatra, Barry Manilow followed with his "New York City Rhythm." Anna slipped right into it and Luke loved watching her hips and thighs twisting and shaking as they both moved across the floor in perfect synch.

The lilting rose essence of Anna's perfume mixed with both their body sweat sent a tingle down his spine as his heart thumped inside, and when the song finished, she embraced him, Luke kissing her cheek, and they laughingly made their way back to the table.

"I haven't danced that way for years," Anna said.

"I should take you more often," Luke admitted.

Anna chuckled. "It's fine. It's fun every once in a while, but I don't need it every weekend."

Luke let out a relieved breath as he helped her into her chair then sunk down in the one beside her. "Good, because I'm exhausted."

Anna chortled. "Don't be such an old man. You'll get your second wind."

Luke reached for a pitcher of water in the middle of the table and poured them both glasses. "Liquid. Need liquid."

"What we need is more wine," Anna said, looking toward the bar. "You just rest your old bones. I'll be right back."

And she was up and hurrying over for two glasses of wine before he could even respond.

THE EUPHORIA, OR "honeymoon period," as Luke referred to it when he recalled it later, lasted only two more weeks. The last weekend of May, Anna's health problems caught up with her again. They were working in her yard, Luke operating a rototiller, while Anna worked ahead of him clearing weeds. The girls were laughing and playing on a swing set and jungle gym they'd bought years before for one of their first Christmases with all three kids. Lee and Ray had helped Anna move it here after the divorce, with Luke's consent. Watching them play as he and Anna worked filled Luke with warm memories of the life they'd once had—one that had now somehow miraculously been resurrected for him. He'd never known such happiness.

It was as he turned back to the rototiller that she fell; as if her knees just suddenly gave out. Anna fell to her knees, crying out in pain. Luke couldn't hear it over the rototiller, but then he saw a flash and heard something as Mandy came running toward them, her mouth forming the words: "Momma! Momma!"

Luke looked then and saw Anna kneeling in the dirt, her face agony. Immediately he released the handles of the rototiller and ran toward Anna. Mandy had already reached her and now Cassie was racing toward them, too.

"Anna, what's the matter?" he called out instinctually, and then he fell to his knees beside her, his hand wrapping across her shoulders. "Are you okay?"

"Help me up," she croaked, and so Luke did, Mandy doing her best to assist from the other side, holding Anna's arm.

Anna struggled a bit as Luke lifted, leaning her against him, but they got her to her feet.

"What happened?" he asked.

Anna shook her head. "I don't know… my knees… this pain…" Again, she cried out.

"Momma!" Mandy cried out, tears forming at the corners of her eyes.

Cassie was sobbing too and repeated, "Momma!" as Luke looked at Mandy.

"Go inside and call 9-1-1, now!" he ordered.

Mandy sobbed openly then, but Anna somehow managed to put a hand softly on her daughter's shoulder and said, "Please honey."

As Mandy turned and raced for the house, Cassie taking her place clasping Anna's arm for dear life, Luke led her slowly, supporting her from the other side, trying to get her to the patio bench on the cement patio twenty feet away.

Less than twenty minutes later, Anna and Kyle were in the ambulance with Luke and the girls following in his Subaru as they headed for the hospital. Luke joined them in the waiting room when they arrived, and it took another two hours before Dr. Sousa came to talk with Luke.

"How is she?" Luke asked immediately, his heart pounding.

The doctor shook his head. "Not good, I'm afraid. She can go home with you, but she'll be back in the wheelchair. The cancer has spread, and she's weak."

"I don't understand," Luke said, not wanting to believe it. "She's been so great the past couple months. She was almost her old self. Yesterday when she fell, we were working together in the garden. We danced at a wedding a couple weekends ago—"

Dr. Sousa put a hand on Luke's shoulder. "Cancer can be a real bastard. It plays tricks. One day you're fine, the next…"

"But she can get better again, right?" Luke asked, his mouth dry and chest tightening, even as he already knew what the answer would be.

"She could," Dr. Sousa admitted, "but I'd be very surprised if that happens this time. She had a brief reprieve, but during that time it seems the cancer was working inside her to do more damage. When it finally became too much, her body gave in, and she collapsed. All too often that's a sign of decline, not a brief setback."

"Do you believe in miracles?" Luke whispered, desperate and scared. He couldn't even hear his own voice over the pounding inside his chest.

Dr. Sousa nodded. "I do, but they're rare, and I think she's already had several. You need to prepare yourself." He lowered his hand and glanced over Luke's shoulder to where Luke was reading to Cassie and Mandy was scrunched up in a chair, her arms wrapped around her folded knees. "And them." He sighed. "I'm sorry, Luke. Truly."

Luke gulped, taking a deep breath. He had to be strong for the kids. "When can we go home?" he finally said.

"She needs a little rest," Dr. Sousa said. "Can you manage her, or do you want the ambulance to transport her home?"

"We can manage," Luke insisted.

"Okay," Dr. Sousa nodded. "I'll go check on her and have them prepared, okay?"

"Can I see her?" Luke asked.

"Just for a minute," Dr. Sousa said. "She really needs rest to build energy so you can take her home."

Luke nodded and then followed the doctor through swinging wooden doors into the ER treatment area. Dr. Sousa pointed as he spoke to a nurse, and soon the nurse was escorting Luke past several treatment rooms to a room around the corner.

"The doctor said five minutes," the nurse instructed. "I'll be back in six, okay?" She offered a sympathetic smile before turning and hurrying off the way she'd come, leaving him staring at the heavy, oversized wood door with a small window through which he could see Anna laying tucked under white sheets in a large, railed bed—tubes attached to her wrists and arms as well as her nose. IV bags dripping. With even a mere glimpse, she looked a lot worse than she had in the garden.

"Anna," he said as he rushed into the room and let the heavy door slam shut behind him with a thump and click of the metal knob. The bright glare of fluorescents overhead filled the space, reflecting off the bare, white, antiseptic walls as he crossed the room to stand beside the large, railed bed where she laid, the hiss of the breathing machine attached to her face ominous in his ears.

"Hi," she said, almost a whisper as her eyes met his and she tried to smile.

"You look pretty," he offered. The smell of antiseptic and chemical cleaners filled his nose. He supposed it was better than a lot of other fluids one might smell at hospitals but it still gave him the same urge he'd always felt to get out as soon as he could.

"I look awful," Anna said. "You always were a terrible liar."

"I never know what to say in hospitals," he said and leaned down to gently brush his lips against her cold left cheek.

"Well, thanks for attempting to encourage me," Anna said. "I can go home tonight, they said."

"Yes, but lots of bed rest and the wheelchair await," Luke added.

Anna sighed but looked resigned.

"You need to rest a while first, okay?" Luke said. "I just wanted to check on you so I can go back and reassure the kids."

"Oh my goodness, they must be so frightened," Anna exclaimed, looking ready to jump out of bed and run to her babies.

Luke patted her arm. "They're fairly calm now. Just hoping you're okay."

"For now, Luke," Anna said. "But I don't know how long I have."

Luke choked up so instead of speaking he simply grunted and gave a slow nod. "I'd best let you rest," he added when he'd finally gathered his words and emotions both. He patted her arm again and leaned in for another quick kiss of her cheek.

Anna's eyes followed him to the door but as he turned back for a final goodbye, he saw she'd already drifted off, so he carefully opened the door and closed it behind him before hurrying back down to the waiting room to tell their kids.

CHAPTER 28

ANNA HAD BEEN home a week, when Luke rolled her out onto the backyard patio to watch the stars. The gentle breeze took away some of the sting of the warmth and humidity of an early Missouri summer. Luke had set a chilled bottle of wine and two glasses on the patio table.

"Wow. What's this?" Anna teased, her eyes sparkling with delight. "So romantic."

Instead of responding, Luke positioned the chair carefully so that Anna would have the clearest view of the horizon over the fence and around the trees and shrubs.

"Great view, too," Anna teased then shot him a sideways look. "Did you arrange this too?"

Luke gave what Anna took as a forced smile and poured them each a glass of red before grabbing another metal patio chair and positioning himself close by on her right. As he sat, he handed her the wine. As she watched him, his movements were short and jerky, and there was a tightness around his eyes, and he took quick breaths and bit his lip.

"You okay?" she asked, her brow furrowing.

Luke nodded, his smile more sincere. "Yes, sorry. Just thinking." He took a deep breath and looked at the dark sky filled with sparkling stars. "Beautiful night."

"It's perfect," Anna agreed.

Luke remained silent again, sitting beside her, lost in thought. His shoulders were relaxed but his fingers kept tapping the arms of the chair, like he always did when he was debating his next words or making a decision. Swiveling in her chair she caught the bags around his eyes. Had he slept? He was spending a lot of time commuting between work and two houses. She knew caring for her on top of the kids was a full-time job, let alone managing his company, and her chest tightened with guilt at the thought she was causing him such stress.

"Luke," she said softly, "you look exhausted."

"I'm fine," he countered, shaking his head.

"No, you're stressed. It's a lot to take on with two houses, me and the kids, work."

"I'm doing what I have to, and I have no regrets," he said, finally looking at her.

Anna nodded and gave him a soft smile. "I know, and I'm so thankful. You've been terrific. But that doesn't mean I don't want to do what I can to make it easier."

His eyebrows drew together, brow wrinkling, and he leaned forward to clasp her hand on the arm of the wheelchair. "No, Anna. I'm fine. You need to focus on rest and keeping your energy."

Anna glanced over and saw the candle flickering in her bedroom window. She frowned.

"What's the matter?" Luke asked.

"My prayer candle is lit," Anna said. "I didn't light it."

Luke nodded, smiling. "Cassie and I have been lighting it every day since you were first admitted to the hospital."

Anna looked shocked. "Really?" Anna's brow furrowed. "I stopped lighting it after that."

"I know, but Cassie reminded me, and I figure hope is never something to give up on, even if you're hoping for someone else."

Anna's mouth fell slightly open, her fingers going up to touch her bottom lip. Her eyes appeared wet and dull, a tear starting to form as she crumpled down in the wheelchair.

Luke's neck stiffened, his hands rubbing absently against his thighs as he hurried toward her and knelt beside the wheelchair. "Anna, are you okay—"

"I think you should move back in," she burst out. Then her eyes sparkled as she wiped away the tear and offered a warm, loving smile, her eyes meeting his with adoration.

Luke froze, looking stunned. It was clearly not what he'd been expecting her to say.

"You're here most of the time anyway," Anna said. "You've spent way too many nights in the guest room. And the kids know we're a couple again. They won't mind. Why don't you bring what you need here, and we'll find a. space for it so you can be here full time?"

Luke's eyes widened and his cheeks glowed as his mouth formed a silly grin. "I love you, Anna."

"I know, Luke. I love you, too," she said, closing her eyes as her emotions surged.

In an instant, Luke stood, reaching into his pocket for some small object, and then went down on his knees facing her. When he raised his right arm, holding up the object, Anna saw it was a black velvet ring box and gasped.

"Anna," he said, opening the box to reveal a gold band with a lovely heart-shaped diamond that literally sparkled under the patio lights, "marry me. I mean, will you marry me again? I love you. I need you. And I haven't been this happy in years. I promise I'll never abandon you or the kids again. I'm gonna be there every second—"

Anna thought her heart would burst as he spoke. Even though they'd done this before in a different place, at a different time, her heart surged so much she felt a lightness throughout her body, almost as if she might fly out of the wheelchair at any moment. "Yes!" she cried out interrupting him and leapt forward in the chair to grab his shoulders, pulling him into her arms.

Luke responded by wrapping his arms around her and sliding forward as their lips met with a sensation that moved her heart and soul—two people deeply in love who belonged together. And she wondered how they'd ever let that love escape.

As they finished, gasping for breath, Luke slid the ring on her ring finger and smiled, his stress and exhaustion gone, replaced by sheer joy and excitement. "I thought I'd have to convince you more," he confessed.

She shook her head and held up her hand, admiring the ring in the light. "Biggest star in the sky," she joked, and she realized the answer had been so obvious she hadn't hesitated. Months ago, she'd have pushed him away, scolded him even, but now here she was wanting to be his wife again, wanting to spend whatever days she had left in his arms, as his. It seemed so natural. They were a family again.

"I love you, Luke," Anna said. "Thank you for finding your way back to me again."

Without a word, Luke took her in his arms again, kissing her passionately like they were a couple of teenagers. They kissed a few more times before he slid back onto his chair and held her hand as they gazed up at the beautiful night sky. After a few moments, when thoughts of the wedding itself began filling her head, she tensed, but Luke responded right away—clasping her hand tighter and leaning his shoulder against hers.

"I'll take care of everything, don't worry," he said. "Ray and Grace and your friends will help; We'll have it here in the yard. Maybe put in a small gazebo. Close friends and family. It'll be beautiful, I promise."

As she scanned the constellations in a clear black sky, she saw Orion's bow and catch shining brighter than she ever remembered it, his sword sparkling a little as it hung from his belt. It was the most complete picture of the great hunter she'd ever seen in her lifetime. And from that moment, Anna had no more doubts about it. Like Orion, her life finally had all the pieces again.

Knowing they couldn't be certain how long she'd even be able to participate fully in such an event, Luke kicked the planning into high gear. There was no time to plan anything as elaborate as their first wedding, but then neither felt the need. They kept the invitation list down to fifty of their closest friends and family and planned a ceremony in Anna's back yard. Luke rented a tent and chairs and brought in flowers and extra lights. Anna's sister's family flew in from Ohio. Her brother and his wife and kids came in from California. Even her closest cousins and a couple uncles and aunts drove in. Ray and Grace came with their families, as did Lee. Brenda and Bekah helped Luke with the planning, and with their husbands, served as hosts and hostesses to ease the burden for Luke and Anna.

For Anna, it all brought back memories of their first wedding. That wedding had been a real event. Anna's mother had insisted upon it. There had been almost three hundred guests, and her parents had rented the clubhouse at the Ladue Country Club for the reception, which was catered by a five-star Italian restaurant located on the Hill. They'd also hired a full band for the reception and hired members of the Saint Louis Symphony to play the wedding. It had been much more than Anna had ever dreamed, and far more than she and Luke could have afforded on their own. The only similarity, other than a few attendees, was that because the weather was good, the country club had set up the reception on the clubhouse lawn, next to the golf course. Anna had to admit it had been like a fairy tale wedding, but she also remembered being very relieved when it was all over. Those few weeks leading up to it had been the lowest point in her relationship with her mother. If they hadn't been so close before that, she doubted they would have ever recovered.

Luke was so great through the whole thing, offering his

opinion, only when asked, and listening quietly for hours while she complained about her ridiculously overbearing mother. Thinking back now, she realized overbearing was the last word she would have used to describe her mother under any other circumstances, but Anna's wedding had definitely brought out the worst in her. Their parents even paid for a full honeymoon in Europe, and that had been a wonderful time of relaxation and romance, before the drabness of ordinary life settled in a few weeks later. Anna remembered walking hand in hand on the Champs Elysees past the Arc de Triomphe, riding to dinner in a gondola through the amazing waterways of Venice and waking up in a chalet in the hills of a Tuscan vineyard. Their honeymoon had been a whole month of one amazing place after another, yet even now her fondest memories were of the time they spent together just talking, holding hands, and making love.

After they told the kids and Luke and Grace launched into preparations, Mandy and Cassie seemed thrilled to get to be a part of a wedding. Neither had ever been asked before, and Cassie looked so adorable in her flower girl dress. Mandy made a wonderful bridesmaid along with Brenda, Bekah, and Anna's sister, Kate. Kyle was a groomsman, along with Ray, Lee, and Brenda's husband Dave. Bekah's husband John served as the photographer. He was a talented amateur, and photography took up most of his spare time, so they knew the pictures would turn out well.

The short and sweet ceremony was officiated by the pastor of the church they had always attended in Clayton. Anna insisted on leaning on Luke, so she wouldn't have to rely on the wheelchair. "I want to get married on my own two feet," she'd said, and no one could bear to argue when it meant so much to her.

Despite her previous reservations about finding romance again with Luke, she now felt like things had returned to the way they had always been meant to be. Luke had already moved a dresser and some other items over from the old house along with most of his clothes and a few newer appliances. They'd discussed it early on and decided Anna's new house was nicer anyway, and they didn't want to disrupt the kids again. Plus, with Anna being in a wheelchair, the old house just wasn't going to work. It's split-level design was just not wheelchair friendly, and besides, they'd installed ramps and railings here already. No, they'd rebuild their life together here. The old place no longer felt like home to either of them. It was also the same distance from the office as the old house, so Luke's commute was about the same.

Anna's health miraculously seemed to stabilize during the rushed month of preparations, so she found herself participating far more than she'd expected she could, and that made her happy. In the end, as the day approached, she found herself anticipating it with a peace she'd never experienced the first time around—the certainty that this was God's will for them, and the best way to spend whatever days she had left was by Luke's side with their kids.

WHEN THE DAY of the wedding arrived, things couldn't have gone any better. The weather stayed in the seventies, a rare break from the summer heat. The bright blue skies remained cloudy enough to dampen some of the sun's rays, making the outdoor setting idyllic. They'd hired a trio of jazz musicians to play for the ceremony, whose music provided just the right ambiance. It became a wonderful, romantic celebration of their reunion.

Anna thought often about the power of forgiveness, amazed she had arrived at the place where she was now. She had once thought she could never forgive Luke for breaking up their family, and now, she couldn't be more grateful that he'd brought them back together. She felt grateful to God, too, for working on his heart because all that had occurred happened because of a change in Luke's heart, and only God could make that possible.

All three kids beamed with joy as they watched their parents take their vows for the second time. Even Kyle seemed to have left behind any reservations, at least for that day. When the pastor finally announced, "Ladies and Gentlemen, Mr. and Mrs. Luke Morrison," no one cheered louder than their own kids. Almost as amazing, Anna found herself feeling full of energy standing there. She had worried that after the ceremony, she would be exhausted and needing her wheelchair, but she felt fine—more alive than she had in months. As they kissed each other in front of witnesses, the joy she witnessed in Luke's eyes surely equaled her own. Nothing else mattered—not her illness, past hurts, or wrongs—because in that moment, she knew they belonged together.

Afterward, they danced with each other to a soft bossa nova song, then split up to dance with their children, who smiled even bigger than their parents did. All in all, Anna considered it the perfect day. No matter what lay ahead, it would be a highlight of their lives together, and it made her glad knowing the kids would be left with such a memory when she was gone; that they'd be able to say their parents had been married when she passed. Somehow, she felt convinced that stability would help them through the grieving process.

At well past nine, when she finally sat down in her wheelchair to catch her breath, she couldn't stop smiling, unable to recall the last time she'd felt so happy and peaceful about everything.

LUKE WATCHED ANNA and the children with amazement. They seemed as happy as he did, which seemed hard to imagine. None of them had lost as much or gained as much as he had during the past three years, and yet it was thrilling to know that the reunion of their family could mean as much to them as it did to him. He said a silent prayer of thanks to the God for the forgiveness and healing which had occurred. His own little miracle, no doubt. Perhaps not on the level with the biblical miracles, but a miracle nonetheless—something special and unique few people would ever experience.

He'd been very concerned about Anna despite knowing she wanted to marry him again as much as he wanted to marry her. The ceremony would drain her, and hers was in short supply these days. God provided a miracle there, too, because Anna stayed on her feet the entire ceremony, and even danced for over an hour before she finally sat down. Even now, she only looked like she was catching her breath, as if she might spring back to her feet at any moment for another round.

Oh Lord, how I love her, Luke thought as he smiled at her. *I am the luckiest man on Earth.* The most amazing miracle of all was his certainty that Anna was thinking the same thing as he at that moment.

He felt so grateful to all the friends and family who had worked so hard to make the wedding possible on such short notice. Everyone had been totally supportive, as if the events of the past three years had never occurred. Many of them knew details which they likely hadn't approved of, especially Anna's friends and family, but none of that became apparent in anyone's face or tone of voice. They all remained totally present in the moment, celebrating with Luke and Anna. For Luke, it was a lesson in the power of love and forgiveness he'd read about in the Bible but never really experienced in his own life. Even the kids seemed to have put aside their own issues at least for the day. Kyle was smiling as big as his sisters and interacted with Luke so joyfully that Luke thought, *who is this kid?* A part of Luke wished the evening could last forever, but then he saw the wheelchair again and a sense of impending loss came over him again.

Later, Ray pulled him aside. "I don't know how you did it, big brother, but you pulled it off."

"Yeah, well, two weeks wasn't very long, but we kept it simple," Luke said, nodding.

"I don't mean the wedding, bro," Ray said. "Honestly, Julia and I thought you'd really blown it for good when Anna left you. She and the kids were so angry and hurt. We never imagined you could ever make it work again. But here you are. It's like a miracle."

Luke smiled. He couldn't disagree. "I'm lucky."

"From what Anna tells us, I'd say you're all lucky. Lucky that you found whatever it was you needed to recognize what you were losing, and lucky that you did what it took to fix what you'd broken," Ray said. He squeezed Luke's shoulders, smiling. "We're proud of you."

"Thanks, Ray. And thanks for spending time with my kids when I wasn't around."

"Are you kidding? I love those munchkins," Ray said.

Luke laughed. "Not going to be able to call them that much longer, you know?"

Ray shrugged. "That's why I'm making one of my own. Besides, Cassie's got a while yet."

They stood together watching his kids dancing with Anna. Kyle twirled her around in the wheelchair to the beat of an up-tempo jazz number as Anna and the girls laughed and chatted. They were the picture of pure happiness.

Yeah, Luke thought. *I'm really lucky.* You know, I'm going to need you guys," he finally said to Ray.

"We'll need you, too. We don't know anything about raising a kid," Ray said. They both laughed.

"Scary thought, little brother," Luke replied.

"Yeah, I know. Thank God I've got Julia. She's like my Anna—keeps my head on straight," Ray admitted.

"I hope you know you don't deserve her," Luke teased.

Ray shrugged. "Tell me about it, but then again, I've always been lucky." He smiled cockily, patting Luke on the back and hurried over to Julia. Her face lit up as he dragged her out to dance.

CHAPTER 29

TWO WEEKS LATER, the hot sun beating down on the window like a laser beam trying to burn through a barrier, Luke sat at the desk in his office, catching up on some of the work that had been piling up needing his attention. He'd put it off as long as he could, and Elise and the new Vice President had been diligent about pulling out things they could handle themselves. That day, after lunch, while Anna was napping, he came in to try and get through as much as he could. It was one of those sultry St. Louis summer days—heat bad enough alone but then, being Missouri—because ninety-five Fahrenheit wasn't miserable enough—ninety percent humidity had been heaped on top.

He asked Elise to hold all calls except from his family, so when Mandy called, he took the call right away. "Hi, sweetie, do you miss me already? I miss you."

There was silence for a moment, then: "Daddy, I'm sorry to bother you at work."

"Oh sweetie, you can call me any time. You don't have to worry about that anymore," Luke assured her.

"There's something wrong. With Mommy. Can you come home now? Please, daddy." The urgency in her voice sent chills down his back.

"Sure, honey. I'll be right there," he replied, heading for the door. He stopped only long enough to tell Elise "Family Emergency" and then ran for his car. He didn't even notice the heat, but the sweat was soaking his clothes by the time he slid in his car and started the engine.

He fought all the way home to keep the speed limit which, given his normal propensity for a lead foot and the memory of Mandy's urgency, posed a real challenge. The tires squealed in the driveway as he pulled up to the house and ran for the door.

Mandy opened the door as he reached the stoop, crying.

"What happened, sweetie?" he asked as she took his hand and led him toward their bedroom. *Oh God, please! Not yet!* he pleaded silently.

Before he even reached the room, he could hear the labored sound of Anna's breathing. Cassie and Kyle stood crying beside the bed. Cassie was holding Anna's hand. She was clearly making an effort to comfort them, but the smile was forced, and she struggled to speak between breaths. The room had an eerie feel and a slightly unpleasant smell that reminded him of death. Soiled sheets? He'd just changed them. *Oh God.*

As Luke entered, Kyle turned to him, eyes full of worry. "Why'd you have to go to work today?"

"Anna, are you okay?" Luke asked, ignoring the question and focusing his attention on his wife. "Did you guys call an ambulance?"

Mandy nodded. "Kyle dialed nine-one-one."

"Good," Luke said, smiling reassuringly at them. "Honey, the ambulance is coming. Just relax and breathe."

Anna nodded almost imperceptibly. Clearly it was all she could manage. Her eyes told him how much pain she was in. He reached up and put his hand gently on the side of her face, softly caressing. "I love you."

Her eyes changed, sending the same message back to him. Luke fought back tears. He'd just gotten her back. He couldn't lose her now. God had given him a miracle. He just needed one more.

Sirens sounded from the distance, growing louder as the ambulance approached their street. "Kyle, go wait for the ambulance out front. Hurry!" Luke instructed. Clearly, Kyle didn't want to leave his mother. "Hurry, son!"

Finally, Kyle turned and hurried for the door.

"We heard her breathing," Cassie said.

"You did? That's why you came to her?"

"We came to check on her. We thought she was napping, but her breathing was so loud," Mandy explained. "We were worried."

Luke reached over and put a hand on her arm, winking at Cassie. "You did good, girls. I'm proud of you."

"Is Mommy going to be okay?" Cassie whimpered.

"I hope so, baby," Luke said, as much for himself as them, as the Kyle led the EMTs into the room with their gurney.

"What happened?" one of them asked.

"My wife has cancer," was all Luke replied.

They hurriedly took her vital signs, then called in to the hospital.

THE MOMENT ANNA awoke early from her nap she knew something was wrong. She couldn't seem to catch her breath. She breathed and breathed, but it took a lot of work to take in any air. Her body didn't ache more than usual—usual for cancer, that is. But she felt numb, and she couldn't move. She also couldn't talk. She was too busy breathing. When Mandy and Cassie rushed in, she couldn't even answer their questions. Seeing the worried looks on their faces, Cassie's fear, she started to cry. She felt so helpless. She was their mother, for heaven's sake! She was supposed to be the one who comforted them at times like this! Things had been going so well. What was happening?

As Mandy ran to get Kyle, the thought occurred to her: *I'm dying! The time has come!* She wanted to scream: "No! I'm not ready yet! I need more time!" But she'd already had almost a year longer than the doctors predicted. A lot of people given months to live didn't even make it that long. God had blessed her with extra time. She'd been very lucky. At that moment, her heart filled with gratefulness.

Kyle came in, trying to speak to her, asking what was wrong, but speaking between breaths remained a struggle. She did her best to tell him with her eyes to call for help, and was relieved a moment later, when he picked up her cell phone and dialed nine-one-one. She heard him answering their questions, giving the address. Help would be here soon. *Please, God, just let me hold on a little longer!*

Luke wasn't home. The realization hit her like a bullet. She had to see Luke again, at least one last time. She had to thank him for the way he'd put their lives back together; to tell him she knew he would take care of the kids and raise them well. She had to tell her kids she had always been proud of them and always would be. There was so much she still needed to say. Why had she waited so long?

Luke arrived and she still couldn't speak. The next thing she knew, the EMTs were loading her on the gurney. She said a silent prayer for God to give her just a few more moments to spend with them before she had to go. *Please God!* she pleaded.

Then she was in the ambulance, still struggling for breath, as the sirens wailed and she felt them moving.

LUKE PACED IN the waiting room at the hospital as the kids sat silently on chairs nearby. He didn't know what to say to them. What could he say that would make any difference anyway? He didn't even know what to say to himself. *Oh God, this is so hard!* He'd known all along there would be a moment like this, but he still wasn't ready. So much had happened since she told him about the cancer. This couldn't be it. *She can't die now!* He prayed the hardest he'd ever prayed that God would give them yet another reprieve. *Just a little longer*, he begged.

Suddenly, Kyle stood and rushed Luke, punching his chest with both fists. "You should have been there! You promised! No more work first!"

Luke's tears burst. "I know, son. I'm so sorry."

"I need her." Kyle looked at his crying sisters. "*We* need her."

"I need her too," Luke croaked. He took a deep breath, trying to gather himself as Kyle pounded his chest again and again. "I'm so sorry." He looked at Kyle, who wouldn't meet his eyes, and then he looked down at the girls huddled on the couch. "I'm so sorry. I need her, too. I wish it was me."

Cassie and Mandy just sobbed harder.

Kyle broke into sobs too then and Luke wrapped him tight with his arms, pulling his son's face against his chest. "I'm so, so sorry," he said again. He didn't know what else to say.

Moments later, Doctor Sousa appeared and motioned to them, sadly. "You should come and see her now." Luke nodded, trying to determine if he meant all of them or just him. "All of you," the doctor added.

Luke reached for Cassie's and Mandy's hands. Kyle followed along behind them as Doctor Sousa led them into the treatment room. There were so many tubes coming out of Anna, sounds of machines, oxygen. And that damn smell of antiseptics mixed with industrial cleaners. It terrified Luke. He couldn't imagine how the kids felt. He tried to smile, looking at them reassuringly.

Anna turned her head as they came in, extending her arms. She was clearly anxious to have them near her.

"Can she talk?" Kyle asked Doctor Sousa, who stood on the opposite side of the table.

"Her breathing has improved. Maybe." He wasn't sure. "Anna, do you want to say something?" He leaned over her. She turned to him, her eyes saying 'yes.' He reached over and gently pulled the oxygen mask to the side.

Anna turned back to her family, smiling weakly. "Hi." It came out as a raspy whisper, as if just one word took all the strength she had.

Through sniffles, the kids greeted her. Cassie tried to smile, too.

"I love you guys," Anna said, slowly making eye contact with each of them. "I'm so proud of you." Tears poured down her cheeks now.

"We're proud of you, too, Mommy," Mandy sniffled. Luke felt his own eyes tearing up.

"Kyle, you know your dad loves you. Don't you be angry with him now. You need each other," Anna said, looking into Kyle's eyes.

Kyle looked stunned, like she'd seen everything that had just happened, then nodded and looked away.

She turned to Luke. "I knew when I married you, you were amazing."

Luke started to sob. "I'm not ready yet," was all he could say.

Anna closed her eyes and reached over to weakly squeeze his hand. "Me either, but we don't have a choice." She tugged at his hand, pulling him to her.

He leaned down, kissing her desperately. "I need you so much."

"You'll be fine," she said and started coughing.

Doctor Sousa hurriedly put the oxygen mask back in place.

"You're the best part of who I am," Luke said. "I can't imagine my life without you."

Anna motioned for Doctor Sousa to remove the mask again. He hesitated, and she motioned again with intensity. He reluctantly pulled it away.

"I can't imagine mine either," she managed as her fingers entwined with his. "I love you." She coughed again, and Doctor Sousa put the mask back in place.

Luke kissed her cheek again, tears flowing. "I love you, too. Forever."

She nodded, weakly. It was obvious her strength was fading.

Luke looked at the doctor, his eyes pleading. He could see from the way Doctor Sousa looked back that there was nothing to be done. He stood there holding her hand and motioned for the kids to come closer. They huddled together with him, watching her breathe for the last time. The only sound in the room other than the oxygen and machines was the sound of their sobbing. Two minutes later, one of the machines started beeping loudly and the dreaded long tone filled the air.

She was gone.

CHAPTER 30

AN HOUR LATER, Luke stood numbly in the waiting room again. He couldn't believe she was gone. He looked over past the sympathetic glances of the nurses to the stunned faces of their children. Lee, Grace, Charlie, Ray, and Julia were gathered around them, offering what comfort they could. Luke still couldn't find any words to comfort them himself. He wondered what that meant. What kind of father was so terrible at comforting his children? What kind of father was he going to be without Anna to keep him on course? He felt so completely overwhelmed and lost.

Finally, he went over and knelt on the floor, looking up at them. "Mommy's with Jesus now." It wasn't much, he knew, but it was the most important thing. He hoped they would understand how wonderful that thought was from Sunday school. He searched his mind for something, anything.

"But we still need her," Mandy said through tears as she clung to Julia's side.

"I know, sweetie. We all still need her," he said, reaching out to hug her. Cassie sniffled too from Gracie's lap, and Luke pulled her into the hug, too.

Kyle sat there with his arms crossed, looking away. It must be hardest for him, because he was older and understood more, Luke thought. "But just because she's gone physically doesn't mean she's gone from our hearts," Luke finally said. "We'll always remember her and love her."

Cassie and Mandy nodded, hugging him again. Luke reached out and put a hand on Kyle's knee.

Kyle looked at them, tears flowing. "Why'd God take her?" he finally asked

"I don't know, Kyle. I don't know," Luke said, wishing he had a good answer. "I think sometimes God needs another angel." It had been off the cuff, but he liked it. *Where did that come from?* "But I'm sorry. I'm so sorry."

Kyle bolted from the chair and joined the embrace, his shoulders shaking as he sobbed. They all just sat there holding each other and crying for a long while, as life went on around them.

OVERWHELMED, LUKE LEFT the kids with his family, who promised to take them home, and fled to the hospital chapel again. Making his way down the aisle, he slipped into the second pew and fell to his knees. His fists clenched as tears and grief changed to anger.

"WHY?! WHY?! I'd lost everything. We had a deal. I changed, I did my part. How can you take her away?!" he cried out, not quite shouting. Not that he cared if anyone overheard. He felt betrayed, broken, destroyed. God had answered every prayer except this one—the one that mattered most.

"I love her. I need her. I can't do it alone!" He shouted now, and then tears overwhelmed him and he sobbed again. His chest was so tight he wondered how he could breathe, his body stiff, finger nails tearing into his palms. "What kind of God would do this? A loving God?" He shook his head and then his whole body, until he had to reach up with both hands to steady himself on the back of the front pew to keep from falling over.

"It's a farce! A cosmic joke! All we have to do is pray and God will grant it?" Luke chortled in fury. "Bullshit!"

He pounded his fists on the back of the pew, and then he heard something—a footstep, a rustling of clothes. Was someone here? The chapel had been dead quiet and dimly lit when he entered, and it still was. One of the chaplains perhaps? Surely they'd heard him.

He turned and saw Kyle standing mid-aisle, watching him with a look somewhere between surprise and pity.

Luke sniffled, collecting himself as he stood. "I thought you went home with Aunt Grace."

Kyle shook his head. "Grandpa's waiting. I told him I needed to pray."

A flush creeped across Luke's cheeks. How much had Kyle heard and seen? He tried to hide his wince, unclenching his fists as he took a deep breath, and shoving his hands in his pockets. "You came to the right place. I can leave you alone."

Kyle shook his head again. "No, stay."

Luke sighed. "Okay." He motioned toward the pews. "Go ahead."

Kyle nodded, then stepped forward and slid into a pew across the aisle from where Luke had been. He knelt, stopping to pull out the felt-covered kneeling bench first. Then placed his palms and fingers together in the traditional sign of prayer, closing his eyes.

Luke stayed as quiet as he could, sliding back a few steps in the aisle as he did his best not to disturb his son. When he looked back again, Kyle was staring at him.

"You don't believe in God anymore?" Kyle asked. It wasn't an accusation. It was confusion.

"Of course, I believe," Luke managed, stumbling a bit over the words. "I'm not sure what I feel. So many emotions."

"You blamed God," Kyle said. "Called Him a joke."

Luke shook his head. "I was angry, son. Venting my emotions without thinking about what I'm saying."

"So you didn't mean it?" Kyle asked, eyes locked on his father's.

Luke sighed, wincing again. "I don't know what I think, son. I just hurt."

Kyle grunted, seeming to accept that. "I know it's not your fault, dad. I'm sorry I said that." His eyes were so sincere, showing not shame, but resignation, and a confidence Luke had never seen there. Luke was stunned. At a loss for words.

"I didn't mean it," Kyle said. He finally looked away, his head lowering. "I was angry too. Sometimes I don't know what to do about it."

"Yeah," Luke said. "Me either. It's hard."

Kyle closed his eyes a moment, seeming to continue his prayer, then he stood, his hands lowering to his side as he turned to face Luke. "But we have to help each other. We're a family. That's what families do, right?"

Luke fought back a smile. The son educating the father. "Yes." He nodded. "As best we can."

"Okay," Kyle said and bent to slide the felt bench back up before stepping from the pew and walking over to join Luke. "I'll still be mad sometimes. But I'll try to understand better." *God, the sincerity.* When had his little boy gotten so smart? He'd been so busy dealing with Anna and everything else, he'd failed to notice his boy was becoming a young man.

Luke grunted. "I'll do my best to explain better. It's okay to be mad sometimes."

Kyle watched him a moment, letting silence hang between them. "I know you love us, dad," Kyle finally said. "I love you, too."

Luke was stunned. He hadn't heard that from Kyle in so

long. He didn't know what to do. Should he hug him or would that just ruin the moment and set him off? The urge to hug his son was so strong.

Kyle launched himself at Luke, wrapping his arms around his father's belly, his cheek against Luke's chest. Luke returned the embrace, and they held each other in a moment Luke almost wished could last forever.

A WEEK AFTER the funeral, Luke sat in Anna's house, in her favorite chair. He'd lived there three weeks now, and he still didn't think of it as their house yet. Three weeks! The time had flashed by like lightning. The past week had been like passing through fog. He hardly remembered anything except that Anna hadn't been a part of it.

He glanced out the window at the backyard where Kyle and his sisters were playing in the sprinklers. Even in their grief, they were still carefree enough to play. He wished he could still do that, but it was a talent that died with youth. He'd never felt the loss of it until now.

His hand was clamped around the letter. The last words he'd ever hear from Anna. She'd given it to Brenda just after the wedding, and Brenda had given it to Luke, as instructed, after the funeral. The envelope had still been crisp and unblemished, unlike it was now—crinkled and stained with his tears. A single word had been written in blue ink on the front, in Anna's beautiful script: *Luke*. There was no more beautiful sound he'd ever heard than the sound of her voice saying his name. He'd never hear it again, he knew, but as he looked at his name on the envelope, he could almost hear it now.

Anna had written the letter in the aftermath of the wedding, a time when she'd been overcome with emotions. She had clearly chosen her words with great care. And every time he read it, Luke was deeply moved by what she'd written. No one else had seen the letter. Only Brenda knew about it, as far as he knew, and she knew not to ask. It was a private message between two lovers who had known each other for over thirteen years. The last message to pass between them. It was sacred, and Luke now considered it the most precious possession he had.

He opened the envelope, sliding out the thin pages. She'd written it on the kind of glossy, thin stationary used to keep the weight down. It had been written by hand, two full pages. He stared at the handwriting he'd seen so many times over the past fourteen years. The same handwriting he'd seen on so many cards, gifts, even post-it notes. He hadn't recognized its beauty until he saw the letter, but then he realized how much delight he'd always felt when he saw his name written by Anna's hand. He opened the letter and reread the words which continued to move him.

My dearest Luke,

My heart and mind are still reeling from the amazing events of the past few months. Even now, the day after our remarriage, I can hardly wrap myself around them or believe it all possible. It's like I've lived out my own little fairy tale.

From the moment we met, I knew you were special. You were a bit of a loner, for sure, and I knew you hadn't dated a lot. You were rough around the edges, without social graces sometimes, but you were so handsome, so smart, so determined. I admired you then, just as I admire and respect you now.

Despite the roughness, you managed to set my heart aflutter at just the mention of my name, the smell of your cologne, the touch of your hand. All magical sensations which I had long thought lost, until we found them again. Somehow, we rediscovered our lost treasure. How many couples ever get the chance to do that, my darling?

I know you must be in a daze, reading this, because you know I am gone now, and what we shared is just memories. But you must go on, darling. You must draw on whatever strength you have, and the strength only God can give you, and go on, making a beautiful life and future for our precious children. I know you can help them to become the kind of people we would both be proud of. I know they will turn out wonderfully, because I know the kind of man you've become.

I am so proud to be your wife, the mother of your children, your lover, your best friend. I'm so glad God gave me the chance to know you all over again and discover the new you, Luke. You've given me enough joy to make up for any pain or loss I'd ever felt. You made the last few months pass like a dream, even as I was dying. No pain, no suffering could eclipse the wonder of our life together again. Because of you, my last days were magical and wonderful, and I cannot find words to say enough how grateful I am for that gift.

I know you will never let the children forget me, though in time they will forget the sound of my voice. I know you'll hold on to those memories longer, and I want you to know how much I love and treasure you always. Yet I don't want you to ever let those memories keep you from the happiness you deserve. If you're so lucky to find lightning a second time, I want you to take it, embrace it, with my blessing. Fall in love, get married, build a life together. All of these are things you deserve, Luke. You're still young, with a long life ahead of you.

> *Don't let yourself live isolated and lonely because of me. You gave me my last wish of knowing my children would be happy and well cared for. And my last wish for you, darling, is that you would also be happy and well cared for. I can no longer do that, so please, allow yourself to find another, if it's God's will.*

> *Words can never say how much you will always mean to me. Words could never express what's in my heart. You are the great love of my lifetime, Luke Morrison, and I am so thankful God gifted me with your presence in my life these wonderful years. I'm eternally grateful to both of you.*

> *With all my love,*
> *Anna*

Luke still couldn't get through it without turning into a vegetable. He wiped his tears on his sleeve, carefully folding up the letter, and sliding it back in the envelope.

He'd never imagined a love like this, when he met Anna all those years before. He'd been drawn by her beauty, her brains, and her heart. All the things she'd written about their life together—he felt the same and so much more. Anna was his life. He would have had nothing without her. His friends had often reminded him he'd caught above his limit. Anna was like the pot of gold at the end of his rainbow, and he could search the rest of his life and never find another like her. He was just so grateful to have been given the chance once.

He put the letter back inside his Bible, where he kept it. Together, they were the most treasured words he would ever read, so it seemed fitting. He watched the children again, laughing, joking, enjoying each other, and said a silent prayer that God would help him to enjoy them as they were enjoying each other now. He still questioned his faith. Things felt different now. He'd always been told bad things happened because God allowed them for reasons we might never understand. and God had allowed Anna to die. He wasn't ready to forgive that yet. Still, he prayed for his family, because that's what Anna would want, and he knew it's what he needed most right now. It was the best way he could love them as she had always loved them, and the best way to capture for his heart, some of the spirit they already had—carefree and hopeful. He needed that hope for the future.

He stepped out into the musty air of the backyard to join his kids. Thankfully the humidity and heat had both dropped a bit by early evening. It wasn't pleasant. The air still felt stuffy and thick like the weight of his grief, but it was tolerable, mostly because as a lifelong Missourian, he was used to it. As he crossed the yard he glanced over and noticed the flickering candle still in Anna's window where he'd continued lighting it every day. Anna might be gone, but his hope remained, and that was something he knew Anna would love, and love, and something they both wanted to demonstrate to their kids.

His kids' laughter washed over him like healing balm for his grieving heart. It reminded him even in remembering Anna that she would live on through her legacy. He had no idea what tomorrow would bring, but he was going to face it head on. He had a mission—fulfilling his love's last wish. And in that, he was bound and determined to make her proud.

ACKNOWLEDGEMENTS

This book you are holding in your hands is a miracle of sorts. My first attempt at a novel was in 2007, when I desperately wanted to write something like Nicholas Sparks whose love stories had so moved me. THE LAST WISH was my first attempt ever at writing a novel, but I didn't really finish it. It had missing parts and I felt it failed in a number of ways. Fearing I was not skilled enough to craft anything of such emotional power and honesty, I put it in a drawer and worked on other things.

Then in 2019 I wrote THE LIGHTHOUSE and realized that I still loved the story THE LAST WISH had told, wondering if I might somehow salvage it into something good. When I went back to it, I discovered that some of the writing was better than what I'd been writing since. There was a purity and honesty there, even though I was quite ignorant of storytelling craft at the time, that just worked magic. Even if the story and characters needed work to flesh out and structure properly. So I set to work.

For the new version of THE LAST WISH, of which I am very proud, I thank my dad Ramon W. Schmidt, M.D. (retired) for talking me through the medical aspects of cancer as needed for the story. I thank my mom, Glenda, for being the first reading way back 17 years ago and giving me advice and encouragement even though it needed a lot of work.

Thanks to talented author Merri Maywether for some great insights and kind assistance.

Big thanks to Claire Ashgrove for editing, and A. R. Redington for another great cover and layout for the e-book as well as touching up the print interior files to perfection from my rough drafts.

Lastly, I thank my family: my wife May, and children, Kishi, and Kenjie for their support and laughter, giving me space to write, and teaching me about parenthood and family in ways that have only enhanced my ability to tell stories like this. And most of all for a second chance at being a dad and husband.

Thanks to God for His Son, and to you, the readers, for taking a chance on my work. I hope it reminds you of the power of family, love, and hope I still believe in.

MA Lanham
Ottawa, KS
November 2024

AUTHOR'S NOTE

Thanks for reading *The Last Wish*. I hope you enjoyed the story as much as I enjoyed writing it. To find more of my work, you can follow me on my socials:

https://www.facebook.com/malanhamauthor

https://www.x.com/malanhamauthor

Or on my website at https://www.malanham.com.

I'll have more books out in 2025. In the meantime, please take the time to spread the word. Posting your review to Amazon and Goodreads is a huge boost and, of course, tell your friends.

And check out the sneak peek of my other novel *The Lighthouse* which follows.

With sincere thanks,

M.A. Lanham

Excerpt from

THE LAST WISH

by

M. A. Lanham

CHAPTER 1

JACK PACE'S NIGHTMARES always started the same way. The '98 Toyota Camry's radio was too loud. Abby grimaced as the song finished and Caroline stopped belting the latest K-Pop hit from the back. She reached down to lower the volume.

"Again, mommy!" Caroline cheered. It was a conversation they seemed to repeat day after day.

"On the way home, baby," Abby said gently as she reached up and tucked a loose strand of her brunette hair back behind her ear. "Mommy needs a break."

"Awwwww," Caroline whined, making a sad face.

Abby laughed and shook her head. "It's not going to work. You sing that song a hundred times a day already. You'll survive giving your mama a break."

Caroline frowned and bulged her upper lip in a pouty expression, but Abby wouldn't budge, so moments later, her daughter sighed and grinned, her hand reaching for the silver plastic tiara resting atop her head. "Mommy, do I make a good princess?"

"The best," Abby said and meant it.

Abby slowed the car to a stop at a stop sign and waited to turn left off Belmont Boulevard onto South Ohio Street. Ah, Salina. The only home she'd ever known. It was small, and she'd wanted desperately to get out when she was a teenager but now all her best memories, and everyone she loved was here. What else could a woman want? She'd told Jack those very words more than once.

The trees looked great with their reddish orange and yellow Fall colors. Soon, the leaves would begin to fall as the weather went from pleasant to cold with the approach of Winter. A mother robin flew down from its nest to peck at worms in the grass, the movement of her babies' heads barely visible above the walls of the nest as they chirped and called.

As Abby waited for several cars to pass, she glanced in the rearview mirror at her daughter. Seven years old going on twenty—or at least it seemed like it at certain moments. Wisdom from the mouths of babes, her mother would say. While Caroline was all girl with her blonde curls and spunky, giggly personality, sometimes the things she said just hit home as beyond her years. The flowery scent of her daughter's Disney Princess Perfume drifted to the front and tickled her nose.

Jack had objected at first when her parents gifted it the past Christmas. "She's too young for makeup!"

Abby agreed about makeup but this was a child's perfume, hardly as potent as the adult kind. It smelled, at best, like a scent a teenager might wear. Caroline play-acted at being older. To Abby, that was normal. As a little girl Abby had liked imagining herself as older too. Perfume was not makeup, as she'd made sure Jack understood. In the end, they'd struck a deal with Caroline: she could wear the perfume but no makeup until she was thirteen. Period. But Jack wondered if that agreement would last that long.

"Mommy, were you a princess when you met daddy?" Caroline asked, her blonde head bobbing in excitement, pigtails bouncing on either side. It was a question their daughter asked Jack, too, whenever they were alone on a drive. Oh to be a child and live in a world of fairy tales again.

Abby smiled. "No, but I felt like I was meeting a prince."

"Really? Daddy was a prince? Did he have a white horse?"

Abby laughed then slowly accelerated as she took advantage of the opportunity to turn and headed north on South Ohio, moving right into the outside lane which connected to the parking lot at their destination. Dillons, their local grocery chain, lay a few blocks ahead on the right. "No, babe. No white horse," Abby said, pausing a moment as she pondered how to answer. "Oh but the way he looked at me... It made me feel so special."

"Really? How did he look at you, mommy?" Caroline asked.

Just that morning, he'd come up and wrapped his arms around Abby from behind. As always, her cheeks reddened and her body responded at the touch of his body to hers. He'd leaned over and kissed her cheek. She'd reached back and caressed his hair, then rested her open palm against the side of his face. "I'm grateful every moment," he'd said as he spun her around and they kissed again.

"Ewwww, gross," Caroline whined, making a face as she all but danced into the kitchen and interrupted them. "Too much love."

"I can never have too much love for my girls." Jack smiled, his eyes locked on Abby's.

"I hope your day goes well," she'd said as she pulled away and stepped to the counter to fix their daughter's breakfast. "It sounds stressful."

"Nah, Barry Kline is a bit of a micromanager, but it's early enough the changes he wants aren't going to necessitate a lot of adjustments," Jack had said. "The toughest part is listening to him bitch. The rest is easy."

"Ummmmm," Caroline scolded. "Language, daddy."

"Sorry, pumpkin," he'd said and kissed his daughter on the

head as he sneakily reached down to tickle her. For the next few moments, they'd dissolved into silliness as Caroline screamed and made to escape but Jack kept after her—another morning ritual Abby secretly adored. After a few seconds, Abby arrived to set a plate of scrambled eggs and bacon in front of their daughter and shoo Jack away.

Jack's cell phone beeped as a text message arrived. He read it quickly and grimaced as he skidded back loudly in his chair and stood. "Crap! Barry moved the meeting up. I'm late!"

"But you promised you'd have time to eat with us," Abby had objected, frustrated. He'd promised to make time this morning. These were the kind of promises he always struggled with. It had been the source of several fights over the years

Noting Abby's frown, Jack leaned and kissed Caroline on the forehead then turned and kissed Abby on the cheek, his hand caressing her cheek. "I love you," he'd said, meaning them both. But his eyes had added "I'm so sorry" just for her. And she knew he always meant it. Somehow they'd get through this.

"We love you, too," Abby and Caroline said together, their daughter adding "daddy" to the phrase, and then he'd run out the door.

He got the call thirty minutes later when he was hurrying down the hall to the conference room for the meeting with Barry and the client. He almost ignored it until he saw "Emergency Services" scrolling across the caller ID.

"Mister Pace, I'm very sorry to bother you, but there's been an accident," the 911 operator said in a voice that was way too calm and gentle for what she was about say. Forever after, he couldn't remember her exact words. What he could remember was falling to his knees in the hallway and the feeling as if someone had slammed into his chest, pushing all the air out. Something about a truck barreling through the intersection. The big industrial kind—the kind the Toyota was no match for.

And then time stopped. His world ended. Everything that mattered gone in a flash. As usual, he awoke gasping, his heart pounding and jagged pain throughout his body. Why? Why God, why?! his internal voice always demanded. And for the thousandth time he echoed back, I'd trade places with them in a minute. It should have been me. And then dissolved into sobbing as coworkers rushed toward him with concerned looks, asking what was wrong.

CHAPTER 2

TWO DAYS LATER, the restaurant was a gem, the blind date sitting across the table, a horror show, and Jack wondered how in the world he'd let his younger sister, Josie, talk him into this.

"What part of mineral water with lemon did you not understand?!" his date scolded, glaring at the waitress who had brought her a Dasani with lemon included, not a mineral water with a slice of lemon on the rim as she'd asked. Of course, Jack wondered how a slice of lemon was supposed to actually fit on the rim of a bottled water, but his date, Linda's, instructions had been quite explicit.

"The lemon is included," the waitress explained, her eyes strained as she lost patience. "We ran out of lemons. The owner sent someone to the market." Glasses clinked and silverware dinged against plates around them as the other diners enjoyed their meals, oblivious to the "lemon crisis" occurring in their midst.

Linda crinkled her nose with distaste. "It's not the same thing," she strained to read the waitress's name tag, "Sarah." Linda wasn't even his type. She was in many ways the opposite of Abby—short blond hair, pale white skin, almost six foot, whereas Abby was a tanned auburn-haired beauty of five feet three. But most of all, Linda was very outgoing and type A. Abby had been introverted and gentle, the perfect wife and mother. Jack couldn't imagine living with this woman in a house.

"It's the best I could do, I'm sorry," Sarah replied. "I'll bring you another in a few minutes when John gets back from the market." Sarah looked about fifteen, though Jack was pretty sure she had to be a bit older to work in a place serving alcohol. She was pretty, blonde, not too much make-up—reminding him of how he'd imagined his nine-year-old daughter Caroline might grow up to look one day.

Linda scowled. "Who runs out of lemons on a Friday night?!" She looked at Jack. "The talk was this is a classy place, but I'm not seeing it."

As far as Salina went, The Scheme was classy. But it was a pizza joint, not fine dining. Founded in the late eighties by one of Jack's parents' neighbors, The Scheme was downtown on North 7th Street, its red canopy a local landmark. The interior had dark wooden tables, and a bar with classic gold-embossed chandeliers overhead that left all the right shadows. Soft eighties music played from speakers overhead, taking Jack back to his first time here during high school with his family. He didn't glance around the crowded dining room—it usually was—afraid of seeing someone he knew from his job at Kline Architects, instead staring at the painting of a scene from a Marilyn Monroe movie that hung on the wall above a nearby table.

He blushed, turning to Sarah, and sighed. "I'm so sorry."

"What are you apologizing to her for? I'm the one who was wronged," Linda snapped, expanding her glare to include him.

"My four-year-old daughter has better manners," Sarah said, finally fed up, as she shot Jack a look of thanks.

"My nine-year-old, too," Jack agreed, then winced as he thought of Abby and Caroline. They'd been dead a year now, and he mourned them every day. Why did he still think of them as if they were alive at home, waiting for him? Why was he even here?

Linda grunted. "My brother said your daughter had died. Did he lie to me? I hate kids!"

Jack just scooted back from the table and motioned to Sarah. "Check please. We're leaving."

"What?! I want my water!" Linda protested.

"It's three dollars for the water, and your soda's on the house," Sarah said and smiled.

Jack handed her cash, including a tip equal to the bill, and headed for the door. "You can find your own ride home," he said, slapping another twenty down on the counter in front of Linda then kept right on walking.

"OH MY GOD!" his sister Josie exclaimed as he related the story to her an hour later on the phone. "What the hell was Ben thinking?" Linda's brother, who worked in the office next to Jack's at Kline, had set up the date.

"I don't know, but that was the worst one yet," Jack growled. "I wish everyone would just stop trying to set me up and leave me be." He ran a hand through his hair and leaned back on the sofa, groaning, then took a big sip from the Budweiser he'd opened as soon as he walked through the door.

"We just want you to be happy," Josie reminded him.

"I don't know if I can be without Abby and Caroline," he said for not the first time. "They're the loves of my life, and they were stolen from me. You can't fix that. So please stop trying."

He could almost hear Josie throwing up her hands. "I get that, and yet I refuse to believe Abby would want you to stay at home like a hermit. She'd want you to move on, and at least get out and live, Jack."

"I will when I'm ready," Jack snapped. "This is not when."

It was Josie's turn to sigh. "I gotta get the boys to bed. I'm sorry it went badly. I'll call you tomorrow, 'kay?"

He grunted. "Good night, sis."

"I love you," she said as she hung up the phone.

The accident, on what Jack Pace had come to call "the day that changed everything," came out of nowhere like most of them do. And even today, a year later, most of it was still a blur. He'd laughed and joked with them both like always that morning, snuggling both his wife and daughter—one of his favorite ways to start any day. He'd been preparing for an important new client all week and had to miss Caroline's dance recital and their meals together, but that day he'd promised to make time, and he did... until Barry texted. He'd moved the meeting up last minute at the client's request, and Jack had to rush out the door. He'd seen Abby's displeasure on her face. He'd kissed his wife and daughter and apologized, but even as he headed for the door, he knew it would take more to make it up to Abby. He'd let her down. And he'd fully intended to come home early that night and take a day off the next Monday so they could have his full attention for the next three days. When the police called two hours later, nothing was the same anymore—his job, the house, food... everything—and he doubted it would ever be the same again. Time stopped that day his life ended.

He had been smitten the first time he set eyes on Abby in her Roosevelt Lincoln Junior High School cheerleader outfit— her long, smooth tan legs sending thoughts through his adolescent hormone-ridden brain that would have made him blush if anyone could hear them. He admired her curves, especially the curve of her breasts and that small patch of cleavage the sweater she wore on top revealed every time she did a dance move or bent to twirl or spin. She had beautiful, long auburn locks, and that adorable smile. Jack had never met a girl who'd had such an effect on him. He literally had to remind himself to breathe whenever he looked at her, and that one time when her bright blue eyes caught his... he was pretty sure his heart had stopped, frozen in time, for at least a minute or two. Neither the fact that he was still alive or that the idea defied the laws of physiology didn't change his mind.

It was love at first sight. But it had taken him a while to not only win her over but be ready for their relationship. He was a bumbling, pimpled, geeky ball of hormones, a farm boy, and she was the popular, sophisticated girl from the Hill, where all the wealthy families lived. Abby had been friendly but kept her distance. Jack had never worked so hard in his life as he did winning her over. And by the time they reached high school, they were inseparable.

Abby Brown, she was the one for Jack Pace for sure. And from that day on, his whole life had been about winning her over, and then keeping her happy, no matter what it took. She was the only woman he'd ever loved. And as far as he could imagine, the only woman he ever would. That she loved him back was the greatest gift he'd ever been given, because Jack knew he didn't deserve her, and she'd put up with her share of frustration from him over the years as he tried to find balance between work and home—something he was bad at from years of working ever spare hour helping his parents on the farm. Work was their life back then, and they'd engrained that work ethic in their children, but Abby's dad had come home every night for dinner and family time, despite his well-paying job and great success. That was her role model and had set her expectations. She loved Jack and he loved her, but Abby wanted a husband who made time for his family like her father had, especially after Caroline was born. Jack's career was ever rising and with it, new demands on his time. He did his best, but he knew it had never been enough.

Abby had followed Jack to Lawrence to attend the University of Kansas where he majored in architecture while she studied history. They'd married at First Baptist Church in Salina a week after his graduation, then returned to Lawrence where he'd interned with a local firm until she graduated a year later. Jack accepted the job back in Salina with a firm owned by friend of his father's, and the years before the birth of their daughter had been like an extended honeymoon. Abby took a job teaching history as an adjunct at Kansas Wesleyan, and outside work, they pretty much spent all their time together. With the exception of a few close friends they occasionally spent time with, there was no one else they wanted to be with, and that didn't change for the twelve years before the accident.

The second love of his life, after Abby of course, had been their daughter, Caroline. For seven glorious years before the accident, their life had been as close to perfect as Jack had ever imagined life could be. Not really perfect, but damn close, and he couldn't have asked for a better daughter. She had all the good qualities of her mother, and few of Jack's faults, thank God.

But then that day came. The accident. The hospital. A walking nightmare.

The other driver was a man named Mitchell Bass. He drove a red Chevy Silverado 5500 Crew Cab platform truck bearing the emblem of his employers—Zimmer Industrial. He'd been checking something on the clipboard beside him and failed to stop at what he presumed was a yellow light. When Abby crossed the intersection under a green light, he T-boned her white Toyota Corolla square on the driver's side at a mere thirty-five miles per hour, a mistake that took all of five seconds to destroy everything that had ever mattered to Jack Pace. Bass walked away with a few cuts and scrapes. And for the first nine months after the accident, Jack had thought about killing him every single day.

"Just get up and breathe," Josie and others had told him. "That's your only job right now. It'll take a while, but you know Abby wouldn't want you doing anything to seek revenge. She'd want you to go on, try to find a way to carry on somehow."

He'd listened in silence usually, but most of the times it was because he was fighting the urge to laugh in their face and scream, "What do I have to live for?! I've lost everything! And that bastard doesn't deserve to live for taking it from me!"

The accident occurred at eight-thirty a.m., and Jack had been in a meeting for thirty minutes already. Abby died instantly, the car crushed so quickly it was almost a Z when the emergency crews used the jaws of life to extract her and Caroline, only to rush them to Asbury Hospital downtown. Caroline survived the crash, though critical and in a coma. Jack had never prayed or cried so hard in all his life as he did those two days. Josie and Abby's parents, Grace and Paul, did their best to keep him comfort, offering what comfort and conversation they could, but Jack was like a zombie—reliving over and over all the moments he'd missed from meals to school events, the recitals, and the second honeymoon he'd promised Abby for over a decade. He'd made lots of promises how they'd do it one day when things slowed down, only life never did, and now all he wanted was his life rewound to that terrible morning like it never happened. He hoped Abby's two surgeries would bring her back to him, but she died three days later, leaving Jack to sleep in a chair next to Caroline's bed, squeezing her tiny, precious hand as if it was keeping them both breathing. But Caroline herself had finally succumbed to her injuries the following Friday, and his family was gone forever.

Jack kept it together as best he could, making funeral arrangements, notifying his family and hers, and hosting everyone as they gathered for the funeral a week later at First Baptist, presided over by Pastor Jim Owen, a family friend. The church called in a "Celebration of Life," but Jack could think of nothing to celebrate. He made it through somehow, and as the guests went home, her parents and his—Ken and May Pace— and his sister Josie turned the donated casseroles, the spiral ham, the trays of dinner rolls, three cherry dump cakes, and the reams of noodle salad into freezer-trays-for-one his mother said should feed him for six months. Each kissed him good-bye while Jack held to Josie's sleeve, willing her at least to stay. Abby's mother, Gloria, lingered long enough in front of Abby's closet that she had to be led outside crying into a sweater she'd given her late daughter for Christmas. Each voice flew away with the prevailing winds blowing over Kansas until the house fell silent, leaving Jack alone with hundreds of cards and letters from friends and strangers expressing condolences and sympathies for loss of two people most of them barely knew.

Jack's fall into darkness pressed him into an obsequious square of deep overwhelming sadness, sliced up by a pain that haunted his every waking hour. Missing both of them seeped into his sedated sleep where he relived the accident and its aftermath over and over again. The nightmares began a week after the funeral. Perhaps it was a result of so much speculation and discussion with family during the wake about what Abby's and Caroline's final moments might have been like. Or perhaps he bore some guilt in how he might have rearranged their morning to keep them out of the path of Bass. To Jack, it hardly mattered. There was one thing they all had in common: they were all torture. Who would enjoy reliving their great loves' final moments over and over again—in various scenarios—with no way to distinguish between fantasy and truth? For all Jack knew, it was all fiction—the product of his warped, guilt-ridden mind. Yet it seemed so real when Caroline and Abby were crying out to him for help while he went on at work oblivious, never helping or even being aware of their need for him. He hadn't been aware, he feared, and he became tortured by the fear he'd been a bad husband and father, one who wasn't there when he should have been. A man who had the wrong priorities—too focused on work and not what really mattered.

In the end, he just wanted it to stop. And yet he didn't. At least this way they visited him every night. He heard their voices, their laughs, saw them happy in the moments leading up to their deaths—animated and whole just as they were in life. If that was the only way he could see them, he didn't want to give it up, did he? If nightmares were the price, he'd gladly bear it. Whatever it took to keep the memories of who they were and what they had together alive. He lived in a constant state as if a vise were pressing on the sides of his chest, permanently squeezing it tight. It was a feeling he'd learned to live with and figured would never go away. This was his life now.

HE AWOKE THE morning after the bad date at The Scheme, from yet another night terror that left him gasping to breathe as he always did after reliving the accident. He hadn't been there, and other than traffic cam footage and security footage from the Dillon's Supermarket, like the police, he'd only picked over eyewitness testimony from Bass and other drivers to fill in what happened. For obvious reasons, he refused to rely on Bass' word. Although he'd been tested on site for drugs and alcohol and a lab had cleared him, Jack didn't care. He'd be damned if he let the man who'd murdered his family—stolen them from him—be the narrator of their final moments.

Over the next few months, there were three more failed dates—three more blind dates, two of them just as horrible, and one with a woman who felt more like a friend than anyone he could get serious about. The most horrible had been at Guiterrez Mexican Restaurant, one of his and Abby's favorites—his date's choice, not his, because too many memories. He'd gotten along with the date, Erin, just fine but there was no passion. Then he'd looked across the dining room to see Abby's parents, Grace and Paul, staring at him. The final straw. He wound up excusing himself to go over and apologize to them, and then, when he got back to the table, he told Erin something had come up and left cash on the table, offering her a ride home and food to go. She had accepted, totally confused, and he'd never seen heard from her again. He'd insisted from then on that everyone to stop setting him up. But his aunt and a couple co-workers weren't easily discouraged, so finally, he began wondering if he might actually have to move away to escape, to just get some peace.

At first, he'd started looking at job and real estate listings out of idle curiosity. But as time went on, he became more and more intrigued with the idea of starting over in a new place. Yes, Salina was home. He'd lived there since he was six except for his college years. He knew its every nook and cranny almost everyone who lived there it seemed—he'd dated enough of them, right? This is where his memories of Abby and Caroline were strongest—their stuff, their favorite places, the world they'd shared—could he really leave that behind? Then again, the memories were his wherever he went, and after taking a couple of business trips, and then a week-long vacation spent in Colorado with his sister's family hiking the Rockies, he realized he'd never leave them behind, so why did he have to feel stuck in the same place? Maybe a fresh start somewhere new was exactly what he needed. He'd always mourn them, but he didn't have to wallow in it. Maybe he could find some place isolated enough that he wouldn't be surrounded by people. That would ease the pressure and allow him to escape the most painful reminders he encountered almost daily.

They'd been gone eighteen months now, and he wasn't sure he could ever move on, but that didn't mean he enjoyed the daggers of pain that struck every nerve each time he passed the Southgate Dillon's Supermarket or Salina Central High School where he'd met Abby, or her parents' house, or any of a dozen other places seared with memories of time spent together. No, a fresh start was sounding better and better the longer he considered it, and one day, he spotted the job at a remote lighthouse in Florida. That night, when he went over to Josie's house for dinner—a weekly tradition since the accident—he asked his sister about it to see how she'd react.

"Well, isolation's what you're after, right?" his sister, Josie, asked when he told her about it as he helped her with the dinner dishes.

"Yeah," he said.

"You should check out Kansas City or Chicago, see how you like it," she said, handing him another pan to scrub as she continued rinsing plates and silver before loading them into the dishwasher. She said it more than once every time they'd talked since the accident.

"You know how much I hate cities," Jack reminded her yet again.

"Live in the suburbs like we did," Josie said. "It's almost like a small town."

"Yeah, sure," he said, not really believing her. Usually she argued, offering examples, but this time she let it go. "You went there to start a family and for Andy's career. I don't need that." Josie and Andy were also high school sweethearts who'd met their senior year and fallen hard, getting engaged just after Christmas and planning a wedding right after graduation. Though their parents had worried a little, especially their mother, May, Josie and Andy had moved off to Chicago that July to seek the bigger life together they'd always dreamed of and only come back when Andy's company downsized him, leaving them forced to start over again on a much lower budget.

"Yeah but people move to cities for lots of reasons," Josie countered. "They're crowded, for one. And they're busy. Easy place to get lost in the crowd if that's what you want. Or you can meet more and interesting people from all over the world. A lot better dating pool than what we have around here."

He rolled his eyes. "For God's sake, you know that's the last thing I want."

She chuckled and offered a shrug. "Just pointing out options, bro."

He finished scrubbing the pan and handed it to her. She accepted it and placed it precisely along one side of the lower rack of the dishwasher, then said, "Well, maybe this is your opportunity."

"Opportunity?"

"To downsize. Get rid of some things that remind you of what you lost. I mean, do you really need a little girl's bedroom set? What about Abby's old clothes or Caroline's toys?" Josie suggested.

He sighed. "But that's theirs," he said. He'd locked most of it away in a spare room he refused to enter since a month after the accident, but could he really bear to be without it?

"It'll cost a lot to move everything," Josie said. "Do you even know if the new place has room for it? Besides, you said you wanted a simpler life."

"You're the one who wanted a simpler life," Jack reminded her. "That's why you moved back to Grandma's house, remember?" Their grandma had left it to May in her will when she'd died two summers before Andy lost his job. May had been about to sell it when Josie and Andy found themselves needing to relocate and start over, so she'd gifted it to them, and they'd lived there ever since.

"But Florida is so far away," Josie said, shifting him back onto the topic of his own career change decision. "And the job—lighthouse keeper—it's so random. How'd you even find that? I didn't think they had lighthouse keepers anymore."

"Well, in the U.S, no. This is a rare exception, but in Canada and other places around the world, they're still quite active," Jack said, having done a bit of research. "The Keys look beautiful, and I probably would never spend the money on real estate in a place like that, but the house comes with the job. I'd live in the lighthouse. And you know I like the outdoors."

"It's a big pay cut from architecture," Josie said. "You spent all those years getting a degree and building your reputation. Can you really leave that behind like it's nothing?"

"I can always come back to it," Jack argued. "Anyway, utilities are included with the house, I don't have a family to support. The salary's more than sufficient for my needs."

"But it's on some small island. I know you want privacy but do you really want to be that alone?" From the way she scrunched up her face when she said, Jack knew Josie had a hard time imagining such a life. But for Jack, the isolation was one of the job's biggest appeals. Moving his possessions would get a big complicated, with only private boats to ferry things over. And he'd have to find somewhere to park his car safely on the main island for when he needed it. But…there were really nice advantages. "No one trying to set me up on blind dates every other day. Limited space, so people can't just surprise visit me. I have to get permission from the Coast Guard and only a few at a time. No more finicky or demanding clients." He ticked them off on his fingers as he said them, smiling at the thought, especially of the last.

"Well, it sounds crazy to me, Jack, and you know the kids and I will miss you like crazy," Josie said as she finished loading and bent over to retrieve a pod of dishwashing soap from a box under the sink. She deposited it in the soap holder of the dishwasher and slid the door shut, then closed the outside door as her eyes met his. "But it's your life. If you're really that unhappy, and this is what you need, you know I'll always support you."

"Thanks," Jack smiled and hugged her.

In truth, Jack had already called and been interviewed over the phone twice. His future boss, Warren Gregg, was an interesting older man and Coast Guard veteran with a million fascinating and entertaining stories, and Jack would be working alone there except for days off, so except for the a few scattered tourists, he knew he'd have the time he craved to just mourn in peace and figure out what the future held if anything. No matter what he got out of it, at least he'd have peace from everyone trying to push a future on him he didn't want.

The following day, he'd gone to Barry's office and quit. He put the house on the market and held a garage sale. He needed a clean break and moving all their stuff made little sense, especially when all it did was remind him of his heartache and loss. He kept a few little reminders, like Caroline's Disney Princess perfume, and the engagement and wedding rings he'd given Abby. Most of the rest sold so quickly, he didn't have time for regret. He had to get away from this town and these people, and especially the memory of Michael Bass and the accident. Oh, it'd be with him the rest of his life wherever he went, but that didn't mean he needed constant reminders. He no longer wanted revenge. He supposed that was progress, but as for the rest he needed to start over. Afterward, his head was spinning and he was terrified he'd made the wrong choice. How much did their possessions have to do with the strength of his memories? But those possessions were gone. and there was no going back. He was headed to Florida to start a new life, and he could only hope and pray that somehow it would be the right choice.

*THE LIGHTHOUSE is available
wherever books are sold…*

Please don't forget to leave reviews. Amazon, Goodreads, TikTok, everywhere—Reviews are what help other readers discover my books. Thank you.